GATES OF FURY

KEEPERS OF THE GRAIL 5

TAMAR SLOAN

KEEPER
CHRONICLES

CONTENTS

CHAPTER 1

REIGN

"**S**o, where do you think the Grail is?"

Reign grits his teeth as he looks up from the book he was reading aloud. Simon, the youngest Potential, pushes his glasses up his nose, not seeming to care that he just interrupted Reign.

Again.

Pushing to his feet, Reign scans the five young men and women sitting around the table in the basement, books scattered amongst them. Three days ago they'd sat down, eagerness and hero-worship lighting up their faces. He'd never felt more uncomfortable.

Luckily, the following day their expressions had dulled as he'd used their hours together to review the first two books. The second day they'd read some more, and more, and more. Boredom had crept over their faces as they'd realized this was all stuff they— other, more distant descendants of the Keepers of the Grail—knew.

By the third day they'd realized what Reign was already well aware of—he doesn't know shit about the Grail. In fact, they probably know more about the mythical artifact than he does.

That's when they started asking questions with a vengeance.

Seiko leans forward, brushing her black waterfall of hair back over her shoulder. "Surely you have some idea where the Grail might be."

"Yeah," says Laila, "You're the Grail Keeper, after all."

"It's why we came here," huffs Simon, crossing his arms and leaning them on the table.

Reign glances at the others, seeing if they have something to say. Tariq, the tallest and oldest, simply sits silently, his eyelids hooded as if he's hiding his true thoughts. Or he's barely awake. He spent most of the three days like that. Bryn moves the sucker in her mouth from one cheek to the other, sitting on the edge of her seat as if something awesome is going to happen any second. She's also spent most of the three days like that.

"If I knew where the Grail is, we wouldn't be sitting around this table, having this chat, now would we?" says Reign, trying not to grit his teeth. "Now, as I was reading from this fascinating book on the Knights Templar, once strongly linked with the Keepers of the Grail—"

"We want to know about the Grail," Seiko says, her black brows crimping with impatience.

"Yeah," says Laila, and Reign wonders if she'll back Seiko up every time she says something. "We should be out looking for it. That's what Grail Keepers do, isn't it?"

Reign pulls in a slow, steady breath. "There are others out searching for the Grail as we speak," he says, hoping to get them off his back.

"Ooh, who?" asks Bryn, her butt barely making contact with the chair anymore.

"Mac, my best friend, Gabby, Arielle's cousin, and Sierra, her mom. Last I heard they're in Rome."

Tariq's brows compress half an inch, but he doesn't say anything. Seiko and Laila glance at each other.

Unfortunately, it's Simon who decides to voice what they're all obviously thinking. "So, other people are out looking for the Grail, and you're not?"

Reign nods, not backing down from the implication in those words. Going to Rome means leaving Arielle, and he has no intention of doing that. Ever. "Essentially, yes."

"Great Grail Keeper, you are," Simon mutters.

A shimmer of movement flickers in Reign's periphery, but he doesn't move even as he braces himself. He doesn't need another Grail fanatic on his back.

Joseph stops beside him, scowling at Simon. "This one is insolent. I suggest reminding him exactly what happens when someone questions the Keeper of the Grail."

Reign ignores him, even though he's sorely tempted. In fact, if Joseph wasn't a part of his reality, he'd question the whole destiny that's been imposed on him whether he liked it or not.

He pushes to his feet, splaying his hands on the table. "You're welcome to go looking for it. In Rome, Reno, or even the Republic of the Congo for all I care. I'll be here, dealing with the death and destruction being meted out by the Sins."

Simon crosses his arms even tighter. "I just think that if there's a lead, you—we—should be following up on it."

Seiko nods her agreement, Laila quickly joining in. Reign's not sure, but he thinks Tariq's eyelids drop a millimeter. Bryn pulls the sucker out of her mouth, licking the sweetness off her lips as if she's ready to go pack right now.

Joseph scratches his beard. "They are right. You should be seeking the Grail."

"We're not going anywhere," Reign growls, keeping his gaze on the Potentials even though the words are just as much for the man beside him no one else can see. "We don't even know what the Grail looks like!"

"We won't find out sitting here, reading books that we've read a thousand times," Seiko points out.

Joseph draws back a little. "Those tomes have educated Grail Keepers for centuries. Their value should not be underestimated."

Laila flops back into her chair. "We were told we'd be out there, actually looking for the Grail once you came along, oh great Keeper of the Grail."

Joseph frowns as he takes a step forward. "I do not like her tone."

Reign turns his head toward the old man. "You're not helping, Joseph!" He yanks his gaze back to the Potentials, angry that he now not only looks incompetent, but also crazy. "Until a few days ago, most people assumed I was the last of our kind." Including himself. "If we go out there, we risk being caught. What do you think Cain and his demons will do if that happens?" He doesn't mention that Cain recently seemed to actually help him. Reign doesn't trust that demon as far as he can pole drive him into cement.

Simon's eyebrows clench and compress so hard Reign wonders if they're about to pretzel around each other like his arms. "You just don't want to leave your precious girlfriend," he mutters, sneering the last word.

Reign draws in a sharp breath as the words are catapulted at him. More than just words. The truth. He has no intention of leaving Arielle. Especially not when she's admitted she feels the same for him as he does for her. Those sorts of miracles don't happen to guys like him, and he's smart enough to know it. Except remaining here makes him the worst Keeper of the Grail in history. And the Potentials are realizing that.

Anger at the injustice of it all simmers through Reign's

veins. He's finally found something that's been scarce all his life —that illusive, life-changing emotion love—and he's supposed to turn his back on it.

Not. Happening.

He doesn't care what Joseph says. What this room of future Grail Keepers expect. In fact, once they're trained up, *they* can go hunting for the relic themselves. For some reason, that final thought only has the anger flaring hotter. Maybe it's the frustration that he's letting them all down.

Maybe, secretly, he'd always hoped he'd find the Grail himself.

Before Reign can stop it, two lines of fire streak down his shoulder blades. There's an explosion of heat, a rush of power, and two blood-red wings appear in his periphery. It feels good for all of a second, then he registers the horrified—or is that terrified?—expressions of the Potentials.

Simon squeaks and runs, Seiko and Laila right behind him. Tariq shakes his head then stalks after them. He looks the least scared, but still takes a wide berth around Reign as he walks the fastest he's ever seen to the door.

Bryn sighs as she pushes to her feet, popping the sucker out of her mouth.

"FYI, they'll come around a whole lot quicker if you do less of that," she says, waving a finger to indicate Reign's wings.

"You're assuming that's my end game," he snaps, even as he tucks his wings back in. He wants them even less than he does to be the now-appointed leader of Potentials he didn't know existed. Especially if his wings are going to pop out if he gets worked up.

Bryn angles her head, her purple hair tied up in two buns like Mickey Mouse ears. "You know, we've been waiting for you for a long time."

Reign resists the need to wipe his hand down his face. "I never asked for this, Bryn."

She shakes her head. "That's not why I'm telling you. They want to believe in you, Reign." She steps away from the table and heads to the door, stopping to look over her shoulder. "You just need to give them a reason."

Not waiting for an answer, she covers the remaining distance, only to stop when she reaches the door. Reign braces himself, ready for another well-aimed bunch of words, when she steps back to let Arielle through.

His body instantly unwinds. Oxygen reaches his lungs. His heart has room to beat. He watches her walk toward him, everything else forgotten. The corn silk hair brushing past her shoulders. The features that were sculpted by beauty. The eyes that mirror everything he's feeling. He must've been one heck of a person in a past life, because he's not sure he deserves her in this one.

Although that doesn't stop him from opening his arms and hauling Arielle against him. She fits into him like the missing piece of his soul, smiling up at him. "You finished earlier than I expected."

He sighs. "Boring them to death is still taking longer than I was hoping."

She giggles, then presses closer. "Not that I'm complaining. I was hovering." Her eyes light to an electric blue. "I missed you."

Reign's grin is reflexive. "We've been down here an hour."

"And?" Arielle's hands climb up to cup his face. "It was a *really* long hour."

A low groan rumbles up his throat. Admitting the truth and saying those three magic words opened up a world he could only dream of. Arielle, open and affectionate. Arielle, cute and captivating. Arielle, sweet and sensual.

And he can revel in every side of her, never having to hold back.

He grips her face back, vowing to never do that again. He'll give everything to Arielle. His heart. His soul. His life. Her eyes flutter closed as his mouth descends on hers, her body melting into his in a way that's fast becoming familiar. They kiss, and Reign fills his senses with Arielle. Her smell, feel, taste are his Holy Trinity.

Her hands slip to his shoulders and she tugs herself up, pressing her mouth harder against his. Reign groans again, then willingly leaps into the heat that's climbing up, engulfing them. Their hands move of their own volition, find heated skin beneath shirts, caressing ridges and curves, passion leaving scorching trails.

They pull back simultaneously, sensing they're reaching the point of no return. The chemistry between them has been simmering for a long time now. Once the inferno starts, there'll be no stopping it.

"I love you, Ari," he murmurs, tucking a strand of hair behind her ear.

Her responding smile tugs at his chest. "I love you, too." She glances around the room, her gaze taking on that perceptive edge that still makes him a little nervous. "Now, why did you finish early?"

Reign steps back as he jams his hand through his hair. He promised himself no more hiding. "They want something I don't have, Ari."

"Did you use to say that about me?"

He clamps his mouth shut. That's exactly what he believed —that he couldn't be what Ari needed. And although he's still not sure he can, he's here, giving it a red hot go.

He sighs again. "How do I lead a group of teens barely

younger than me to find an ancient relic that's never been seen?"

Arielle steps in again, slipping her arms around his waist. "I have no idea. But one thing I know about you, Reign, is that you'll find a way. You were chosen for this task for a reason."

The depth of faith in her eyes takes his breath away. But then he narrows his own eyes. "You're not going to suggest I go on a wild Grail chase, too, are you?"

She wrinkles her nose. "Hell no. I want you right here with me." Her face settles into sobering lines. "When everything is so...wrong, this feels right."

Reign pulls her into a hug as if he can protect her from world that's falling apart right now. The layers of Hell are progressively being peeled back.

Two Sins are loose in Mercy City, planning who-knows-what.

And if the remaining three Gates open, Lucifer will be free.

"That's why I'm not going anywhere," he says against her hair. Arielle needs him as much as he needs her.

She pulls back enough to look up at him. "Good." She grins. "Because I want to check out the new bagel place I was telling you about."

His eyebrows shoot up as he grins right back. "Do they do cinnamon and walnut?"

"Yep," she says, clearly pleased he remembered. "I checked their website."

Reign takes her hand and pulls her toward the door. Some time with Arielle, including a bagel or two, and suddenly things feel possible again.

THE BAGEL TEMPLE has an *Opening Day* banner across the front window and Reign glances down at Arielle as he gives her hand a squeeze. "We're here on opening day?"

She shrugs as her blue eyes twinkle. "What are the chances of that?"

He shakes his head, grinning. "My guess is pretty high."

Giggling, Arielle tugs him toward the front door, her anticipation at eating something that would be far better if it were a donut putting a spring in her step. But the giggle dies away as they come closer to the shopfront.

There's no glass in the large windows and the inside of the shop is in chaos.

Reign and Arielle break into a run and as she dashes through the open door and he leaps through the smashed window. Glass crunches beneath their feet as they skid to a halt. Sirens wail somewhere in the distance.

"They're all dead," gasps Arielle.

Bodies are littered around the bagel shop, decorated with a variety of gunshot and stab wounds. Blood pools on the tiled floor, is streaked on the tables, and splattered across what's left of the display case that once housed bagels.

"Here, take it!" screams a voice as a hand darts up and throws a roll of coins at them.

Reign yanks Arielle out of the way and the roll hits a statue of a multi-armed god holding dozens of plastic bagels. The roll breaks open, showering quarters over the dead bodies beside it.

"It's all I have," the man shrieks. "I swear!"

"We don't mean any harm," Reign says calmly, even as he makes sure they keep their distance. "We just came for a bagel."

The top of a balding head appears near the cash register. "That's what the others said."

Arielle smiles gently. "We won't hurt you." She angles her

head as the sirens become louder. "And it sounds like the police are on their way."

The man stands, pushing round-rimmed spectacles up his nose. One lens is cracked. "Too late now," he mutters. "They took everything."

"Who did this?" Reign asks as he glances at Arielle. It's clear what's happened here.

Wrath.

And Greed.

"They were like animals," the man says, swallowing. "No, ravenous beasts. One woman came in, demanding all the bagels, then a kid no older than fourteen grabbed her purse as she pulled it out. Next thing I knew, chaos had broken out."

"I'm so sorry," says Arielle.

The man blinks as if he's still trying to process it all. "It was...awful. Someone said the woman had no right to take all the bagels and jumped her. Someone else shot the kid and took the purse he just stole. Another guy shouted there's more money in the cash register but was stabbed before he could move." He shakes his head. "They became so angry, so quick. And they wanted...everything."

Reign takes Arielle's hand. There's nothing they can do about the massacre that just happened here. "Stay out of sight until the police are here," he tells the man, then looks down at Ari. "We're going to do what we can to stop this."

She nods, face pale but determined.

They leave the bagel shop, the weight of what they have to achieve to uphold that promise leaving them both silent.

End Wrath and Greed.

And find the next Innocent before they release another Sin.

DINAH

Dinah stands outside Veritas Library cloaked in darkness, just the way she prefers it. The black outside matches the blackness within her.

Eldritch, the obsidian hisses. *Endless power. Boundless potential.*

And you are the one who can harness it.

Dinah rubs her forearm absentmindedly, as if she can slow the raw energy coursing through her. The obsidian is exponentially more powerful than she expected, even when she knew it would be a force to be reckoned with. But it's far more compelling than she anticipated. Consuming.

Keeping it under control often has her skin coated in a sheen of sweat and her breaths puffing from exertion. There's one thing it wants.

Eldritch.

The only entity that can match the obsidian is its capacity to wreak chaos and evil.

You're fighting the inevitable.

And it will be the beginning of the end.

Which is also something Dinah has been working toward since the start. She'll give the obsidian what it wants when she knows what she's dealing with.

Her decision hinges on finding out exactly what Eldritch is.

Dinah probes her surroundings with her senses. A truck rumbles down the street at the other end of the block. A rat scurries along the wall behind her, its heartbeat leaping when it discovers it's darker in this spot beneath the tree for a reason. Evil is lurking.

But apart from that, there's nothing. Dinah studies the door to the library, nothing but an old, rusted entrance to an abandoned building. Nim had worked late, which was annoying, but she left almost an hour ago. There's been no movement since.

Moving silently, Dinah makes her way toward the entrance. Even the extensive library of the Tenth Legion didn't have much information on Eldritch. Definitely not anything she didn't know already—a dark power that countless have thirsted for over the centuries. She needs to know how to control it. Just like she does the obsidian.

A low chuckle ripples through her psyche.

Your control is an illusion.

You'll learn that soon enough.

Dinah ignores it, even as sweat beads on her upper lip. She wipes it away impatiently. She's strong. She wouldn't have taken the obsidian from Arielle if she wasn't.

A quick wave of her hand over the door and it opens soundlessly. She'd expected stronger magic, but maybe her own has grown far stronger thanks to the obsidian. Either way, Dinah enters and closes it behind her. Veritas is the only place she knows that could give her the information she seeks.

Inside, muted light gently tumbles from the chandeliers, giving the library a warm, welcoming feeling. Dinah's lip curls in satisfaction. This is going to be far easier than she'd expected. She closes her eyes, connecting with the magic that imbues the air. It instantly swells, the expansion inflaming the obsidian.

Yes, it hisses. *More.*

Dinah tries to push away its greedy malevolence, wanting to focus on finding the right book. But the obsidian continues to rush to the forefront, as if Dinah poses no contest. Her brow furrows. She can't lose control. Not here.

"Hello, Dinah."

Her eyes fly open, quickly glancing down to find she's not

alone. Nim angles her head, her hands holding the wheels of her wheelchair as if she's ready to steamroll her.

Almost glad for the interruption, Dinah crosses her arms. "I saw you leave."

Nim rolls her eyes. "I thought you of all people would know nothing is as it seems. Veritas has more than one entrance." She rolls forward an inch. "And I sensed the obsidian the moment I stepped out."

"Actually, I'm glad you're here." Dinah hardens her features. "Take me to the books on Eldritch."

"You don't want those."

Dinah takes a threatening step forward. "Yes, I do. And believe me, it's in your best interest to take me to them."

"Eldritch is even more powerful than the obsidian, Dinah. You have no idea what you're messing with."

"Exactly," she snaps. "It's the only thing both angels and demons fear." It's the only way to stop the war that's coming.

Nim shakes her head. "Except it can't be controlled."

We can.

"*I'll* find a way," Dinah snarls, emphasizing the first word just as much for herself as for Nim.

Pity, maybe disgust, fills Nim's eyes. "You're a fool. And if you think I'm going to—"

Dinah moves faster than even she expects. She grips the arms of Nim's wheelchair and leans over the seer ominously. "Take me to a book on Eldritch," she growls. "Now."

Hurt her! Make her tell you!

Dinah's hands tremble as she holds on so tight her knuckles go white. She knows her eyes are as black as the entity she's carrying. She can feel it. When the obsidian is this close to the surface, it ices her veins and fires her magic. The power is raw. Breathtaking. And terrifying.

Nim's smart enough to realize she won't stand a chance

because she shrinks back into her chair. "Fine," she says in a small voice. "I'll show you."

Dinah presses her face close, breathing in the seer's fear. "No tricks or you'll regret it."

And we will revel in it.

Nim glares at her sourly. "I won't. I have too much to live for."

Dinah steps back and Nim yanks her wheelchair away. With a sharp turn, she heads to the rear of the library. They pass a dozen towering mahogany shelves but Nim doesn't slow.

"If you try anything, I won't even attempt to control the obsidian," Dinah warns, conscious they're heading further into the bowels of Veritas.

Blood, it pants hungrily. *Pain.*

Nim snorts softly even though she doesn't look over her shoulder. "The fact you think you have it under control is the height of ignorance."

"You're still alive, aren't you?"

Nim ducks her head as if she's trying to make herself small again, once more smart enough to shut up. She passes more bookshelves, and although they look the same, Dinah can sense their content is...darker. The shadows are deeper, seeming to cling to the leather-bound tomes with more determination. The shift in energy calls to the obsidian and Dinah realizes she's the one panting now, and not with exertion.

The hunger belongs to her.

Or does she belong to the obsidian?

Before the disturbing thought can spark any more terror, Nim takes a sharp right down a row of shelves. She stops only a few feet in, then flicks her hand. A book floats down, large and dark brown, a skull embossed on the cover. It descends and Nim turns to face Dinah, the book remaining in front of her.

"The Book of Monsters," she says somberly. "It has everything you need to know."

Dinah extends her hands, a frantic bead of sweat zigzagging down her spine. Yet her mouth is dry. Her skin feels hot.

The Book of Monsters floats toward her, only to stop midair. Dinah scowls at Nim. "Release it."

"You don't want to do this," Nim says, her gaze intense.

"Yes, I really do," Dinah grinds out.

She's doing this so she can learn how to control Eldritch and the obsidian.

She's doing this to prevent an apocalyptic war between angels and demons.

Nim sighs and releases her hold on the book. It continues its slow flight to Dinah, the pages fluttering impatiently. The Book of Monsters wants to share its dark secrets as much as she wants to read them.

It opens like a ghostly flower as it nears Dinah, the thick vellum pages rustling softly. Bold, black writing decorates the pages, strange-looking illustrations flicking past too fast for her to understand what they are. Finally, it settles about half-way open, and these pages are all black. Dinah steps forward, drawn to the color that now taints her soul.

Get away! the obsidian screams. *Run!*

But it's too late.

There's a rushing pull, like the power of the tide has been compressed into a split second.

And Dinah's sucked into the Book of Monsters.

CHAPTER 2

ARIELLE

Arielle can feel herself being carried, and the sensation is heavenly. She snuggles deeper into the warm chest and the strong arms around her tighten. She feels protected. Cherished. Loved.

And the fact she can feel that way after what she and Reign saw this afternoon is a testament to the power of their love.

After they'd returned to the farmhouse, Arielle hadn't been able to chase the images from her mind. Almost a dozen people had killed each other, driven by pure anger and greed. The deaths were brutal and swift...and bloody.

After informing Marlowe and Rachel of what they'd seen, and the agreement that the Knights Templar would be on the lookout for the Sins, it was Reign's suggestion that they watch some trashy TV while eating ice cream, and Arielle had welcomed it. They'd curled up on the couch, and although she couldn't focus on the TV, she felt safe. Protected.

She must've fallen asleep because the next thing she knows, Arielle's being carried to bed. She breathes in a contented breath, drawing Reign's scent deep into her lungs. A part of her wants to turn her head and nuzzle the throat that's only a few inches away. The other part of her refuses to move, just wanting to soak up the moment. There's only one thing for certain right now.

More trouble is coming to add to the already overwhelming tasks before them.

They reach her room too soon because then Arielle's being carefully placed down on her bed. Her head sinks into the pillow as her duvet is tucked around her shoulders. Reign presses a soft kiss to her forehead and her heart simultaneously swells and constricts. Could this guy be any more perfect for her?

She wraps a hand around his wrist, keeping her eyes closed as sleep tugs at her, wanting to drag her deeper into its depths. All she needs now is for Reign to curl around her and for his soothing heartbeat to be what counts out the seconds to oblivion.

But then he's pulling away. Walking away. Opening and closing the door almost silently.

Arielle's brow furrows. He just left.

Taking the warm, achingly beautiful feeling with him.

She sits up, her frown deepening. "Does he have to be so freaking noble?" she mutters. For a guy who thinks he's bad to the core, he sure doesn't act it. In fact, every night he's insisted they sleep in separate rooms. Something about wanting to take it slow. Arielle waits for a few minutes, hoping he might come back. He doesn't.

"Take it slow, my ass," she grumbles as she pushes the duvet aside. "Worst idea ever."

She and Reign have spent too much time apart as it is. Plus, she's wasted enough time regretting not telling him how she felt, she's not going to regret slowing things down, too. She loves Reign. She wants him. And he's not here. It's time to rectify that.

Arielle pads down the hallway, trying to keep her footsteps silent. Rachel's light is off, as is Marlowe's in the room adjacent to hers. Arielle rolls her eyes. She doubts those two are apart. They were far smarter in admitting how they feel about each other. There's no way they've relegated themselves to separate beds.

Arielle reaches Reign's door and hesitates, wondering if she should knock. What if he's in the shower? Or getting changed? Or already asleep, stretched out in bed, shirtless...

Each one of those images has her turning the knob, not caring about caution. She's more than ready to take their relationship to the next level. She peeks inside, noting the soft glow coming from the lamp on the other side of the room that she hadn't noticed underneath the door. Then she sees Reign.

He stops halfway across the room, still towel drying his hair from the shower. All he's wearing are a pair of low-slung tracksuit pants. "Ari?" he asks, looking delicious and concerned. "Is everything okay?"

She slips inside and closes the door. "No. It's really not."

Reign throws the towel aside as he stalks toward her. "What is it?"

Arielle's breath stutters in her chest, making it hard to talk for long seconds. Reign's muscled chest is only a couple of feet away, the low light sculpting the ridges and valleys. She's never seen anything so mouthwateringly beautiful.

He takes her shoulders. "Ari?" Now he sounds worried.

She holds his gaze. "I don't want to sleep alone."

Reign's breath exhales in a whoosh. His hands slip away from her shoulders but Arielle steps forward, pressing her palms on the warm skin of his chest, not wanting to lose contact. He freezes. "I don't think that's a good idea."

"It's the best idea," she shoots back.

"Ari," he says, his voice sounding strained. "If we spend the night together, I can't just...sleep. And I don't want to pressure you."

Slowly, enjoying every inch of skin she touches, Arielle moves her hands up Reign's chest to his shoulders. She molds her palms to the chords of his neck, her fingers brushing strands of damp hair. "I'm pretty sure I'm the one pressuring you right now." She mock frowns. "Because you keep running away."

A groan rumbles through Reign. "Ari...there's so much going on, and I want you to be sure."

"And I appreciate that," she murmurs, pushing up so their mouths are only inches apart. "When everything is so unsure, this is one thing I've never been more sure of. I want you, Reign. In every way."

This groan is deeper. One that seems to vibrate right through her. One that rockets the heated pool low in her belly straight up to molten. Reign's hands spear into her hair as his lips crash down on hers. Arielle opens her mouth, just as hungry and urgent. They kiss, no devour, each other, hands already restlessly moving.

Arielle skims her palms over Reign's chest, roaming down his corrugated stomach, then around to the muscles of his back as they flex. He's so smooth. Hard. Scorchingly hot. She can't get enough, can't keep still. She wants to touch him everywhere, commit these ridges and dips to her memory, sear them alongside everything she knows about this amazing man.

A moan climbs up her throat, the sound husky yet primal. She meant what she said. She wants Reign.

In every way.

Reign's mouth tears from hers, trailing fiery kisses down her throat. Arielle's head tips back in heady pleasure. His hands bunch the material of her tank top at her waist, something rippling through his body. One last ditch effort at self-control?

Or preparing to remove the annoying barrier that clothes have become?

Yes! Her heart shouts the word. Her body screams it. Her soul demands it.

A knock on Reign's door has them both stilling, their panting breaths filling the silent room. "Ignore it," Arielle whispers.

But the knock comes again, louder and more insistent. Reign heaves a frustrated sigh then steps back. "We can't," he says, regret making his voice rough. "It could be important."

Sins.

Innocents.

Gates of Hell.

And that's just the beginning of what they're facing. New Grail Keepers. Dinah possessed by the obsidian. The threat of Eldritch. An apocalypse breathing down their neck. Arielle also sighs as she crosses her arms. The ones that feel empty without Reign.

Running a hand through his mussed hair, he walks to the door, opens it, then looks down. "Nim?"

She doesn't wait for an invite, simply wheels forward, forcing Reign to step back. "Sorry. I know I'm interrupting."

Arielle flushes. This is her mother's best friend, and she was doing her darndest to seduce Reign. "We were just talking."

Nim arches a wry brow. "The spirits were worried they were going to combust."

"They were watching?" Arielle squeaks.

Nim snorts. "They have better things to do, but they said the temperature spike in the room just about blistered them."

Reign walks over to a chair and picks up a t-shirt to put on. "What's up, Nim?"

She winks at Arielle once Reign's chiseled chest is out of view. "That's disappointing isn't it?"

Arielle isn't sure whether to laugh or flush with mortification again. Nim is practically an aunt to her, and her pointing out Reign's hotness is weird. Or maybe it's because flashes of how that chest felt are searing her palms... Arielle clears her throat. "You wouldn't be here if it wasn't important."

Nim's playful expression falls away. "Yeah, it's important. Dinah came to Veritas."

Reign's whole demeanor hardens. "Did she hurt you? Where is she now?"

"I'm fine," says Nim. Her lips tip up. "I've trapped her in the Book of Monsters."

"Seems fitting," says Reign dryly.

Arielle frowns. "Tell us what happened."

"She came looking for information on Eldritch," says Nim, adjusting her wheelchair so she's facing both of them. "The obsidian wants it. So I gave her the book, and it trapped her inside. She needs to learn exactly how dangerous Eldritch is."

"And this will do it?" Arielle asks.

"It will. The Book of Monsters chronicles the history of every terrible fate man has endured. It's the only way she'll see that Eldritch can't be released."

Arielle nods. "That's good," she says, hoping it doesn't sound like she's trying to convince herself. "Well done."

Reign steps closer. "What's up?"

She sits on the edge of the bed, no longer surprised by his perceptiveness. "It's a good thing, really."

Even Nim must pick on something, because she angles her head. "But?"

Arielle sighs, knowing she's being selfish. Dinah being trapped somewhere where she can learn the truth of Eldritch is definitely a good thing. Arielle knows, she's lived with the obsidian inside of her, too. It twists everything in its thirst for power. "It's just that she's the only one who knows the truth about my father."

Nim picks up her dog tags and presses them against her lip, suddenly looking thoughtful. Almost straight away, she looks up, her face hardening as if she just made a decision. "I can tell you about him."

"You can?" Arielle blinks, trying to confirm she heard right.

"I always wanted Sierra to tell you the truth, but she was adamant you should be protected from it." Nim's dark gaze sharpens. "I suspect you already have your suspicions."

Arielle nods slowly. "I know he's connected to Xeven somehow."

"You know it's more than that," Nim says gently. "Deep down, you've figured out Xeven is your father. His true name is Ryder."

"Xeven?" Reign asks, shocked. "Are you sure?"

Nim nods. "Very. But he's been under the influence of Cain since before you were born, Ari. Those things he's done, they weren't his choice."

Ari studies the floor, conscious that Reign comes to sit beside her. Her father's name is Ryder. And Cain stole him from her.

She looks up at Nim. "How do I free him?"

He deserves to be reunited with her mother.

She deserves to know her father.

Nim shakes her head sadly. "I don't know, Ari. All I do know is that whatever magic Caine is using, it's powerful." She frowns a little, then digs into the pocket of her army pants. "And that it might have to do with this note that fell from Dinah's pocket just before she was sucked into the Book of Monsters."

Nim holds it out and Arielle walks to her, taking it. She unfolds the piece of paper, noting how worn it is, the folds deeply creased. All it holds are a few confusing words, but ones Arielle knows are the answer she's been looking for.

The Hell Masks are the key.

RACHEL

Rachel stares at the ceiling of her bedroom, realizing sleep isn't going to come anytime soon. She huffs out a breath, fluffing her bangs out of her face, but they just drop down again, annoying her. Shoving them out of her face, she sits up, pushing away the covers. Sitting up, she glances at the door that leads to Marlowe's room, but quickly changes her mind. He works so hard, taking care of everyone. Leading the Knights Templar, helping Arielle and Reign, looking after her.

A smile ghosts over Rachel's lips.

He does all of those with his trademark exceptionalism, and it touches her heart deeper and deeper every day. He's attentive. Affectionate. Always there when she needs him. He was the one who broke Wrath's hold on her, replacing anger with love. She owes him everything. Her life. Her heart. Her hope.

Poor guy doesn't need her crawling all over him in the middle of the night. Especially when the one line he's drawn is how far their relationship goes physically. Turns out Marlowe is a Knight to the core. No premarital hanky-panky for him.

The least she can do is let him sleep in peace, even if there's nothing more she'd like to do is see how hard it would be to break that golden rule.

Rachel sighs, picking up the photo of her parents sitting on her bedside table. That still leaves her with the question that's taken root and won't go away. She runs her finger over her father's laughing features, then her mother's softly smiling ones. The image was taken when Rachel was a baby, back when her parents were still together. Before the fact they're both Innocents tore them apart.

Before their hidden angelic truth had them killed.

The familiar twist of grief has tears stinging Rachel's eyes, but that's not what's keeping her awake. The weight of loss is one she'll always carry. No, it's the knowledge that angel ancestry runs through her own veins that won't leave her alone. Her conversation with Marlowe is stuck in a loop in her head.

"Reign's just discovered he's far more than he ever imagined," he'd said, his blue eyes twinkling with certainty. "Just like you are."

"Me?"

"Yes, you. The daughter of two Innocents." He'd arched a blond brow. "Which makes you an angel."

An angel. How can she be an angel? Rachel glances over her shoulder, almost as if she expects white wings to sprout out. But there's nothing there. Just like she can feel nothing inside of her. No power. No proof that she's anything more than human.

Picking up her cell phone, she taps on the screen with no real idea what she's going to do. It's not like there's anyone she can call at this time of the night. Suddenly, an idea has her straightening. It's a long shot, but that's never stopped her.

Scrolling through the names, Rachel finds the one she's looking for. With a quick tap of her thumb, she calls Gabby. Arielle's cousin has barely been in contact since she left to search for the Grail, largely because reception is terrible in the strange corners of the globe the quest is taking her. But she's an angel. The only person who might be able to give Rachel answers.

The phone rings once. Twice. Then three times. Rachel tries to tell herself she's not disappointed. The chances of Gabby picking up were slim at best. Maybe she can see if there's some other random angel hanging around—

"Rachel? Is everything okay?"

A smile flashes across her face. "Hey, Gabby. Everything's fine. I didn't actually think I'd get hold of you."

"Reception is patchy, but it seems this call was meant to be. What's up?"

Rachel considers making small talk, maybe checking in on how Gabby's search is going, but she decides to get straight to the point. This call could drop out at any moment. "I need to ask," she says, adjusting herself to sit more squarely on the bed as if she's bracing herself. "Could you feel that you were an angel? Did some part of you know?"

There's crackly silence for a few moments. "I did, but I didn't want to face it. I'd been doing things that weren't possible for a human from a young age."

"Oh." Rachel's spine curves, not sure why she's disappointed.

"But then again, I was a full angel and I didn't know that until Mom was killed because she's an Innocent."

Which makes Gabby the daughter of an archangel and an Innocent. Rachel sighs. "If I'm the daughter of two Innocents, what does that make me?"

"I'm not sure," Gabby says carefully. "It's possible that you have Grace within you, just like your parents did. And that it's dormant for you, too."

Her father never knew he was an Innocent. Her mother didn't realize until she was married and had a child.

"So it may never express itself?" Rachel asks. Several of the Innocents have lived in ignorance of their heritage.

"Maybe," Gabby says gently. "Although if there's Grace within you, it'll come out when it's ready. Believe me, I know."

"Okay, thanks Gabby." Rachel tries to infuse her tone with

gratitude, but she's pretty sure she fails. If she did become a full-blown angel, maybe she could save future Innocents. Not keep failing like and having to watch others die as another Sin is unleashed on the world.

"Focus on what you can do, Rach. That's where your power is."

The line cuts out and Rachel hangs up, staring at her screen until it turns black. She's not sure if she has answers or not. Or maybe she does, and she just doesn't like them. It's possible she's an angel, but she won't find out unless the Grace within her decides to make its presence known. And it may never.

Essentially leaving Rachel a human.

"Which is what I've been all my life," she says to herself. "Which is what Arielle is, too."

And although Rachel carries the guilt of all the Innocents they've failed to save, Marlowe would point out they're part of the team that killed two Sins already.

Gabby's right. Rachel may not have powers or wings, but she has brains and technology. She picks up her laptop and opens it.

It's time to find the next Innocent.

CHAPTER 3
REIGN

"**G**o," Reign says, giving Arielle a gentle push toward the door of the farmhouse. "There's nothing we can do until there's a sighting of a Sin or Rachel tracks down the next Innocent."

Arielle chews her lip as she turns toward him. "I don't know. I think I should stay here."

Reign rolls his eyes. He's spent the morning convincing her to go to Veritas to research how to free her father, and it looks like they're going to have to go through it all again.

He grips her shoulders and turns her back to the door. "Get whatever books you can find with a vague mention of Hell Masks then bring them back and add them to the stacks of books already filling up this place." He presses a kiss to her temple. "Now, go. The sooner you leave, the sooner you'll be back."

Arielle spins around, clasps him and a quick hug. "Thank you," she says softly. "I love you."

"I love you, too," he murmurs. "Stay safe."

She pulls back, smiling even as her eyes shine with emotion.

"Hell yeah, I will." She leans in, dropping her voice. "We have unfinished business."

With a delicate blush and a flicker of lashes, she's gone, leaving Reign trying to find his breath again. Arielle coming to his room last night was like a dream come true, quite literally. His nights have been filled with images of him finding all the ways he can make her gasp like she did before Nim interrupted them. Turns out, Arielle wants this, too. And he's not strong enough to turn her away.

No more waiting. No more holding back.

It's time for Arielle to know without a doubt that she's everything to him.

Reign closes the door, sighing as he realizes it's time to go teach the Potentials again. That is, if they even turn up. They've been avoiding him since his demon wings popped out yesterday. It's clear they don't think much of him as the Keeper of the Grail and their appointed leader.

All because he refuses to leave Arielle's side.

He flexes his shoulders, trying to loosen the instant tightness as he makes his way across to the kitchen. Maybe his whole life was a preparation for letting them down, because he doesn't intend on doing anything else but remain with Arielle.

His phone chimes as he's about to pass the marble bench and he stops to pull it out, the frowns. It's a message from one of the Knights Templar. *Sin sighted.* Along with a location.

Spinning on his heel, Reign turns around and heads straight back for the door. He won't tell Ari about this. There's no point in her witnessing what they saw at the bagel shop again. Not when there's nothing they can do.

He's just reached the door when Bryn's voice reaches him.

"Where are you going?" she asks. "We have class."

Reign turns, preparing himself. "It's been canceled. A Sin has been sighted."

To his surprise, Bryn tosses her blue hair over her shoulder and strides toward him. "I'm coming with you."

She stops beside him, one eyebrow raised in challenge. But Reign has no intention of arguing. He doesn't have time. Plus, it might be good for one of the Potentials to see exactly what they're up against. Then they might start to understand why he won't—can't—leave. This isn't just about Arielle. This is about the people of Mercy City.

The location turns out to be one of Mercy City's few casinos. The way there is dotted with the remnants of Wrath's rampage. Buildings and cars and trash piles in varying stages of singed to burned out, broken street signs, benches, cement, the odd flapping length of police tape. It makes the trip to the casino a subdued one. The trail of devastation is something Reign can't stop looking at, even as he wants to look away.

Hugging the outskirts of the city, the neon signs advertising roulette and poker only highlight the cracked white paint and the fact people have used the fake pot plants out the front as ashtrays. The two floors above are a cheap hotel for those who want to drink and gamble then disappear into oblivion, the white paint progressively peeling to reveal sooty gray concrete the higher the building goes.

As Reign climbs out of his car, he notes the place is quiet.

Bryn angles her head. "Too quiet?"

"Yeah," he says, noting the unbroken front windows, but that the front sliding doors are stuck on open. "Too quiet. Stay alert."

"There goes the nap in the backseat," she says dryly.

Shooting her a glance, Reign leads the way, approaching the casino cautiously. "Greed might still be here."

Because he has no doubt that's the Sin who's been here. A casino is prime picking to feed an out of control thirst for money. The sign saying *99c Shrimp Cocktails* wouldn't have helped, either.

Reign pauses at the open doors, listening, but it's still eerily quiet. Shouldn't there be some music? Slot machines chiming or something? He steps through into a foyer with faded green carpet and trashy gilded columns looking as if they're the only thing holding up the ceiling. Still nothing.

With a short hand movement, he indicates for Bryn to keep moving forward. A tall archway with a flashing *Win Here* sign above it leads to the casino playing area ahead. Muscles coiled and ready, Reign makes his way toward it. Within a few feet he smells two things.

Blood. And sulfur.

"Demons," he mutters.

Bryn wrinkles her nose. "FYI, you don't smell like that."

Reign doesn't glance back, nor does he point out he's the only demon he knows with red wings. At least he doesn't smell like burnt matches crossed with charred eggs.

One more step forward and any other thoughts are halted in their tracks. A hand is wrapped around the base of the arch. A bloodied hand. One attached to a dead body.

The woman stares at them with sightless eyes, her face frozen in a snarl.

Bryn draws in a sharp breath as she stops behind Reign. "Brace yourself," he says roughly, already knowing what they're about to walk into.

The casino widens out, garish light exposing what it now holds. Overturned slot machines. Scattered cards. Broken chairs. And everywhere there's blood, chaos. Death. Bodies are lying on the floor, over broken tables, one leaning against a gaudy column, looking as if he was trying to use a roulette wheel for protection.

Once again, they're too late.

"Now do you see why?" Reign chokes out. "This is what the Sins are wreaking on Mercy City. These people did this to each other."

Bryn drags her gaze away from a man and a woman in matching plaid shirts who have their hands wrapped around each other's throats. Although the wounds to their heads appear to be what killed them, they didn't let it stop them from trying to strangle their partner. "I'm starting to get an idea," she says hoarsely.

"I need to check for survivors," Reign says. There's no sound of sirens yet, which means no help on the horizon. "You can wait in the car if you like."

"If you can do it, so can I, Grail Keeper," she responds resolutely.

He's about to argue, but changes his mind. He wanted Bryn to see this, and although this massacre is even worse than the bagel shop, she wants to stay. He can respect her for that.

They make their way through the death and destruction, avoiding pools of blood or looking too closely at still-open eyes or still-seeping wounds. People killed each other with whatever was handy, a gun, a chair leg, the glass from a shrimp cocktail. It makes for a gruesome scene.

But they don't find anyone alive. Greed, possibly Wrath, too, have been thorough. Reign looks at Bryn across the room, noting she looks as green as he's feeling. The need to get out of here and breathe fresh air again is overwhelming. He's about to suggest they get the hell out of here when a movement in his periphery catches his attention. He spins, wondering if some crazed human was still hiding.

Cain arches a brow, but it's not just his appearance that's surprising. It's the fact he can see straight through him. "Hello, Reign. I hope you're looking after my Mark."

Reign turns away. Hallucinating Joseph of Arimathea is

more than enough right now. But Cain appears in front of him. "I'm dead, by the way. Abel finally got his revenge." He glances down at Reign's arm. "That's why you have it."

As if on cue, the Mark heats up, feeling like it's branding Reign's skin. "Get away from me," he hisses, stepping around him.

But Cain once more appears in front of him. "It's in your best interests to listen to me. The Mark is dangerous. It's what brought out your suppressed demon qualities."

Determined to get back to Bryn and to get the hell out of here, Reign doesn't even bother going around Cain this time. He steps right through him, an instinctive ripple of goosebumps crawling over his skin.

"The Mark is powerful, and dark," Cain warns from behind him. "If you don't listen, Reign, you'll become the very thing you hate."

Reign spins around, two scorching lines spearing down his shoulder blades. He clenches his fists, trying to get the anger under control. "I will never be like you," he growls.

Cain opens his arm. "And you think I chose this?"

Before Reign can respond, a scream rips through the air. He turns back, already running as another cry erupts from Bryn. She's holding a chair out in front of her as a large man swipes a blade back and forth erratically.

"It's mine!" he shouts. "All mine!"

"You can have it, you crazy asshole," she shouts back, swinging the chair in a wide arc.

It smashes across the man's chest, but the only acknowledgement is a brief shake of his head. Then he's moving again. Lurching at Bryn. Jabbing the knife.

"No!" shouts Reign, his wings erupting as he covers the distance between them.

But even with flight, he doesn't get there in time. The man

slams the knife into Bryn's shoulder, pushing it to the hilt. He yanks it out, wrenching a cry from her, then brings it down, ready to do it all over again.

Reign reaches them before the knife can slice Bryn again. He shoves the man away, grunting at the brute strength vibrating through him. Judging by the mottled red of his face, it's fueled by rage. The man stumbles then rights himself, now slashing wildly at Reign. He leaps, using his wings to gain extra height, sailing over the knife and powering his knee into the man's nose. His head snaps backward, his body going instantly limp as if a rope was just severed. He drops to the ground, probably dead.

But Reign doesn't have time to check. He pushes away the searing flush of guilt. Bryn staggers backward, her hand covering the wound at her shoulder. Blood oozes from between her fingers, bright and copious. Reign catches her before she collapses, carrying her to a nearby lounge, brushing away the cards and poker chips with his boot.

Bryn grimaces as he puts her down. She tries to adjust herself, but the grimace deepens. "Okay, so this hurts. Like, a lot."

"We need to get you to a hospital," Reign says tensely. "I'm calling 911."

She bites her lip. "I'll just lie here and wait."

Glad she still has her sharp sense of humor, Reign pulls out his cell and dials, impatiently waiting for the efficient voice saying "911, what's your emergency?" To his shock, he gets a recorded response asking him to hold the line for the next available responder. He yanks the cell back to glare at it. Since when did 911 have an answering machine?

An uneasy feeling coils in this gut as he hangs up, opening the app that Marlowe installed on it, then returning it to his ear.

The radio frequency that the emergency services share crackles into his ear.

"Disturbance at City Mall. Send all available cars."

"Gunshots reported at Meyer and Dawes Law Firm."

"Mercy City Hospital at capacity. Send Level 1 patients only. Repeat. Life-threatening injuries only."

Reign's frown deepens as he realizes why 911 isn't able to take calls. They're being overwhelmed. The next crackly voice has him freezing.

"Riot on Wells Street."

The casino is on Wells street.

"Reign? I don't suppose you have any Advil on you? Maybe some morphine?"

He turns back to Bryn, his mind working overtime as he tries to figure out what to do next. "Keep up the pressure on the wound." He tries for an encouraging smile. "You're doing great."

She glares at him. "I'll feel great when I get some serious opioids in my system."

Ones that aren't coming any time soon.

A crash from the archway has him spinning around. A voice carries through the blood-soaked casino.

"He's in here!" screeches a woman. "The guy who stabbed my husband just cause he won big in blackjack!"

Knowing there's no time to explain, Reign scoops Bryn up. "What the—" Her words are cut off by a hiss of pain as he breaks into a run, heading to the double doors he sees at the back of the room. Spinning so his back barrels them open, Reign finds they're in a corridor. Stairs are to his right, another set of double doors that say *Staff Only* to his left. Making another snap decision, he goes left, once more barreling through the door.

Reign finds himself in a large, industrial kitchen. "Bryn," he says, looking around, trying to figure out what their next move should be. He glances down when she doesn't answer, discovering she's unconscious, either from blood loss or pain. Or both. "Shit."

Sweeping a nearby bench clear of metal bowls, he carefully places her down, wincing at the clanging and banging. Finding a nearby stack of clean tea-towels he presses one to the wound at her shoulder. Blood is already trickling onto the bench.

Voices reach him from within the casino. "Let's clean this place out!" someone screams.

"They've got to be hiding their money somewhere!" shouts another.

Adrenaline pumping through his veins, Reign pushes a glass fridge in front of the doors. Then another table. Then some sort of giant mixing machine. He steps back, realizing there's a screen above the door projecting the hallway on the other side of the doors. Probably so servers don't run into each other as they come in and out. But now, they show him who he's just barricaded himself against.

A mob of people rush into the corridor. One is carrying a street sign. Another a shotgun. They're all carrying the rage of Wrath on their faces.

One of them tries the doors to the kitchen. "They're locked!"

"Let's try the stairs!"

The mob go right and scramble up the stairs, shoving each other hard enough that someone falls down with a cry. Someone else tramples over them, uncaring that they fall silent.

Reign takes a step backward as if he can put distance between himself and the situation he's found himself in. He returns to Bryn's side, putting pressure on the tea-towel, registering that it's now blood soaked.

He needs help.

And it has to get here before the mob decides the kitchen is worth breaking into, no matter what.

DINAH

Dinah spins one way, then the other. "Nim!" she screams, furious. "Get me out of here!"

But silence is all that greets her. Silence and darkness.

Hands fisted at her sides, Dinah stops, realizing something else. The obsidian is quiet. There's a stillness inside of her she hadn't appreciated until it was gone. What's more, the relief is overwhelming.

"Hello, Dinah."

Startled and ready to fight, she spins back around to find a young woman standing a few feet away. Outlined by soft, white light, she's small, with pale blonde hair in a short pixie cut framing her pretty features..

She smiles. "I've been waiting for you."

"Stay away from me," Dinah snarls. She's in the Book of Monsters. There's no way that angelic looking girl isn't a threat. Except all that surrounds her is endless black. There's nowhere to run to, nowhere to hide.

"My name is Emma," says the woman. "And I'm here to give you what you seek."

Dinah watches her suspiciously. "Which is?"

"To know about Eldritch, of course."

"Thanks, but I'd prefer to read it for myself. I don't need to experience it, nor do I need some real-life narrator." She should never have trusted Nim.

Emma walks, more like floats, closer. "I'm more of a guide."

"I don't need one of those eith—"

Emma clicks her fingers, and their surroundings flicker, as if a page was just turned. Dinah quickly registers the vast expanse of blue ocean in front of them, gentle waves lapping just beyond the reach of her feet. A seagull caws somewhere high above.

"What am I here for?"

But then she sees it. A massive island out on the horizon, almost as beautiful as the city sprawled across it. Bright white, it practically sparkles in the sunlight, a fascinating mix of ancient Greek coliseums and futuristic curves and spires. Thick columns hold up arches and bridges, while rounded domes and graceful towers look as if they're trying to touch the sky.

"The city of Atlantis," Emma says.

"So it's beautiful," Dinah snaps. "We both know it's heading for the bottom of the sea. So what?"

"Yes, it is beautiful, isn't it?" Emma doesn't take her gaze off the sight of the pearly city. "It's why it sank that is of importance."

Emma clicks her fingers again, and this time, there's even the rustle of paper. Dinah finds herself flying across the water at an alarming speed. Frustrated that she has no choice but to endure this, she crosses her arms. Ahead, a mermaid leaps from the crystal blue water, arcs, and dives back in, scattering diamond droplets into the air. The scene is so idyllic, it almost makes Dinah wince. This civilization had a long way to fall, literally and metaphorically.

They rush at Atlantis, now weaving amongst the soaring arches and emerald gardens and serene vistas. Dinah realizes the island is circular, and so is the city, a grand temple in the center. And that temple is where they're heading. They land on shiny marble and glide through more arches, past ornate columns, straight into the inner sanctum at the center. A priest wearing purple robes is standing in front of a stone table. On it, lies a girl. Dead.

"She was sacrificed," says Emma. "One of many."

"What for?" Dinah finds herself asking before she can stop

herself. A heavy feeling in her gut tells her she can already guess.

"Why else?" Emma asks as the priest raises his arms and throws his head back. "For power."

Suddenly, a sound like thunder, but a thousandfold louder, booms. The earth beneath them shudders. The marble cracks. Screams tear the air.

"I don't want to see this," Dinah says through gritted teeth. This part has been documented in more than just the Book of Monsters—Atlantis ends up at the bottom of the ocean.

"He caused more than just the sinking of Atlantis," Emma continues, ignoring Dinah. "The priest used ancient spells, primordial spells from the time of Gaia and the universe's creation. It created a breach between what scientists of today would call matter and antimatter. The impact was catastrophic."

The screams increase, clawing at the air and drenched with terror. A flash of something has Dinah spinning around, although the being moves too fast, the flash of blood-stained claws, inky tentacles, and gaping, ravenous mouths is enough to send a shudder rippling down her spine.

"Untold horrors were released onto the world," Emma says gravely.

Eldritch.

Dinah raises her chin. "But they were trapped."

Emma inclines her head. "Yes, they were," she murmurs, clicking her finger again.

The page turns, and a circle of Greek Gods appear, standing around the same stone table, but everything is different. They're underwater, for starters, their hair and clothes swirling around them even though they stand stoic and silent.

"The Titans closed the breach. They weren't able to stop

Atlantis from sinking, but they could save it by relegating the city to a pocket dimension. One that was hidden from the rest of the world, but safe. The priest was cursed to a painful existence by creating a separate dimension called Purgatory, which is now his eternal prison." Emma indicates toward the stone table. On it is sitting a silver box. "And yes, Eldritch was contained."

The box that would become Pandora's.

Dinah mentally shakes off the melancholy of the scenes she just witnessed. "Sure, it's a sad story. And it explains how Pandora's Box came about. But I'm not here for a history lesson." She's here to learn how to control the obsidian.

Emma smiles. "I was told you were stubborn."

That has Dinah tensing. "By whom?"

Emma doesn't respond, instead clicking her fingers again. "This page is found only in the Book of Monsters."

Bright light has Dinah squinting, then raising her arm to shield her eyes. Through the protected slits, she sees a large set of white wings. "An angel," Dinah growls. What are those meddlesome beings doing here?

"An archangel, to be precise," Emma says. "He watched the whole thing."

The archangel hovers mid-air, his back to them, then lifts his hand. Black, inky smoke writhes around his fingers, fangs and scales and sinews flashing in its depths, as if it's trying to form into something. The archangel catches it in his palm then clenches his hand so tightly that veins and tendons ripple across his skin. His aura brightens and pulses, his arm trembling with the force.

"What is he doing?" Dinah asks, not sure she wants the answer.

Emma doesn't respond. The archangel opens his hand, then lifts the object now sitting in his palm. He raises it, as if to glory in what he just forged. A small, unevenly shaped piece of death-colored stone.

The obsidian was just created.

Dinah blinks, processing what she just saw. The obsidian is part of Eldritch. No wonder it wants to reunite with it so badly. This is the edge she could use to control it.

She turns to Emma. "Tell me more."

CHAPTER 4
ARIELLE

Arielle taps her fingers on the steering wheel as she sits outside Veritas Library. The old, abandoned storefront stares back at her, providing as many answers as her mind.

With everything that's going on, should she be here? Is it even possible to save her father?

What if it's too late? What if Cain's influence has corrupted her father beyond repair? It's been almost twenty years of control and manipulation. And her father has committed some horrible deeds during that time... Something spasms in her chest as at the thought. A person can't do those sorts of things without it staining their soul.

But how can she not try? Her mother hasn't stopped loving him. Believing he'd return. Turns out, he was never far away.

Yet, the Sins... The Gates. Shouldn't that be her focus right now?

Arielle's phone rings, jolting her out of the endless merry-go-round that her mind has become, Reign's name flashing on the screen. "Hey," she says warmly. He's the one that insisted she take some time to do this. "I'm just outside Veritas."

"Ari, Bryn's been hurt. I'm trying to get a hold of Marlowe, but—"

She's already turning the keys in the ignition. "Where are you?"

"The casino, but we're surrounded by rioters. You can't come without a few Knight Templars."

"Marlowe's not answering?" she asks, jamming the car into gear. There's no way she's sitting here, waiting.

"I only tried once. We also need a medic."

That has Arielle frowning. Bryn's injury must be significant. "I'll keep trying," she says, navigating her way out onto the main road that leads to Mercy City's center. "Just hold on."

"Are you driving?" Reign asks, a frown obvious in his voice.

"Of course, I'm driving."

"There are angry, greedy people everywhere, Ari. You can't come on your own."

She rolls her eyes. "Would you come on your own?"

Silence is her answer, telling her she's made her point. "I can't bear the thought of you getting hurt," he says with a quiet intensity.

Arielle's heart almost aches, it feels so full. "I feel the same." She takes a right at a set of lights. "Which means we'll always have each other's backs."

There's a soft sigh on the other end of the line. "We're in the kitchen of the casino. There's a back door, but I've barricaded it. Knock five times when you get here and I'll let you in."

"I'm sure Marlowe won't be far behind," she assures him.

Hanging up, Arielle focuses on getting to the casino as quickly as she can as she dials Marlowe's number. It's around the next corner that she discovers neither of those are going to be as straightforward as she'd like. Marlowe doesn't answer. And traffic slows as it banks up, although she can't see far ahead enough to know why. When the sounds of sirens reach her, the sinking feeling in her gut only drops lower. This isn't peak hour. The riots are more widespread than the casino.

Ahead, the traffic comes to a standstill.

Arielle's cell rings and she quickly picks it up through the car's speaker. "Marlowe?" she asks, hoping she's right.

"Sorry, Ari," he says. "I was training with the Knights. What's up?"

"Reign's trapped in the casino with an injured Bryn. Can you send someone?"

"They're on their way," he responds instantly. "And I'll send Pan, he's one of my best medics."

The knots of tension in her stomach unwind a little. "Thanks. I'm on my way there now."

"They should be right behind you."

Arielle hangs up with another genuine "thanks," then focuses on how to get to the casino. The road ahead is a gridlock of cars. There's no way to turn around and the only place she can see to turn off is an alleyway up ahead. Although it's only two car lengths away, it may as well be a mile seeing as she's not moving. Plus no one has turned down it, suggesting it's blocked. Arielle's hands clench the steering wheel. Does she run the remaining blocks to the casino? Somehow, the thought of losing the protection of her car makes her uneasy. And what if Bryn needs a way to be transported?

The SUV in front of Arielle honks loud and long, then the driver of the hatchback in front of it shoves an arm out and flicks the bird. The next honk lasts long enough that Arielle screws up her face at the obnoxious sound. It stretches her nerves taught.

Suddenly, the SUV revs its engine and nudges forward. The arm juts back out of the hatchback, aggressively waving a fist. The SUV's engine roars even louder as it rams the hatchback, shoving it into the car in front of it. A Mercedes.

The driver of the Mercedes shoves her head out and screams obscenities, but that just seems to anger the SUV driver more. It launches forward with more force, this time ramming the hatchback hard enough that it twists sideways before slamming into the Mercedes. The crumpling sound of metal can be heard over the blaring of more horns.

The Mercedes door flies open and the driver climbs out, her face clouded with fury. "What the fuck is your problem?" she screams, kicking the hatchback.

"Don't get pissed with him, bitch," the SUV driver screams back. "I'm the one you want!"

As the woman marches toward the SUV, Arielle realizes their anger has created an opening. The SUV shoved the hatchback, leaving a narrow gap leading to the alleyway. Arielle jams the car into gear and hits the gas. The three divers who looked ready to brawl spin around at the sound of another engine. Ignoring their furious faces, Arielle swerves around the SUV, driving fast despite the close confines.

Bryn's life may depend on this.

The hatchback driver's head snaps toward the alleyway, realizing what Arielle's intent is. "Oh no you don't!" he shouts, running toward it.

Gripping the steering wheel and locking her arms, Arielle doesn't allow herself to slow down. She can't. It's the only way to get there before the guy does. Pressing her foot down on the gas, she pretends she's Rachel and the rules of physics don't apply when she's behind the wheel. The car accelerates.

The man's brows shoot up when he realizes she's not stopping. Then he puts his head down and runs faster.

"Please, please, please," Arielle mutters as they both beeline for the alley.

She reaches it a second before he does and yanks the steering wheel down. The car careens right, for a split-second spinning out of control. The man's eyes widen as he quickly changes trajectory, now running for the protection of a nearby bus shelter.

Arielle yanks at the steering wheel, scenes of the car continuing to spin and crashing into the wall, possibly taking the man with her, flashing through her mind. But the wheels gain traction again and the car straightens, jerks too far the other way as she over-corrects, then straightens as Arielle does. She finds herself in the alleyway, now faced with a double wire gate.

Pressing her foot back on the gas, Arielle considers closing her eyes as she powers toward them. There's a thud. A crash then a scream of tearing metal and the gates are ripped off the brick wall they were attached to. One flies over the top of the car, the other slams into the wall and ricochets back. Arielle swerves as it lands on the bonnet and bounces over the roof. She instinctively ducks, but there's no more bangs or clashes. She's through.

Taking a left at the end of the alleyway, she finds herself back out into flowing traffic, breathing hard. Not giving herself time to think of the series of narrow misses, she focuses on getting to the casino. To Reign. And Bryn.

It still takes longer than she'd like. The moment she sees a series of brake lights ahead, Arielle takes a turn, opting for the narrower, less frequented side roads. It means a sinuous, indirect trip to the casino, but she gets there eventually, in one piece, without killing anyone, and still in possession of her car.

The front doors of the casino are gaping holes, the neon signs hang from wires, and large plant pots are overturned and smashed. Arielle drives around the back, her stomach tight. If there are rioters there, she's not sure how she'll get in.

But the rear is as empty of people as the front is. Arielle parks beside a loading dock and rushes to a metal door that she hopes leads to the kitchen. She knocks five times and waits.

Precious seconds pass but she doesn't hear anything. Glancing over her shoulder, she pulls out her cell phone. She'll have to talk quietly but hopefully Reign will hear her. She can't afford to bring attention to herself standing here.

A scraping on the other side has her straightening. Then the door's opening and a muscled arm streaks out and yanks her in. She tumbles into Reign's arms, gasping with relief. He somehow manages to hold her tightly against his chest as he closes the door. Allowing herself a second to revel in the contact, she pulls away so they can both shove the metal lockers back across the door.

Reign grabs her hand. "Quick. I can't leave Bryn alone."

He pulls Arielle through the industrial corridor and the moment it opens out to a large kitchen, she suppresses a gasp. Bryn is lying on a metal table, blood-soaked tea towels scattered around her. Reign rushes over and presses a folded one against her shoulder. "She's been unconscious for a while now," he says tensely. "Did you get a hold of Marlowe?"

Arielle rushes closer, wishing there was something she could do to help. She's never felt more human. "He's sending some Knights and his best medic." She glances up at Reign. "But the roads coming into the city are gridlocked."

His lips thin even as he looks unsurprised. "Did you park close by?"

"I did." She glances at Bryn, chest constricting at the thought of moving her when she's already lost so much blood. "And I couldn't see anyone around."

A thud echoes above them and Reign's lips become a tight line. "That's because they're inside."

Another crash sounds to Arielle's left and she sees two doors, more metal furniture stacked against them. A gritty screen above shows someone dart past, carrying a television. Arielle moves closer to Bryn, registering that Reign's strapped up her wound with what looks like the contents of a first-aid kit. It'll have to do. They can't stay here.

Reign moves to the other side of the table, and Arielle can see the weight of his Grail Keeper responsibilities weighing on him as he squeezes Bryn's hand. A Potential was hurt on his watch. "If I carry her, do you think you can move the lockers and get us to the car?"

Arielle nods resolutely. She'll have to.

Reign's face is pulled into tight lines as he prepares to lift Bryn. Just slipping his arms under her has her moaning in distress. But before he can pick her up, a louder crash sound from beyond the door. A closer one.

They violently rattle, knocking the table and refrigerator leaning against. "The doors are locked!" someone shouts.

"That means there's something good in there!"

Arielle and Reign glance at each other. They've run out of time.

Before either of them can speak, there's a similar thundering from the back door. A moment later, a methodical thudding sounds.

"They're trying to break it down," Arielle gasps.

"Change of plans," Reign grinds out. He comes around the table and glances around. Opening and closing a couple of drawers, he finds what he's looking for. His face grim, he holds up a large knife and a cleaver. "We have to protect Bryn."

Swallowing, Arielle takes the knife, the weight in her palm making her feel sick, even as she knows Reign's right. The mob beyond the doors are rabid with fury and greed. They're going to need to defend themselves and Bryn.

They stand back to back, ready for when one of the doors finally caves in. "I can't let anything happen to her, Ari," Reign says in a low voice.

Arielle's heart cracks. He wants so bad to be a good Keeper

of the Grail. A leader. Yet he takes responsibility when things go wrong, and refuses to claim when things go right. She lifts the knife a little higher, the knowledge there's nothing she won't do for Reign settling in her chest.

"We'll do this together," she promises him.

Suddenly, the double doors crash open, scattering the furniture that was barricading it like it belongs in a dollhouse. Reigns spins around, coming to stand beside Arielle so they can face the first onslaught. Arielle blinks in surprise. Relief is an instant rush.

Alexandra stands in the doorway, bodies scattered around her. She strides in. "I heard you needed help." She scans the room and registers Bryn on the table. "What happened?"

Reign joins her beside the table, looking pained. "She was stabbed by a rioter. She's lost a lot of blood."

Alexandra's silver-gray eyes turn assessing as she scans Bryn's inert form. "I've learned some healing skills at demigod camp. I can at least take away her pain."

Her hands skim over the blood-soaked bandages as her brow pinches. Arielle holds her breath as Alexandra closes her eyes, her lips moving silently. Within seconds, color slowly suffuses Bryn's face. Her body unwinds as pain releases its grip.

Alexandra steps back, her arms dropping as if they're suddenly heavy. "I've done all I can."

Reign checks under the bandages and his shoulders sag with relief. "The wound isn't completely healed, but it's closed over. We should be able to move her now without doing more damage."

"Thank you," Arielle says, her own relief rushing out on a huff.

"I would've come sooner." Alexandra's gaze flickers. "But the spirit world is becoming restless. An ancient, dark power has been awakened in Purgatory."

"Of course it has," Reign mutters.

Arielle goes still. "Because of the obsidian, isn't it? That's what woke it up."

Alexandra nods grimly. "Yes, because of the obsidian."

"I should never have touched it," Arielle whispers.

"I've told you, it was drawn to you," says Alexandra. "I doubt anyone could've resisted its call."

Arielle looks away, still not convinced by that explanation. There's nothing special about her for the obsidian to be drawn to. And all she had to do was not touch the black stone.

Reign wraps his fingers through hers. "If I'm not allowed to regret decisions when I didn't know any better, neither are you."

She gives him a wan smile. How can she ever show this guy that although he's not perfect, he's perfect for her?

Alexandra picks up the knife Arielle put down, flicking it several times as if she's carried it all her life. "We need to get to the farmhouse."

Reign glances at the scattered bodies beyond the door. Faint sounds of more ransacking carries through the open space. He reaches down and picks up Bryn's limp body. "Then we need to stop the Sins."

Arielle's lips twist as they make their way to the back door. If they're going to list everything on their to-do list, then they've left something off.

They need to find the next Innocent.

RACHEL

Rachel taps on the screen of her laptop, frowning. "Surely not..." she murmurs to herself. But more tapping reveals the same outcome.

A sound has her looking up from where she's curled up on the couch in the den. Marlowe enters, his golden waves darkened with sweat and his shirt molded to his chest. The sight has her mouth going instantly dry. The guy is downright delicious.

"I just heard from Arielle and Reign," he says, his somber tone cooling her heated thoughts. "They were trapped at the casino by rioters. Bryn's been injured."

Rachel doesn't move, but every muscle coils, ready to go. "And?"

"Alexandra turned up just in time. She's also healed Bryn enough so they can move her. They're on their way here."

"That's good," Rachel says, unwinding a little. "Well, as good as it can get," she adds dryly.

Marlowe perches on the sofa beside her, his handsome face looking as unruffled as usual. "We'll win this. I know we will."

She almost shakes her head at his undying optimism. Especially when she's about to feed it. "I've found the next Innocent," she says, pushing the laptop toward him.

He takes it, looking far less surprised than she's feeling. "I knew you would."

Rachel leans in, pointing at the image on the screen. "After I made sure the rootkit Quan had implanted is definitely gone, I ran the algorithm three times."

"Dr. Renata Melendez," he reads aloud. "A doctor at Mercy City General Hospital."

"What's the bet she was Shell's or my mother's physician?" Rachel says, trying not to get excited. "We need to pay her a visit."

Marlowe passes her the laptop back and picks up his own tablet. "Let me see which ward she works on."

Rachel waits as he taps away, a small furrow forming between his brows that she can't help but notice is rather cute. This nephilim has layers of adorable that she's relishing as she discovers each one. She resists the urge to touch him, anywhere, everywhere, conscious this is important. And she has no doubt Marlowe will find out where Dr. Mendelez is. Nowhere is safe from his hacking ability.

He looks up a few minutes later, but the frown hasn't gone. "She's not in Mercy City."

"What?" Rachel gasps, sitting up so she can see his screen. "Where is she?"

"On medical duty with Doctors Without Borders," he says heavily. "In Kabul. Afghanistan."

Rachel's spine curls as she sinks back into the couch. "Well that's freaking great."

Marlowe pushes to his feet. "I need to go talk to her. It'll be faster."

Rachel slowly does the same, knowing he's right but not liking it. Nephilim can blink all over the globe in the same way angels can. Marlowe could be in Kabul before she or anyone else could check where their passports are.

Her hands float to rest on his chest. "Stay safe," she says, hating the vulnerability that's crept into her voice. Losing both her parents has undermined any certainty this world used to hold.

"I will always come back to you, Rachel," Marlowe vows, cupping her face with tender hands. "No matter what."

"You'd better," she whispers. "I need you, Marlowe."

He presses an achingly sweet kiss on her lips as if he's sealing the promise. She melts into him, clings to him. Wishes she could take this kiss to the next level in the hope she can convince him to stay.

Marlowe pulls back, his blue eyes twinkling as if he can guess where her thoughts are heading. "I'll be back as soon as I can."

Rachel sighs and steps back. "Preferably before that."

Marlowe steps away, smiling a little even as she catches a glimpse that this is just as hard for him in the depths of his beautiful eyes. "I love you."

Her heart swells and compresses all at once. "I love you more," she says, her own smile climbing up. Then she reaches out and playfully slaps his butt, wanting to give him the same joy he brings her. "Now go get me an Innocent."

CHAPTER 5
REIGN

Reign stands at the end of Bryn's bed, staring hard as if that alone can speed up the healing. Propped up on pillows, she's deeply asleep, just like Marlowe's medic, Pen, had predicted. He said Alexandra's healing had closed the wound well and now all they had to do was the one thing Reign's not so good at.

Wait.

Bryn lets out a soft sigh, the white bandage wrapped around her shoulder peeking above the sheets then sinking back down out of view. She looks...peaceful. Probably the most relaxed he's ever seen her.

Or maybe he's just trying to find some way that this is okay.

Sighing, Reign turns away. Some leader he is. The first time he takes a Potential out and she's seriously injured. In part because he's a Grail Keeper with demon blood. And a Mark.

He glances down at his forearm, his jaw tensing at the sight of the L-shaped brand with two small dots tucked inside it. He wouldn't have been distracted if Cain hadn't turned up, saying words that tugged at his deepest fear.

If you don't listen, Reign, you'll become the very thing you hate.

The same denial he'd voiced at the time roars through his mind. He will *never* be like Cain. Yet Cain's response, both sad and yet defiant, slice through it as effectively as when he'd said them the first time.

And you think I chose this?

How the hell did he end up with it, anyway? And why? And where the fuck did this demon heritage come from? All questions that have been demanding answers he doesn't have. He's an orphan, with no way of knowing his roots. Reign rubs his fingers over the Mark, the familiar self-loathing corroding at his insides. There's only one person who keeps it at bay, and right now Arielle is talking to Rachel after she pulled her aside the moment they returned.

The door to Bryn's bedroom opens and Reign drops his arm, wondering if it's time to start wearing long-sleeved shirts. When he sees who enters, he wishes he already was.

Simon storms in with such force that he has to push his glasses up. "What happened?" He gasps when he sees Bryn in the bed. "What did you do?"

Reign straightens slowly, hating the guilt that flashes through him. "We were investigating the Sins when she was attacked. She's going to be fine."

Laila and Seiko enter next, both paling when they see Bryn. Tariq isn't far behind, his low-level frown sinking into a mid-level scowl.

"She was stabbed," Reign says, hiding his wince. "But she's been healed. She just needs some rest and she'll be fine."

"Poor Bryn," murmurs Laila.

"Yeah, poor Bryn," echoes Seiko.

Tariq's gaze falls on Reign. "This is because of the Sins?"

"Of course it's because of the Sins," Simon explodes. "Because Bryn was trying to do the right thing and helped Reign. Rather than what we're supposed to be doing."

"Keep your voice down," Reign warns. "And we're supposed to protect people, which is exactly what we were trying to do."

Simon's mouth twists. "We're supposed to be finding the Grail."

Reign takes a step closer to the surly young man. "Isn't that the whole point of the Grail? To protect humankind?"

Simon's mouth snaps shut. Then twists. He looks like a surly toddler. "I'm going to go read the books again."

Reign bites back a good-luck-with-that retort. By the time they find the Grail, Mercy City will be ruined. Countless lives will be lost.

Laila and Seiko glance at each other and then follow Simon out. Tariq spends long seconds gazing at Bryn, his face as unreadable as always. "She believes in you," he says quietly, almost to himself. Then, without looking at Reign, he leaves, too.

Reign's shoulders sag. Yes, Bryn believes in him. And look where that got her.

Wondering where Ari is, he turns toward the door just as his cell rings. Frowning, he registers a silent number. No phone call from one of those has ever been good, and telemarketers or bearers of bad news share the number-one slot on his list.

"Hello?" Reign answers, bracing himself.

"Hello, Reign."

"Colt?" he asks in surprise.

"Yes, it's me. Everything's fine," he assures. "I heard you recently had some news."

Reign sighs. "Turns out we have more in common than we thought," he mutters. Turns out they're both demons.

Colt chuckles. "I'm not sure who's happier at that news, you or I."

"Although my wings are red," says Reign. Like blood. "Yours are black." Like every other demon.

"So? My hair is red, yours is black," Colt responds. "What's your point?"

Reign huffs out a grudging half-laugh. "If only it were that simple."

"The way I see it, it is," says Colt, his voice deepening as if he just got his serious pants on. "The Grail Keepers need a leader, Reign."

"I'm well aware of that," he grinds out. "But they also need someone who can do it."

"What they need is someone who believes they can do it."

Silence stretches out over heart beats as Colt's words crawl through Reign's mind, looking for a way in. They don't succeed.

And somehow, Colt senses it. "You wouldn't be here if others didn't believe you could, Reign. Arielle does. Rachel does. Marlowe. Gabby. Even Dinah has worked with you, and she wouldn't do that if she didn't believe it was going to ensure she wins."

Reign's teeth are set on edge at the mention of the traitorous witch's name, but he finds himself listening to Coal's words.

"And personally, I don't think being a demon is so bad," Colt adds, humor lightening it tone. "It might give you an edge? Maybe it doesn't matter. What does, is you doing your part to stop this."

Reign lets out a long breath. "I'm trying, Colt. I really am."

"And every success we've had, you've been part of."

Reign pauses again, realizing Colt's words are no longer bouncing off his defenses. They're sinking in, almost seeming to make sense. "Is this a demon thing?" he asks. "Being able to sense when another needs a pep talk?"

Colt chuckles. "No. I've just learned that defining ourselves too narrowly is a mistake."

Because he's a demon. And Gabby is an angel. A union that

should be impossible, yet Reign's never seen two people more devoted to each other. Seems they decided that labels wouldn't get in the way of what they wanted. What their heart believed is right.

But then something strikes him. If this is another "go get the Grail, big boy" talk... "I'm not leaving Mercy City," Reign growls. "I'm staying here with Ari, taking down the Sins and protecting the remaining Innocents."

"That sounds like a Keeper of the Grail speaking. Like *the* Keeper of the Grail speaking."

Reign glances at Bryn. Is it possible he's doing the right thing? That his gut is right?

"Thanks, Colt," he says quietly.

"We need to win this, Reign," he says, his voice low again. "And that means playing your part. Talk soon."

He hangs up, leaving Reign to stare at the screen until it turns black. He's been willing to play his part. Determined to, in fact. The drive comes to him as naturally as loving Arielle.

It's just that he's not too sure what his part is.

The door opens again and Reign tenses, hoping it's not the Potentials again. He's had enough of the what-the-fuck-is-my-role-in-all-this rollercoaster. But it's not Simon or the others. It's Arielle.

And the moment he sees her, the storm in his mind eases. Calms. In fact, sweet sunshine pierces the doubt, chasing it away. With this girl is where he's supposed to be. Protecting her. Loving her.

"Hey," she says, keeping her voice down as she glances at Bryn. "Can you talk? It's about the next Innocent."

Reign jams his phone back in his pocket. "What's up?" The tension in Arielle's face is clear, but he's not sure if it's a good tense or a we-have-a-situation tense.

"I've been speaking to Rachel," says Arielle as he

approaches, closing the door behind him. "She's found the next Innocent."

"And?"

"Marlowe went after her." Arielle's lips flutter, an almost smile, but not quite. "But there's been an issue."

DINAH

A blink is all it takes and Dinah finds herself somewhere familiar. She executes a slow turn while Emma watches her.

"The Crossroads," she asks, noting the barren road they're standing on diverging ahead. "What are we doing here?"

Emma clasps her hands together, managing to look regal despite her height. "As you know, the Crossroads are the pathways between dimensions."

"Yep," says Dinah. "We don't need to go over that."

"What you don't know," says Emma, unaffected by Dinah's brusque tone. "Is it's far more than that."

Considering what Emma's already shown Dinah about the sinking of Atlantis and the release of Eldritch, oh, and its link to the obsidian, Dinah stands and waits. In fact, she braces herself.

"Back when the world was first created, massive amounts of quantum energy was released, creating negative quantum energy at the same time."

"For every action, there is an equal and opposite reaction."

Emma smiles a little. "Something like that. Balance must be maintained for the universe to exist."

Dinah glances around. "And what does this mean for the Crossroads," she asks, even as she knows this is much bigger than these dimensional intersections.

"It means an inverse Crossroads exists, where the negative

energy is stored."

"There's a mirror world," Dinah breathes.

Emma nods. "Yes. We live in the world of light, but there is also a world of dark."

"And that's where Eldritch resides."

She nods again. "The two worlds are linked by the Crossroads. A conduit of sorts."

"Conduit?" Dinah asks, not liking the sound of that.

"Yeah. As you know, dreamscapes also exist within the Crossroads, which is why a person can have good dreams and bad dreams. A nightmare happens when the dark energy seeps into an individual dreamscape."

Dinah looks around again, suddenly feeling like she's standing on a precipice. The dark world of antimatter is far closer than she'd like it to be. "Eldritch isn't far away, is it?"

"Eldritch is the name given to the dark matter. And when it becomes sentient, it creates Eldritch monsters."

Or Eldritch horrors, Dinah thinks, although she doesn't say it.

"They used to terrorize the world back in the time of faeries. It was the Titans who sent them to the dark realm and created the Crossroads." Emma inclines her head. "Well, the inverse Crossroads, too. Everything that exists here, exists there."

But twisted by darkness.

"So that's where the Eldritch monsters are?" Dinah asks. "The inverse Crossroads?"

Emma smiles as if she's pleased that Dinah's such a fast learner. "And that's where we're going next."

Dinah opens her mouth to object as an emotion she hasn't felt often freezes her veins—fear.

But the Crossroads disappear.

And are quickly replaced by their dark reflection in the antiverse.

CHAPTER 6

ARIELLE

Arielle leads Reign to the den, wishing there was time to talk. She'd expected him to join her by now, but he spent longer in Bryn's room than she'd expected. It makes her uneasy. Arielle knows he feels responsible for Bryn's injury. And she knows he worries he's not the right person to lead the Grail Keepers.

When it's as sure as her next heartbeat that he is, demon or not.

Yet, what does that mean for them? He now has a team to lead. And a Grail to find...

They reach the den where they find Rachel pacing. She looks up. "Bryn?"

"Is going to be fine," Reign assures her. "She just needs some rest."

"Good," she says, relieved. "We can focus on the Innocent."

Reign glances between the two of them. "You've found them?"

"Rachel has," says Arielle, watching him closely. "With her algorithm."

"Once I cleaned it up after Quan messed with it," Rachel

adds bitterly. "But yes, I've identified Dr. Renata Melendez as our next Innocent."

Reign nods, even though it's clear the name means nothing to him. "She's obviously linked to one of the other Innocents?"

Rachel glances at Arielle so she can answer. "Renata knew my Aunt Shell," Arielle says, pretending the tightness in her chest isn't growing. "I've met her myself."

Reign's brows hike up a notch. "You have?"

"Yeah. A few years ago now." Arielle moves away, understanding Rachel's need to pace, even if it's for a different reason. Rachel's worried about Marlowe as he goes looking for Renata.

Arielle's worried she and Reign are about to be as separated as they are.

"I was home sick," she says, pushing her hair out of her face even though it's not really bothering her. "We'd all been sick, actually. The flu. And Renata popped in to check on us."

Reign's gone still and Arielle wonders if he's picking up on her tension. Most likely. She takes an extra second drawing in the next breath, trying to calm herself down. Maybe she's wrong...

"Anyway, I was in bed and Renata had left my room after telling me to keep up the fluids and suggesting some zinc supplements." She smiles a little at the memory. "Actually, I got a whole lecture on how zinc helps the immune system fight off invading bacteria and viruses. Oh, and the body also needs zinc to make proteins and DNA."

"Thanks for the info," Reign says wryly.

Arielle's smile broadens. "I know. Renata was a woman of science. And I only remember her telling me that because of what happened next. She had a conversation with Shell outside my closed door. I knew at the time it was odd. Now I know it was significant."

Rachel sits down on the nearest chair. "Significant how?"

"Renata was telling Shell about a friend of theirs who she was worried about. A friend called Evelyn."

Rachel stills at the mention of her mother's name. "Renata also knew her?"

"It appears so. And Renata was worried about Evelyn because she'd started to research the occult. She believed angels exist."

Arielle remembers how she'd lain in bed, wide-eyes blinking as she'd pulled the covers up a little higher. It had definitely sounded like this Evelyn woman had gone off the deep end. It was Renata's next words that had cemented the memory in her mind.

"And Evelyn believes we're angels, too."

What had even been weirder was that Shell hadn't instantly shut it down. All of Arielle's life her aunt had been dismissive of the supernatural. Of course, now she knows why. They were keeping the secret of Gabby's true nature.

Never realizing Shell was an angel, herself.

Rachel rubs at the edge of her eyebrow. "Mom was trying to convince them. She probably knew danger was looming."

Arielle nods. "I'd say so. But when Shell just murmured something about things happening in this world that we don't understand, Renata scoffed. She said that's why science exists, and she wasn't going to listen to the ramblings of a crazy lady." She sends an apologetic glance Rachel's way. "I got the sense she wasn't planning on talking to Evelyn again anytime soon."

Rachel's lips twist. "Mom said she'd tried warning some others but it didn't work. It's one of the reasons she isolated herself."

And yet both Shell and Evelyn both died, sacrificed so a Gate of Hell could be opened.

Which is what will happen to Renata if they don't stop it.

Rachel pushes to her feet, determination settling over her

features. "We traced Renata to Kabul, Afghanistan," she says, glancing at Reign. "Marlowe's gone to talk to her."

"Which is the problem," says Arielle. "Renata refuses to believe in anything beyond the realms of science. I doubt she's going to listen to Marlowe, someone she doesn't know."

Reign rubs his chin thoughtfully. "What does that mean?"

Arielle hesitates, wishing the answer wasn't already alive in her mind, waiting to be voiced. It's the only way, as much as she wishes it were otherwise.

Rachel pushes to her feet, responding before Arielle gets a chance. "I'm sure Marlowe will work his mag—"

The front door opens, revealing Marlowe himself. Rachel is a blur of movement as she runs and throws herself at him. He catches her with a chuckle that quickly dies as she presses her lips against his.

Reign moves over to Arielle and slips his arm around her waist. "So gross," he says, humor glinting in his eyes.

Rachel pulls back but doesn't unwrap herself from around Marlowe. "If you'd kissed these lips, you wouldn't be able to tear yourself away, either."

Reign chuckles as he pulls Arielle closer. "Noted."

Arielle looks up at him, her gaze dropping to his lips. "Good thing you've never kissed Rachel then," she murmurs quietly. "Because judging by Marlowe's expression, it's a struggle for him, too."

Reign's jungle green eyes heat. "Let's just stick with kissing each other then," he says huskily.

"Deal," Arielle whispers, warmth unfurling in her belly, wishing she could make the most of the promise in his sultry eyes.

Rather than considering what she knows must happen next.

"No Renata?" Rachel asks, and Arielle turns to find her looking over Marlowe's shoulder and through the open door.

He sighs. "No. She laughed in my face the moment I mentioned any whiff of dangers to her life that I couldn't explain." He shrugs. "Short of kidnapping her—and a doctor out there is going to be noticed—I had to leave."

"Arielle thought she might not listen," Rachel says with a frown. "She knew her when she was young. Renata is a stickler for science and hard evidence."

"I've left some Knight Templars to guard her in case the Sins figure out she's the Innocent, too. But we need a plan."

Arielle slips out of Reign's hold, wanting to be able to see his face along with the others. "I need to go see her. I'm the only one she might listen to."

Reign tenses as Marlowe and Rachel glance at each other.

"I think you're right," says Marlowe.

Rachel nods. "Learning she's an Innocent from a stranger was obviously too big an ask. She's more likely to trust you."

Arielle nods, having already come to the same conclusion. Except that means leaving for Kabul, as soon as possible. She looks at Reign, finding him watching her, his handsome face pensive.

"You're going to Afghanistan?"

She nods, a lump lodged in her throat. "I have to."

"Then I'm coming with you."

Arielle blinks, having not expected that response, let alone so quickly. "But the Potentials..."

Reign turns to Marlowe and Rachel. "Will you train them while I'm gone?"

They nod. "Of course," says Marlowe.

Rachel grins. "They'll be able to take down whomever they want by the time you get back."

"Just what Simon needs," Reign mutters.

Arielle clasps his hand, conscious that Simon is the Potential who's been giving Reign the most trouble. "I'll take him down if he keeps going the way he is," she mutters herself.

Reign looks at her, surprised, then pleased. "He has no idea what he's going up against."

Arielle turns to face him and takes his other hand. "Are you sure?" she asks, even though there's nothing she wants more. "Are you sure you want to leave?"

"I go where you go," he says, his green gaze darkening. "Always."

She lets out a long breath as she slips into his arms and holds him tightly. That's exactly what her heart wanted to hear, even as her mind shifts uneasily. Reign is the Keeper of the Grail. He should stay here, with the Potentials. Actually, he should be off searching for the Grail itself.

Yet, he's going to leave for the Middle East. With her.

"Thank you," she breathes, then presses her lips against his. She knows it's supposed to be the wrong thing to do, but being in Reign's arms never stops feeling right. The thought of being away from him has her soul crying out.

It's him.

Arielle almost startles as Trinity's voice slips through her mind. Why in the world is her imaginary friend piping up now? With the same words as the first day Arielle met Reign...

Deciding there's no time to try and understand it, only that those two words hold the ring of truth, Arielle takes a step back, still holding one of Reign's hands. Trinity is obviously her subconscious, maybe even her soul. And she knows just like Arielle does.

Reign belongs with her.

"All booked," chirps Rachel, making them both spin around. She holds up a tablet to show the screen. "Two return tickets to Kabul, Afghanistan."

"Impressive, even for you," says Reign, shaking his head. "When do we leave?"

Rachel grins. "In four hours."

Arielle gasps then turns to Reign. "We need to pack!"

His lips twitch. "It seems we do." Then he sobers. "And then we need to succeed."

Arielle presses her palm to his chest, drawing strength from the steady heartbeats she finds there. He's right. They can't afford to fail.

They need to find the Innocent.

Bring her home.

And this time, keep her alive.

RACHEL

Rachel turns back to the front door of the farmhouse, her smile slipping away now that the taxi carrying Reign and Arielle is out of sight. Marlowe told them exactly where Renata is, so finding her won't be an issue.

It's bringing her back, alive, that will be.

But if there are two people who can do it, it's Arielle and Reign. Straightening her shoulders, Rachel makes her way through to the kitchen, following the sound of grunts and cries. Unsurprised, she sees the Potentials in the backyard, training with the Knight Templars. Marlowe's taking his promise to Reign as seriously as she intends to.

Rachel slips through the sliding door that leads to the patio as she registers it's only a small group of Knights out here. Two are still in Afghanistan, tailing Renata, but the others must be in the city, searching for sightings of the Sins. She scans the group, only one Knight that she's looking for. Their leader.

She's surprised to find him on the patio, too, standing aside with his cell phone to his ear. And he's frowning.

Rachel moves toward him, knowing it must be serious if his smile is upside down. He sees her coming and lifts an arm and she easily slots in against him.

"Okay, thanks for letting me know," Marlowe says, hanging up a second later.

Slipping her arms around him so she can hold his lean form, Rachel registers how tight his muscles are. "What's up?"

He glances at the Knights as they train the Potentials. "There was another attack in the city."

Rachel's arms tighten. "Wrath and Greed are an awful pairing." Unfettered anger coupled with insatiable selfishness.

Marlowe sighs. "It wasn't the Sins."

"What?" Rachel pulls back to look up at him. "Then who?"

"There was a massacre in an old warehouse on the outskirts of Mercy City," Marlowe says grimly. "But not of humans, but of vampires."

"Isn't that what your Order does?"

Marlowe's face settles into grim lines. "It wasn't one I'd ordered. And the Knights don't kill for the sake of killing. The last thing we need right now is a war with the vampires."

"You've lost me," Rachel says. "If you didn't order the vampire cleanup, who did?"

His gaze falls back on the Knights and Potentials. Simon just got knocked on his ass by Tariq, but he quickly leaps up again, running at him with more scowl than skill. "Zealousness is dangerous," Marlowe says. "Believing anything too strongly blinds a person to other perspectives."

"Why do I get the sense we're not just talking about Simon?"

Marlowe's blue gaze falls back on her, troubled and dark.

"Ever since Kenna died, a rift has been growing in the Order. Felix believes our role is to exterminate vampires."

Rachel's starting to understand the frown. "It's not that simple, is it?" It never is.

He sighs. "No. We don't kill indiscriminately. Angels would like to see nephilim exterminated, just because they see us as a threat."

Her arms instinctively tighten again. Words such as exterminated shouldn't be used in reference to the beautiful soul she's holding. "Then Felix needs a good kick up the sphincter."

Marlowe sighs again. "I can't. He's disappeared, taking the Knights who are loyal to him and his cause."

Rachel's gaze darts back to the Knights. Simon is once again picking himself up from the ground. "That's why there's less of them here."

"Yes. Felix has diminished our numbers."

"I'm going to kick his sphincter so far up, it's going to become his face," Rachel growls darkly. "Making him a sphincter face."

They're outnumbered already, and Felix disappears with a contingent of the Knights? The need to strangle him, shake him, then strangle him some more is pretty darned strong.

Marlowe doesn't say anything and she looks up to find him studying his men. One ducks beneath Tariq's mighty swing, while two more are taking Laila and Seiko through a punch, punch, kick combo, while Simon is having his legs swept out from under him by another, who grins as she does it. Seems more than one person is keen to take Simon down a notch or two.

But Marlowe doesn't smile as he watches. In fact, the edges of his lips turn down. It's one of the first times Rachel's ever seen him worried.

She slips in front of him, breaking his line of vision. "I just thought you should know, you've got this."

Although he doesn't move, she feels his muscles unwind. Rachel steps in closer, wrapping her arms around his neck. "Oh, and you've got me."

"Rachel," he murmurs in a way she's never heard her name spoken.

Tenderly.

Reverently.

Almost like a prayer.

She pushes up and kisses him, sealing the words, making them a vow. "This hot guy told me once that nothing is as it seems, including times like these."

This time, Marlowe smiles, his lips expanding across hers. "He sounds hot *and* wise."

"It's the wise bit that makes him so hot."

Marlowe's arms tighten as he hugs her hard enough to lift her feet off the ground. "Never change, Rachel."

"Never leave me and you've got yourself a deal," she murmurs back.

"I promise."

They kiss again, even ignoring the disgusted groan that comes from Simon. Rachel meant what she said. This is the reason Reign's not here.

Love.

As long as she has Marlowe, anything is possible.

CHAPTER 7
REIGN

Reign's never been beyond the limits of Mercy City. It means that the moment they land in Kabul, the sights and sounds are almost overwhelming. From the dry heat that seems to stick to your lungs along with the dust, to the frantic roads and never-ending shades of sand and stone, he's never seen anything like it.

He'd hate it if it wasn't for Arielle's fascinated delight with every aspect of this strange country.

As they sit in the cab, she grips his hands as she stares out the window. "There are so many people, Reign!"

All wearing some version of a flowing robe in every color of the sun, although black and white seem to be the staples. The women keep their dark gazes averted, their faces cloaked in more material, while the men glare as their cab passes, many of them clasping machine guns to their chests.

The city feels alien. And dangerous.

Reign shifts closer to Arielle, wondering yet understanding why someone like Renata would make her way here. Flashes of poverty are everywhere—beggars crouching on streets, mudbrick homes are jammed in between buildings and scattered in the rugged hills surrounding them, and children dart between stalls with dirty clothes and faces. War paints this city wherever he looks, leaving behind countless casualties with its broad strokes.

"Here," says their driver as he pulls outside the hotel, the one word thick and guttural, rattling off the cost of the trip almost too fast for Reign to understand.

Arielle passes him some green and red notes etched with mosques and Arabic writing. The man smiles, his gaze lingering on her hair. "Thank you, beautiful lady."

Reign quickly exits, taking her with him, conscious Ari's one of the handful of women not wearing a headscarf, but also the only blonde one he's seen. "Sure, thanks."

Inside the hotel, they're greeted warmly and lead straight to the top floor and into an opulent apartment. The porter smiles and nods his head, leaving Reign and Arielle to gawk at the rooms Rachel booked for them.

Gilded with warm tones of red and gold, the large living room they're standing in is impressive in size as well as grandeur. Deep burgundy Afghan rugs stretch under heavy cream couches, gold lamps sitting next to each arm creating pools of light and cool shadows. Beyond is one of the biggest beds Reign's ever seen, tasseled red, cream and gold pillows scattered artfully along the dark timber headboard.

Arielle moves to a nearby table with a large fruit basket on it. An embossed folder sits beside it and she opens it. "Twenty-four-hour room service, day spa, and two restaurants." She picks an envelope and spills the contents into her hand, her smile growing. She holds up a set of car keys. "Hire car," she says, eyebrows raised. "Seems Rachel used Marlowe's credit card."

"It appears so," says Reign, a little wide-eyed himself. He knew the nephilim has significant resources at his fingertips, but he didn't realize they were *this* significant. "I mean, we may not even be staying here very long."

What would it be like to take Arielle to dinner? To eat-in while they watched foreign television? To send her off for a facial and massage? Except they're not here on a holiday. It was agreed that once they arrived they'd contact the Knights who are tailing Renata to see where she is, then go see her as soon as they can.

Arielle skips over to him, grasping his hands. "Rachel wanted to spoil us. Marlowe probably, as well."

Reign nods, a little speechless. They've been through so much, and are facing even more, it's nice to know their friends are trying to pamper them, even if it's for less than a day. He leans down and presses his lips to Arielle's, savoring their delicious softness. "I want to be able to spoil you, too."

She smiles against his mouth. "Having you here is what makes this special, Reign. Just being able to hold you is a gift I'm grateful for every day."

He groans, sinking into the beauty that is this girl. He never *ever* wants to let her go. Warmth licks at his skin the moment the contact lasts longer than a heartbeat and he pulls away before it can gain life. The passion he feels for Ari is too close to the surface. Too impatient to be acknowledged.

And right now, they need to find out where Renata is.

"I'll call the number Marlowe gave us," he says to her, then clears his throat of the husky note that crept in.

She sighs. "Yeah. We need to do that."

Reign dials the number as Arielle floats around the large room, running her fingers over polished wood or intricate embroidery. The number rings several times, enough for his brows to cinch in.

"Yes," comes a crackly voice that sounds as if it's not even in this country.

"Guy, it's Reign. We've arrived and checked in."

"Good." Guy's voice is even fainter and Reign pushes his cell phone harder against his ears. "You'll have to hang tight for a bit."

"A bit?" Reign asks, not liking the sound of that.

"Dr. Melendez left for a northern province, a little village outside of Kunduz to be specific, this morning following reports of a skirmish and an injured pregnant woman."

"She what?"

Arielle picks up on the surprise and returns to stand in front of Reign, questions clearly stamped across her face.

"She'll only be gone a couple of days, max," says Guy. "She's planning on transporting the woman back to Kabul for treatment once she's stable."

"So we wait?" Until a pregnant woman is stable following an attack.

"Yep. You don't want to be driving around this place without someone who knows the area." There's a scuffling sound. "Gotta go. I'll be in touch."

The line goes dead and Reign resists the need to rub his temple as he tells Arielle what he just learned.

Arielle returns to the table with the fruit basket and folder, which she opens and flips through. "I'm pretty sure I saw a map in here." She pulls one out triumphantly and walks over to the glass coffee table, pushing aside the vase full of fresh flowers and spreading it out.

Reign joins her and they sit side by side, scanning words that he has no hope of pronouncing. Arielle finds the place quickly, tapping her finger on the dot that represents the city of Kunduz. "This is where she is."

"And we're here," he says, pointing to Kabul several inches down. "A couple of hours drive, at least."

Arielle chews on her lip in thought then glances to afternoon sun through the window. "It will be dark by the time we get there."

"Guy recommended we wait," says Reign, not liking the sound of driving off into the sunset in a country they don't know. "And he's probably right."

"I suppose so," she says, still nibbling on her lip.

Reign thinks of the machine guns and the way the driver of their cab looked as if he was losing the fight to stop himself from touching Arielle's hair. "And I think we should stay inside. Lay low. That way we can be ready when she returns."

Arielle's blue eyes settle on him and he can practically hear the cogs turning in her head. "So, we're stuck here for a couple of days?"

"Seems so."

"Just the two of us."

"Yeah." Reign watches and waits, wondering where she's going with this. "Just the two of us."

As he repeats her words, two things happen. Twin blue flames spark in Arielle's eyes.

And the implication of those words sucker punch him to the gut.

Just.

The.

Two.

Of.

Them.

Arielle pushes to her feet with sinuous grace. "Then I know exactly what would make today perfect."

Reign watches, desire winding his gut tight, as she takes his hand and tugs him until he's standing, too. His breath rasps in his throat. Every nerve ending is coming alive, purely because Arielle's looking at him. Like that.

Tugging on his hand, she leads him to the foot of the bed,

then stops, gazing up at him, her eyes darkening, yet full of blue fire. "Fate has given us this, Reign. I know what I want, the question is, what do you want?"

There's only one answer to that. That's all there's ever been.

"You, Arielle," he breathes. "I want you."

CHAPTER 8
ARIELLE

With those words echoing the truth in her heart, Arielle falls into Reign's arms. There's no more hesitation.

No more excuses.

He crushes her to him, kissing her with all the love and passion that's detonating within her. Except the moment their skin, their hands, their mouths touch, it doubles. Quadruples. Amplifies to infinity.

Becomes the inevitable product of two souls finally being given the freedom to fly.

Arielle clings to Reign, her fingers digging into the muscles of his shoulders. She gasps as her head falls back and his mouth trails hot kisses down her throat. Fire is everywhere. Where his lips caress her skin. Licking at her mind. Deep in her core.

She yanks off his shirt, wanting to feel him everywhere, for him to feel everything she is. The afternoon light gilds his tanned skin, creating shadows in the valleys, and smooth edges over the ridges. Fascinated, Arielle runs her fingers over his shoulders, down his biceps, then trailing over to his chest. Everywhere she glides over is hot, searing her fingertips. She presses her hand against his sternum, wanting more of it. His heart thunders against her palm, and his rapid breaths has her own fluttering. But most of all, she loves the way the fire blazes even hotter.

Her gaze travels further down, to the ridged, flat abs and the top of his jeans. The need to keep touching is overwhelming. The need to see it all is even stronger. Her hand twitches, ready to explore the man who has her heart when Reign's hand shoots up to grab hers, stilling it against his chest.

Arielle glances up, finding him watching her with hooded eyes, his mouth parted as he pants ever so slightly. His eyes are the darkest green she's ever seen, a lush, verdant forest of desire. "We need to slow down," he says huskily.

Her response is to kiss him. Deeply. Thoroughly. She doesn't want slow. Nothing about their relationship has been that. The danger rushing at them has never been that.

She wants Reign.

Now.

Impatient, she pulls off her t-shirt, then wraps her arms around him, pulling him close. The moment their skin touches, they both gasp. She's never felt anything more blisteringly right.

Arielle feels this groan as well as hears it. It rumbles through his chest, the tremors echoing deep within hers. "Arielle."

And then Reign's kissing her as if his next breath depends on it. She takes it, glories in it, and gives every ounce of passion back. Their mouths move hungrily, devouring, starving for more contact. Reign's hands roam up and down her back, unclipping her bra, molding her curves to his hot angles.

"So beautiful," he murmurs reverently.

The words fuel the desire that's a molten pool low in Arielle's belly and she stumbles as her legs give out. She doesn't fight it and falls back on the bed, the need to finally have Reign in bed with her leaving her clinging to him.

He braces his fall with his elbows, never once breaking the hold their lips have on each other. Arielle gasps when his weight finally settles on her, pressing her into the mattress. Reign is delicious and hot and all hers. She spears her fingers into his hair, holding him still so she can kiss deeper even as her own body moves restlessly beneath him. Pleasure explodes like a thousand fireworks everywhere their skin presses, molds, grazes.

Tongues roam. Hands explore. Clothes are cast away, a barrier they resent more with each passing second. Gasps and moans fill the room, the sounds doing what Arielle didn't think was possible—soaring the passion higher.

Suddenly, Reign stops. "Ari," he pants, looking pained. "I haven't brought protection."

Either because there was no time to pack that for this impromptu trip, or because Reign is so damned determined to go *slow*.

She cups his cheek, loving him a little deeper. "I'm on the pill."

She doesn't mention she organized it a couple of weeks ago, knowing this is where their relationship would inevitably blossom to. More like counting down the moments, actually.

"I want to be yours," she says, tugging his face down so their lips hover a breath apart. "I want you to be mine."

Reign murmurs, possibly groans, one word. "Always."

Their joining feels like the stars aligning. Like a nuclear bomb of desire. Arielle and Reign move as one. They kiss with abandon. They hold each other's heated gaze, breathe deep as they taste sweat-slicked skin, moan brokenly when a new hidden place of pleasure is found.

They cry out each other's names as they reach the inevitable peak their love has carried them to.

And then they're collapsing into each other, folding arms and tucking limbs. Reign pulls the covers over their sweat-slicked bodies and Arielle curls into him, her heart still a rodeo in her chest. Resting her head on his chest, she smiles as she discovers Reign's is doing the same. She presses a soft kiss right above his heart. She's never been more sated. More...completed.

And downright exhausted.

"I love you, Ari," Reign says, tenderly brushing a damp tendril of hair from her shoulder.

She snuggles more deeply into his arms, a faint smile playing along her lips. "I love you, too," she says, quickly followed by a big yawn.

Reign chuckles then adjusts the covers over her shoulders. "Sleep, Ari. We still have tomorrow."

She wants more than that.

She wants forever.

MORNING LIGHT TICKLES over Arielle's eyelids and she scrunches up her face, trying to deny its existence. She's so comfortable. So content. The last thing she wants to do is leave that feeling. But then something else curls into her consciousness. The sounds and scents of someone else. Warm skin beneath her cheek rather than a pillow.

Her eyes fly open, an expanse of smooth chest greeting her. Heat suffuses her as images of last night climb up with the warmth. It was beautiful. Passionate.

Everything.

She knows the moment Reign's awake because his steady breathing changes, shortening and tightening just like hers has.

Arielle angles her head up as she gently stretches stiff muscles, eliciting a soft groan from him. Even before a word's been said, she's already feeling sexy and loved. The moment their gazes connect, the feelings only intensify.

Jungle green holds the same emotions she's experiencing. Love. Tenderness. Barely banked desire despite their long night of passion.

"Good morning," he murmurs.

Arielle slides up, drawing in a sharp breath as skin grazes skin. "Yes, it is."

Reign's fingers spear into her hair to cup her head as he guides her mouth to his. They kiss slowly, honoring and reveling in this new facet of their relationship. In how complete it's made it. Still, the passion banks quickly, fueled by the knowledge of what's been sparked between them.

Already breathless, Arielle languorously trails her fingers across his shoulders as she molds her soft curves to his hard edges. Pleasure unwinds like a cat in the sun, blossoming in every cell. This time she's willing to give slow a go.

She pulls back, wanting to take in the beauty that is Reign. The breathtaking lines and angles of his face. The tousled hair that her fingers itch to feel. The tongue that flicks out over already-moist lips, as if he's tasting their passion.

Slow may be harder than she'd thought.

But she's up for the challenge.

Arielle's just leaning down when the delicious sight fades from her vision. She startles, even blinks her eyes as she checks they hadn't closed without her knowledge. But Reign, the bed, the room, all slip away from her. Leaving her in darkness.

"Arielle?"

Reign's alarmed voice is the last vestige of reality before she finds herself trapped in a vision. She spins around, already knowing what she'll find. The obelisk is only a few yards away, powerful and straight. But this time, the crumbled remains of the other obelisks surround her like some post-apocalyptic scene. Rubble, ash, destruction.

Except that's not all that's here with her. Renata stands at the base of the obelisk, neck craned as she admires its silent magnificence. The moment she sees her, Arielle breaks into a run.

"Renata, get away from there!"

There's a thunderous *crack* and the obelisk splits, fingers of green light spearing out, hungrily reaching for the Innocent.

"Renata!"

But it's too late. The tendrils wrap around her, clamping onto her hair, her face, then her neck. The next *crack* is far quieter, but no less devastating. Renata's neck twists sharply. Her body goes limp. And she crumples amongst the destruction of every other obelisk they were unable to save.

"Arielle." Reign's concerned voice filters through and she clings to it. "Ari, I'm here."

Her eyes fly open and she finds him gripping her shoulders, face tight with worry. "You saw another vision again, didn't you?"

She nods mutely then climbs into his arms. "I saw the next obelisk." She swallows. "And Renata being killed."

Reign's arms tighten around her, pressing a kiss to her head. "I'm sorry."

Arielle looks up at him. "We need to go to her. Time's running out."

His lips thin as he considers her words, obviously not liking them. They're in a foreign war-torn country, and to go after Renata, they need to drive further away from civilization. There's no way Reign will be comfortable with that. His protective streak runs deep.

But he sighs. "Okay. We'll take the hire car."

Pressing a brief kiss to his lips, Arielle climbs out of bed to shower and get dressed, already sad their escape has ended. But if Reign can put aside his need to keep her safe because he knows how important this is, then she can tuck away the disappointment.

They need to save Renata.

Before it's too late.

CHAPTER 9
REIGN

R eign isn't sure whether he's more comfortable that civilization is far behind them or not. Leaving the city of Kabul means leaving the machine guns and simmering anger behind, but driving into the harsh landscape of Afghanistan, with little more than a map and good intentions doesn't feel a whole lot safer.

Although safety is obviously not at the top of their list right now, which is why he's constantly checking the rear vision mirror, even though the thick cloud of dust behind them obscures anything. There could be a horde of demons following them and there's no way to know.

"So, you're sure you'll be able to find Renata once we get to the village?" Reign asks, glancing over at Arielle. Except the moment he takes his eyes off the dirt track they're on, the SUV jolts over a pothole.

She braces her arm on the door. "Yes, I'm sure. I can sense the Innocents, remember? Plus, I doubt there are many Italian-born women there."

Focusing back on the road, then quickly jerking around a minor crater, Reign nods, not pointing out that they don't speak the native language, so won't exactly be getting directions. He knows his surliness isn't Ari's fault. It's because they're out here, in one of the least-safest places they could be, without any chance of backup.

And because their time at the hotel was cut short.

Last night was...

Was...

Beyond words.

He reaches over and clasps her hand, squeezing it. Last night also cemented that Arielle is his world. His sun. His whole damn universe. There is no future without her.

He's about to bring her hand to his lips when pain flashes up his arm. He hisses, realizing the Mark is flaring, burning his skin. Instinctively, he drops Arielle's hand, as if it might be contagious.

"Reign, is everything alright?"

"Are you going to tell her the truth?" comes a voice that shouldn't be here. "That it's really not?"

Reign puts both hands on the wheel and grips it. "Yeah, I'm just—"

"Feeling the burn of the Mark?" taunts Cain, his face and torso shimmering in front of Reign just beyond the windshield. "It never goes away. Nor do you ever get used to it."

"Reign," says Arielle, concern filling her voice. "What's going on?"

"It's the Mark," he says tightly, dragging his gaze away from the apparition of Cain. "It flares up sometimes."

"It will get worse as time goes on, too," says Cain, seeming to gain more substance the more he talks. "As it exerts its dark influence on you."

Reign shakes his head as if that will rid him of the vision and the words. He will never let the Mark corrupt him like it did Cain. He has too much to fight for. Last night was proof of that.

"It will work faster with you, though," Cain continues. "Because you already have demon blood."

"Reign!"

The alarm in Arielle's voice has his sight refocusing on the road, but it's too late. The SUV drops as it hits a washed-away part of the road. The steering wheel jerks right as the car swerves, yanked along by the deep gouges in the compacted dirt. Reign desperately tries to straighten it but the jarring bumps mean his hands can't gain purchase. The SUV bounces over ruts and rocks, tips wildly as one side of the road drops away, then jars back up as it jolts over a jagged stone.

There's a *crack*. Then a *snap*.

And the car careens to a halt.

Reign turns to Arielle, his heart hammering against his ribs. "Ari, are you okay?"

She peels her hands from the dashboard, looking pale and shaken, but there's no sign of blood, no limbs sitting at odd angles. "Yeah, just got my bones rattled a bit."

"I'm so sorry," he gasps, horrified at what could've happened as he registers the lean the car is sitting on. All because Cain distracted him.

Arielle gives him a shaky smile. "I'm fine, really." She unclips her seatbelt, the one that probably saved her from serious injury, jumping a little when the metal clasp clatters against the window. She puts her hand on the door. "But I wouldn't mind a bit of fresh air."

"Of course," he says, guilt gripping his gut.

Reign jumps out, dropping a couple of feet to the uneven ground below. Behind them is a cloud of dust that's as thick as a wall thanks to their wild careening. He walks around to Arielle's side, opens the door and helps her out. She steps over a deep divot and he watches her every move carefully. There's no favoring of one side or cradling of injured parts.

"I'm fine, Reign, really," she assures him. "I'm not made of glass."

Jamming his hand through his hair, he turns back to the car, quickly realizing it's not a rut that has the SUV on an angle.

"Shit," he mutters, eyeing the wheel that's tucked under the car at an unnatural angle. "We've snapped an axel."

Arielle squats down, frowning at it. "We can't fix that, can we?"

"No, we can't." This time, Reign jams his fingers through his hair and tugs. Hard. "Fuck."

They're stranded in the middle of a desert in a foreign country.

And it's all his fault.

Arielle pulls her cell out of her pocket. "We'll try to ring Guy. I'm sure he can..." She lifts the phone and waves it one way then the other, once more frowning. Her shoulders sag as she stares at her screen. "No reception."

"Of course there's not," Reign mutters, even as he wants to shout the words. Heading out here was crazy, at best. It just became dangerous in a way they really didn't need.

Arielle steps closer to him. "We'll figure something out. What happened?"

He glances down at the Mark. The one he never asked for. The one that seems to have now tied him to Cain. How does he tell Arielle that he's tainted by more than just demon ancestry?

And yet, he has to. She deserves honesty. Right now, it's all he can give her.

"I'm seeing Cain. And I don't know why, but he keeps telling me the Mark has the potential to be a dark influence."

She weaves her fingers through his, gazing up at him the certainty in her blue eyes. "If I can fight the obsidian, you can fight this."

Except Arielle's good. And he's...

It will work faster with you. Because you already have demon blood.

Letting out a harsh breath, Reign looks around, wondering what they're supposed to do next. Waiting isn't his strong point. There's nothing but arid land in every direction. Looking over his shoulder, he notes the dust from their crazy careening and abrupt stop is starting to settle, returning to the dirt it was violently thrown up from. Reign's about to turn away when something catches his attention.

He stops.

Frowns.

A body is materializing from the orange haze. A man.

Reign spins around, fists raised and ready to fight. Someone's followed them and he doubts they did that because they want to make sure they packed sunscreen.

Arielle gasps as Reign realizes who it is.

Xeven walks toward them, the dust settling on his shoulders, his hair, the lines of his scarred face.

This man is Arielle's father. Yet he's not, and has never been. Because Cain's controlling him.

Reign instinctively steps in front of Arielle as Xeven comes closer, only to find her once more standing beside him. "I need to know why he's here."

He had a feeling she'd say something like that.

Xeven stops several feet away, which Reign is thankful for. He's not going to trust the guy just because he donated half the genetic material to make a baby.

The guy's gaze lingers on Arielle, as if he's trying to place her. He frowns before settling his gaze on Reign. "I know how you got the Mark."

"You followed us out here to tell us that?" Reign growls.

Xeven inclines his head. "Among other things." His eyes flick to Arielle before returning to Reign. "Cain is dead."

Reign's muscles remain locked and loaded as he tries to make sense of this strange conversation, out here in the middle of the desert. "I heard." He doesn't mention that it was Cain himself who told him.

"And once he was killed, Aclima, Cain's twin sister, transferred the Mark from him to you."

"She what?" Reign explodes.

"You see, when Cain was gifted his Mark, she was given her own, a counter-Mark, by the angels," Xeven says. "She wanted Cain punished for what he did to Abel, but for her angelic Mark to live on, Cain's had to as well."

Anger flushes through Reign so fast, it almost startles him. "So she thought she'd put the Hell sticker on me?"

Xeven nods. "As you can see, that's exactly what she did."

Before Reign can speak, Arielle steps forward. "But why Reign?"

Xeven's scarred face seems to twist as he watches his daughter shrink the distance between them, even if it was only a few inches. "Because Reign is a direct descendant of Cain's bloodline."

"Like fuck I am!"

Xeven drags his gaze away from Arielle to stare at Reign's arm. "The Mark can only be transferred to a descendant of Cain himself. You have his blood in your veins."

A familiar feeling claws up Reign's ribs, trying to nestle once more in his chest. Self-loathing.

His ancestor was the first murderer.

Xeven looks up, his steady almost emotionless gaze settling on Reign's face. "My loyalty is bound to the Mark. It was how Cain had me do his bidding. Now that loyalty has passed onto you, Reign. I am beholden to keep you safe."

"That's why you're here?" Arielle asks, the hitch in her voice tugging at Reign's chest.

Does Xeven even recognize her?

Reign thought he has a lot to digest, but the father Ari's always wondered about, secretly hoped to meet, is standing a few feet away from them, talking as if he's nothing more than a messenger. One who's more connected to Reign than her.

Xeven's brows twitch. Then he absent-mindedly rubs at his chest. "I don't remember much from before Cain took control of my...mind. I know I was looking for the Holy Grail. I know I met a girl named Sierra and that we...connected." He stops, looking at Arielle. "I didn't know I had a daughter."

Arielle's silent and Reign waits, silently offering support. No matter how she responds, he'll back her up.

She lifts her chin, that one action jolting pride through him. "How do we know we can trust you?"

Xeven, her father, nods slowly. Reign's not sure, but he thinks he looks impressed. "I will tell you everything I know. I want to help."

Arielle narrows her eyes. "Prove it."

Reign wishes he could high-five Ari. Then hug her. Then punch Xeven in the face for putting her through this. She's being so strong, but because she has to. There's no way to tell whether there's any shred of her father left beneath the scarred remains Cain left behind.

Xeven holds her gaze. "Aclima is Mayor Virginia."

Arielle gasps. "That's why she worked to remove Cain's power when we were battling Lust."

Reign snorts. "Seems even humankind's first family had their fair share of drama. They should've had their own reality TV show."

"What's her endgame?" Arielle asks, her voice hardening. "Why has she involved herself in all of this?"

"To put a stop to the war between angels and demons," Xeven says. "And she'll stop at nothing to do it."

Reign isn't sure whether that makes one of the oldest souls on Earth a goodie or a baddie. Extreme measures for any purpose can be dangerous.

"We still don't know whether we can trust you," Arielle says, and there's something in her tone that tells Reign this isn't just about her being cautious.

She wants to believe this man, because somewhere under the scars and detachment, is her father.

But if she trusts him, not only will that mean a risk to their lives, but a risk to her heart.

Finding her father, and then being betrayed by him will slice it to pieces.

Xeven steps forward, then glances down, as if he's surprised he moved. He looks up, his face almost twisted in pain. "I want to help..." He clears his throat. "I want to help, Arielle."

She stills at the sound of her name on his lips. Then literally doesn't move for long seconds. Reign simply holds his breath and waits, ready to pummel this man if he has to, ready to hold her if she falls apart.

"And I can prove it to you," Xeven says. He reaches behind him and pulls something out from beneath his shirt. "I helped Cain collect a lot of ancient artifacts during his search for the Grail. I have the blade that can kill Greed."

DINAH

A shiver ripples down Dinah's spine as she stands somewhere that's familiar, yet nowhere she's seen before.

The inverse Crossroads have all the same building blocks. The packed-dirt road that divides ahead. The strange, clinging mist that stretches to infinity. Energy that ripples through the air.

But that's where the similarities end.

The road here is black. The mist is the color of ash. And evil clings to everything.

Dinah spins around, realizing this is where Emma told her the Eldritch monsters have been relegated to. Visions of teeth and tentacles and terrifying mutants fill her mind and for the first time, she wonders whether she can die here, in the Book of Monsters.

Emma smiles calmly. "They're not here."

"What?" Dinah demands, even as relief loosens her chest. "But you said—"

"No, you assumed the Eldritch Horrors were here. They are in the antiverse." Emma glances around as if that's not all that far away. "Already free. Waiting."

"They're not in Pandora's Box," Dinah mutters, realization once more her new companion. "They never were."

"No, they weren't," Emma says. "Pandora's Box is a key, not a container. It opens, and a breach between our worlds is created, freeing Eldritch."

"They're loose," breathes Dinah, glancing around as if they're still going to leap out any second.

"When Pandora was given the Box, she let the monsters out. The old gods trapped Eldritch in the antiverse, then hid the Box in a pocket dimension within the Crossroads." Emily's lips thin. "There were plenty of warnings that it should not leave there."

Dinah lifts her chin, deflecting the guilt that's trying to creep up on her. The obsidian wanted the Box, and now she knows why.

It wants to reunite with Eldritch.

She was manipulated, but that doesn't mean she can't use

this to her advantage. Her whole life is one long story of overcoming adversity. Of making it work in her favor.

Emma notes the movement and she nods, as if she expected it. "If you open Pandora's Box, a breach will be torn open and the Eldritch Horrors will be unleashed on Earth. Which is exactly what the obsidian wants."

"Maybe it won't get what it wants," Dinah snaps back.

Emma's smile returns, but this time there's the hint of sadness to the soft lines. "How will you know? You thought you wanted Pandora's Box. And if the obsidian wins, you'll become like one of the Sins."

Dinah keeps thinking the surprises are over. That she's heard enough doom and gloom to last her the rest of her witch-long life. But it turns out Emma is far from finished. In fact, the best may yet come.

Because right now, she's suggesting that the obsidian, that Eldritch itself, is linked to the seven Sins.

CHAPTER 10

ARIELLE

Arielle hasn't moved, her father's words that he will give her the blade that will kill Greed still hanging in the air.

Yet the man across from her is a stranger. So scarred she can barely see what he once would've looked like. The man her mother fell so irrevocably in love with is buried so deep, she's not even sure he exists anymore.

How does she know if she can trust him?

Despite all that, Arielle nods. The only way she'll get answers about her father is to keep him close, and for now, that means trusting him. "Thank you."

He blinks. Then blinks again. This close, she can see his eyes are a faded blue, as if a haze is covering them. "Yes, of course," he says, swallowing. "One less Sin would be good right now."

Arielle nods again, recognizing it for the peace offering it is. Her father may just be here because he's tied to the Mark, but he's trying to show he's a man of his word. Now they need to find out if that counts for anything.

Reign's hand brushes her arm. "We still need to get to Renata before either Greed or Wrath do."

Her gaze flickers to the wheel that's lying almost horizontal under the SUV. "Maybe we start walking?"

From memory they're still a couple of hours from the village the doctor is believed to be at, but maybe they'll find some reception along the way to contact Guy. Of course, if he's off rescuing them, he's not with Renata, protecting her...

Xeven—Arielle can't bring herself to call him Ryder, or anything else, yet—turns and indicates behind him. "We can take my car."

A second SUV, this one even larger than the one Rachel booked them, sits several yards away, now coated in a thin layer of dust. Arielle and Reign glance at each other, realizing they're really going to have to trust Xeven if they're going to climb into a vehicle with him.

Yet, what choice do they have?

Reign's lips form a tight line. "Do you want the front or the back seat?"

Arielle's heart warms. Even though he's clearly uncomfortable with this, he's still willing to let her choose whether she sits beside her father or not. And she very much wants to. She turns to Reign. "I call shotgun."

He nods sharply. "I wished I packed one."

Arielle finds herself smiling. "Even without one, I know I'm safe."

"Damn straight," he mutters darkly.

Xeven glances between them, as if their interaction is fascinating. Almost alien. A moment later, he abruptly spins on his heel. "Let us leave."

"Keep your hand close to that knife," says Reign as they fall into step behind him.

Arielle squeezes his arm, grateful he's here with her. "I love you," she whispers.

Ahead, Xeven's head twitches to the side as if he heard her.

Reign notices, because his eyes narrow. "There's nothing I wouldn't do for you, Ari," he says, not bothering to keep his voice down as it rings with truth.

Xeven's shoulders tense as if he's just braced himself and Arielle's not sure, but she thinks she hears a sharp, drawn-in breath. For some reason this gets to her father. But in a good way?

"Cain really did a number on him," Reign mutters under his breath, then frowns.

Arielle resists the urge to glance down at the Mark on his arm. The very same one he inherited from Cain, whether he likes it or not. She knows Reign can fight whatever dark influence it holds, she just hopes he knows that, too. He has a habit of underestimating himself.

They all climb into the car and Xeven cautiously drives through the ruts that have trapped Reign and Arielle's SUV. The moment they pass it, he accelerates, driving with focus and precision. Silence fills the vehicle and Arielle finally realizes the significance of this moment.

She's in a car. With her father.

The man she's spent her whole life wondering about.

For a brief moment, she considers calling her mother, but she quickly discounts the idea. Xeven isn't her father. Ryder is. And they need to find out if Ryder still exists after all this time. It would shatter her mother's already broken heart to know the man she's yearned for is here. But isn't.

Which means getting to know the enigma she's sitting beside.

Arielle turns to her father. "What else can you tell us?"

Xeven keeps his gaze on the road, and she's not sure whether it's because he's uncomfortable with their close proximity, or whether it's the pockmarked road that he feels needs his undivided attention. "I can tell you where the Sins came from."

Reign shifts forward, his head appearing between the two seats. "What about them?"

"Well, they're not demons, as everyone assumes," Xeven says. "In fact, they're a perverse breed of angels, manufactured in factories. And unlike regular angels, who carry Grace, they don't. They were the first prototype of angel clones."

"Angel clones?" Arielle asks, astounded at what she's hearing.

Xeven glances at her, and she catches a flash of intelligence in his hazy-blue eyes. "Gabby didn't tell you? She's faced them."

Arielle's mouth twists wryly. "Things have been kinda busy."

Was it really only not that long ago that she was being protected from the reality of the supernatural? And yet, she couldn't be more involved. In fact, it was the supernatural that forever changed her life when her mother decided to search for the Holy Grail.

Xeven returns his gaze to the road. "Well, they were the first experiments to create beings with angelic power, without any connection to the Grace, although just as powerful. Rumor has it that they were created to be the antagonists to the Grigori."

"You're saying the Sins are pseudo-angels," says Reign, clearly incredulous.

"Yes. They were recruited by Michael to guard Eden and keep Adam and Eve contained. He wanted Earth for angels only. But Lucifer encouraged Adam and Eve to think for themselves, hence eating the apple and discovering how to create children. Michael was furious, and impersonating Lucifer with a magical mask, he cursed the Grigori into seven trees for eternity."

"But then my mom and Blaise created the Tear all those years ago."

Xeven jolts as if they just hit a pothole, even though they've finally reached a stretch of smooth road. "Yes. Because Cain lied to them. He lied to us all."

Arielle holds her breath, realizing that her father's memories are indeed still inside him.

But then his hands clench the wheel. "After the Rebellion Michael wanted to punish Lucifer for everything he'd done. So he created seven more clone angels, but this time he created them in the same way he created the obsidian—by using the dark power that was let through the breach."

Reign frowns. "What exactly are you suggesting?"

"I'm not suggesting anything," Xeven says matter-of-factly. "I'm telling you. Michael created the Sins by channeling Eldritch."

Arielle shakes her head in disbelief. "Cain lied to you about a lot of things," she says, trying to be gentle. "Lucifer is the one who's been sending demons to Earth and getting the Innocents killed."

Xeven glances at her briefly, that flash of intelligence flickering in his eyes. "Have you heard the term 'history is written by the victors'?"

Her brows pinch together. "No." Although she can see that it makes sense.

"Lucifer has been misrepresented through the ages. All he wanted was for the humans to have free will, while Michael wanted them restricted and controlled. He imprisoned Lucifer in the Cage, corrupted Hell and created the Sins."

"From the obsidian," Reign says, looking like he's thinking as hard as Arielle.

"Yes. Luckily Lucifer came to know of the Sins and so created weapons that could kill them before he was trapped in the Cage."

Arielle can feel the knife that can kill Greed digging in her back. She tries to process what her father is telling her. That Lucifer created it to save humanity. That he's been the one wronged all these centuries.

"Cain was the one who discovered that the Sins were controlling and corrupting demons. They're the ones responsible for the demon's image of being evil and dark."

Arielle glances over her shoulder at Reign, wondering what he thinks of this seeing as he has demon blood running through his veins. He's frowning, hard and deep.

"Why would they do that?" asks Reign, looking as if he's trying to see if this story has any holes.

"The Sins believe if demons created carnage on earth, that would draw angels out of Heaven. They are unable to enter Heaven, so they wish to bring the fight to them."

"So this all started with Michael and Lucifer?" asks Arielle.

Xeven nods, smoothly weaving around a large pothole. "Lucifer was God's favorite son and Michael was jealous. He's the one responsible for this. In his bid to outdo Lucifer and become God's favorite, he created all of this mess."

"So it was the rivalry between those two brothers that began this," Arielle says, thinking of Lance and his jealousy of Reign and how far that drove him. People lost their lives because Lance wanted what Reign had. "And where is God in all of this? How can he just watch it happen?"

"God knows, but he also knows the consequences of interfering with the timeline. That's why he has angels. He believes Lucifer can fulfill his vision of Paradise."

"Except Lucifer is in the Cage," Reign points out.

"Yes, he is," Xeven says somberly. "Which is why Cain wanted him freed. Not only to remove the Mark, but also so Lucifer could finally fulfill his vision."

Reign shakes his head. "They'll try to destroy each other."

Just like Lance did with Reign. In the end, the only way to have peace was for Lance to die.

Xeven nods. "Cain knew this. He wanted to see Michael dead. He was the one who influenced Abel, leaving Cain to believe the only way to stop his brother was to kill him."

Thus becoming the first murderer.

Arielle folds back into her seat, trying to unravel the centuries old story of brother betraying brother. First Lucifer and Michael. Then Cain and Abel.

Ultimately, Reign and Lance were the products of hundreds of years of hatred.

No wonder Lance was so twisted.

And what an impressive feat that Reign isn't.

Arielle turns to look at him, wanting to tell him this, but she registers his face. Reign's almost pale with shock, and she suddenly realizes he reached the next conclusion before she did. One question has now risen to the top of all the others.

Should Lucifer be freed?

Except to do that, the remaining Innocents must die.

And all of the Sins will be unleashed on Earth.

DINAH

When Dinah opens her eyes from nothing more than a blink, she finds herself in paradise. An involuntary gasp is wrenched from her throat as she executes a slow turn, hoping she'll never blink again. There's not a millisecond she wants to miss as she tries to absorb the divine sight cradling her.

Azure blue sky stretches for miles. Emerald green grass undulates endlessly in every direction. Mountains are in the distance, some peaked with snow, others covered in lush jungle. Everywhere there's flowers. Trees. Rivers. Creeks. Rocks. Birds trill. Water gurgles. A breeze caresses Dinah's skin, bringing with it a kaleidoscope of nature's scents. Each sweet tendril feels like a gift. The sounds are each a note that's a part of the music gracing her ears. The colors she's trying to absorb are saturated, pure, blazing.

Beautiful.

"Is this Heaven?" she asks in wonder. This is definitely the one place she never thought she'd see in her lifetime.

Emma shakes her head. "This is Hell."

"But..."

Dinah tears her gaze away from the splendor to gape at the woman. "Have you been lying to me this whole time?" There's no way they're standing in Hell.

"I have not lied to you once," Emma says, unoffended. She points over Dinah's shoulder. "The Archangel Michael has arrived."

No. It couldn't be.

But the same angel she watched hovering as Atlantis had sunk is striding toward a small, sparkling creek. The same angel who forged the obsidian from Eldritch.

Michael lifts a fist then opens his hand, revealing the uneven, midnight-colored stone he's holding. The black of the obsidian looks instantly out of place in this world of color and life. His lips climb up as his wings expand, looking every inch the satisfied archangel.

"What is he—" Dinah cuts herself off, not wanting to know the answer.

Even though the dread dragging at her stomach already knows.

"No!" Dinah watches as another man, brilliant white wings outstretched, runs toward him. "No, Michael!"

"This is Lucifer," Emma says quietly, as if it pains even her to watch this, and she's the one who lives among these pages.

Michael snaps his head in the direction of his brother. He swipes his other hand, sending a blast that knocks Lucifer to the side.

Straight into a cage that materializes with an explosion of light.

"No!" Lucifer roars, his hands wrapping around the bars and shaking them violently.

But the Cage remains shut. It means he has no choice but to watch what happens next.

Michael returns his focus to his palm. Slowly, irrevocably, without a flicker of hesitation he turns his hand. Drops the obsidian into the crystal-colored creek. And steps back.

The effect is instantaneous.

Darkness ripples out from the one point of contact, killing, desiccating, annihilating everything in its wake. The grass shrivels and dies. The trees turn into twisted skeletons. Rivers become ash. The sky blackens, becoming a giant bruise.

And Lucifer's devastated wail of denial is the soundtrack for the destruction.

Emma steps into Dinah's line of vision, her golden hair looking out of place in this desolate war zone. "You believe you can control the obsidian within you." She shudders. "What if you can't?"

This is what will happen to Earth.

Just one stone-sized piece of Eldritch can do this.

"What you did, drawing the obsidian out of Arielle, was noble," Emma says. "But now you have a great responsibility. A choice with these consequences." She waves her arms to indicate the ravaged world they're now in but doesn't take her gaze off Dinah.

She's either trying to impress how important this is.

Or she can't bear to see what this magnificent paradise has become.

Dinah crosses her arms, resisting the need to rub away the chill skittering over her skin. She nods, no longer fighting this. "What else is there for me to see?"

Emma's shoulders drop on her exhale. "Come." She swipes her hand. There's the rustle of paper.

And Dinah actually looks forward to wherever they're going next. Anywhere, as long as it's not the Hell that Michael's hatred created.

She doesn't know which was worse to witness. The loss of paradise.

Or Lucifer's grief.

CHAPTER 11
REIGN

Reign sits in the back seat, feeling hot despite the air conditioning blowing cool air over his face.

Arielle is quiet in the front seat, no doubt caught up in her thoughts after everything Xeven told them. Her father drives, just as silent, his gaze never wavering from the road. A craggy mountain range formed through the haze a little while ago. Reign suspects that's where they're heading.

He wipes his hand down his face, registering the fine sheen of sweat stuck to his temples. Surely freeing Lucifer can't be the answer.

Another wave of fire licks up his arm as the Mark flares like it senses what he just thought. Gritting his teeth, Reign presses his other hand over it, wishing out of sight meant out of mind. Lucifer is also the only person who can remove his Mark. He doesn't need to ask Xeven to know. It's half the reason Cain was so obsessed with freeing the archangel.

So he could be free of the constant, low-grade torture the Mark inflicts.

Reign screws his eyes shut for long seconds as the next

inevitable thought slices through him. Maybe he deserves this. This is his punishment.

Cain killed Abel. He was given the Mark.

Reign killed Lance.

And now the same Mark burns away at his arm twenty-four-seven, the fire trying to creep into the cracks of his broken soul, thirsting to corrupt it.

When he opens them, the mountain range has grown closer and Reign makes out mud brick huts scattered at the base, square and flat-roofed, sparse green grass sprinkled between them. Children appear, running to the road and pointing.

Xeven slows the SUV. "Put your scarf over your head," he says, eyes flitting to Arielle.

She nods as she slips the dark material over her golden locks, keeping her gaze on the approaching village and people congregating outside. "We just need to talk to Renata."

The car slows even more as they reach the crowd of about twenty males, from child to old man. Xeven rolls his window down and those closest pull back when they register his scarred face. He either doesn't notice, or pretends not to. "Dr. Mendelez," he says. "We're looking for Renata Mendelez."

"Doctor?" asks one of the men, his face lighting up with understanding.

"Yes, doctor," says Xeven. "We see doctor."

The group of men begin furiously pointing toward a mud brick hut squatting at the top of a gentle slope several yards away. "Doctor! Doctor!"

They make their way to it, the small group following the SUV, shouting "Doctor, doctor," over and over.

A woman steps out of the hut as they approach, wearing the same flowing robes as everyone else, her head covered in a shawl. "Renata," gasps Arielle. "It's her!"

She's out of the car the moment Xeven stops, meaning Reign is a split-second behind her. He hurries to her side, mentally cataloging the group behind them, the other men who are either stepping out of surrounding huts or pushing to their feet where they were squatting beside walls. A few faces of curious women appear in the square windows cut out of the huts.

"It can't be," Renata says, pushing back her shawl so her face is clearer. "Arielle? What in the world are you doing here?"

Arielle stops in front of the tall woman. "Looking for you."

Reign joins her, studying the woman's strong features. She looks as if she's meeting an alien. "I don't understand."

Which is probably fair. Most people don't venture into the far reaches of a war-torn country, looking for a family friend.

Arielle adjusts her own shawl, and a few men murmur behind them, making Reign tense. He glances over his shoulder, noting that Xeven's remained by the car, looking just as alert.

"We came to warn you, Renata," Arielle says. "Your life is in danger."

Renata smiles. "Did my son send you? He's always worried about me working in these places. But I assure you, I'm well aware of the risks. Women here are some of the most vulnerable—"

"No. It's far more than that," Reign says, letting the urgency of the situation seep into his words. Convincing Renata to leave and getting back home is feeling more and more pressing. "The war that's coming isn't what you think it is."

"You don't think I've heard the scare tactics before?" Renata huffs, crossing her arms. "They won't work. The women will have no one if I leave."

Reign and Arielle glance at each other and she nods, making the decision even before he's really asked the question. She turns back to the doctor. "Do you remember when Shell told you about Evelyn believing in angels?"

Renata stiffens. "That was a long time ago."

"Well, she was right," Arielle says, holding the doctor's gaze. "About angels existing, and that she was an angel, just like Shell was. And you are."

"You came here to tell me that?" Renata demands incredulously.

Reign crosses his own arms. "Doesn't that tell you how serious we are? This isn't exactly an ideal holiday destination."

She glares at him. "I'm a woman of science. You can believe what you want. I'm no angel and neither were my friends."

"You mean the ones who were ritually sacrificed because they are?" he throws right back.

Arielle rests a hand on his arm. "Please, Renata. We can explain everything. Just come with us. We can keep you safe."

But the doctor shakes her head. "I can't leave. There's an injured woman who needs help. I'm worried she's going to go into early labor."

Reign clenches his jaw. His gut. His hands. He suspects if he tries something desperate like picking up the good doctor and carrying her to the car it will result in being attacked by a bunch of angry Afghanis. Who no doubt have machine guns. He sighs, trying to unwind his tense muscles. They might have to do it at night.

He's just about to turn to Arielle, suggesting they grab a drink and some shade when Xeven's voice reaches them.

"Arielle. Reign."

Although he says nothing but their names, they both spin around, recognizing the note in his voice. One of urgency. Of warning.

They instantly see why.

Dust billows beyond the car, the pale cloud rising higher than all the others Reign's seen. He narrows his eyes as he registers a flash of something among the rioting flecks of sand. Flashes of black.

Wings.

Demon wings.

The Afghanis break into shouts, scattering into the village and sending the children into the huts.

"Quick," Renata calls. "We need to take cover. It's another attack."

Reign turns to her, pointing a finger at the approaching threat. "Look closer. It's not who you think it is."

Renata looks like she's about to tell him to go shove it but something catches her attention. She frowns, probably not even conscious she takes a step forward as if trying to get a better look. Reign knows the moment she realizes this isn't the usual danger. That it's possibly not human.

"It can't be..." she gasps.

Reign turns to face the oncoming demons. Their wings are visible now as they beat the dusty air, stirring up the earth into a sandstorm. They streak over the ground, more flying than running, coming at them with inhuman speed.

Reign's own wings appearing is inevitable, power rippling through him. The fight is coming to them and he's going to meet it head on. There's Arielle and an Innocent to protect.

"Get her in the car!" shouts Xeven.

Reign's not sure if he's talking about Renata or Arielle, but when he turns back, Renata's gone, her scream ripping the air. Arielle looks from her departing back to the approaching onslaught, clearly torn.

"Go after her," says Reign. "Keep her safe. Xeven and I will take care of the demons."

She hesitates, her blue gaze shooting to his. It's clear she doesn't want to leave as much as she knows she has to.

"Come on," he says, allowing himself a smile. "Give me a chance to test these suckers out." He arches his wings high for emphasis.

Her response is to press a fierce kiss against his mouth, give him a "don't let anything happen to you" glare, then turn and run after Renata. Reign allows himself the space of breath to watch Arielle, to connect with the endless love he feels for her, before turning to face the thirst for Innocent blood coming at him.

Wanting to put as much distance between it and the village, Reign pumps his wings and shoots forward. He aims for the center of the dust cloud like an arrow, finding Xeven not far behind him as he runs with his own supernatural speed. The demons morph from the dust as if a curtain is being pulled back, their eyes gleaming red and teeth bared. They look rabid and feral, and Reign feels his own power swelling. He'll match them, fury for fury.

Determination to kill is about to clash with determination to kill.

He spins a split second before reaching the first demon, his wing slicing through the air like a red machete, cracking across the demon's face. His head snaps to the side, the rest of his body following. Reign kicks him in the small of his back, the snap of his spine almost lost in the demon's cry of pain. He leaps, slamming his elbow into the face of another, then using the demon as momentum to flip in the air and come down on another and crumple him like origami.

Xeven flashes somewhere to Reign's left, a blade in his hand as he slashes, blocks, then slashes again. The taste of blood and dust quickly fill Reign's mouth. He ducks when a blade whips past his throat, discovering Xeven isn't the only one who came with weapons. Another jump, flip, no-holds-barred punch, and the demon is quickly trampled by his comrades as they rush to take his place.

Reign's just landed when he sees four demons coming at him. One throws a knife and he spins sideways just in time as it carves the air past his chest. He breaks into a run, adrenalin spiking when two more lift their arms to throw their own blades. Realizing his chances of avoiding three out of three aren't great, he braces himself, reminding himself he has demon healing. Because he's not retreating.

Suddenly, the four demons twitch and convulse as their torsos are riddled with bullets. The staccato roll of machine guns fills the air. The villagers are helping! Reign launches into the air, giving them unfettered access then diving right back to clean up another batch. They might actually stand a chance.

But the fragile hope of victory is quickly crushed when Reign sees exactly how many demons the Sins have sent. An army of close to a hundred are thundering toward the village, all ravenous for death and destruction.

And Reign quickly realizes they're not just here for the Innocent.

They're also here for him.

Demons attack him in relentless waves, and although he taps into the power that's been dormant in his veins, there's always five more to replace the one he just killed. Rounds of machine gun fire stutter periodically, shredding demon wings or sending some to the ground. But each one is quickly followed by a painful human scream. Then silence.

Reign realizes what he's refused to acknowledge. That he sure as hell wasn't going to let Arielle register. They're outnumbered. By a lot.

Suddenly, one of the demons breaks away from the others, launching high into the air and then angling for the village. Reign tries to intercept him only for another to crash into him, sending him hurtling to the ground. He scrapes and tumbles over the rocky soil, leaping to his feet the moment he gains traction.

The moment he's upright, Reign discovers he's surrounded.

"Xeven!" he shouts, looking around frantically. If there was ever a time for back up, this is it. "Xeven!"

But the scarred man is nowhere to be seen. Reign spins, using his wings to protect himself as he scans the battlefield the outskirts of the village just became. Xeven is nowhere to be seen.

The coward has run? Reign can't believe it!

A demon leaps on his back and Reign throws him off, ripping the knife from his hand and slamming it into the demon's chest. A cry to his left has him kicking out instinctively, connecting with a shoulder. Two more demons rush at him and Reign maintains his momentum, trying to clean them up, only for a third to sweep his leg out. The moment he hits the ground, Reign leaps up again. If they get him down for longer than a few seconds it'll be the end of him.

As he ducks a swipe at his jaw, Reign sees Xeven is a few yards, kneeling with one palm pressed to the ground. His head is bowed and his eyes are closed as if he's praying.

Reign tries again "Xeven! We can't let any more get past!"

Surely the man has some protective instinct toward his daughter buried under the mind warp Cain exerted on him. But Xeven doesn't glance up.

Desperate, Reign decides to use a different angle. "I thought you were tied to the Mark! I could use some help here!"

A snarling demon leaps at Reign. And then another. And another.

He fights them off as best he can, but even with his newfound speed he can't avoid every strike, block every kick. A fist smashes into his temple. A foot plows into his torso. The hard edge of a wing slams across his face, sending him careening backward.

Reign lands with a grunt, already scrambling to get back up except a demon lands on his chest, pinning him to the ground. Eyes alive with bloodlust, she lifts a blade high up into the air, howling with victory.

"Xeven," Reign gasps even though it feels fruitless. But he can't accept the fate the demon thinks is about to play out.

He can't leave Arielle.

There's no response, not that he was really expecting any, which means Reign turns into a thrashing, fighting mass of fury. He kicks, bucks, screams. And becomes a beacon for every demon in the vicinity. They pin his arms and legs, even shove his head back and hold it immobile. It means Reign has no choice but to watch the sun catch on the edge of the knife. To register there's a strange green sheen to it.

To wait for it to come down like a guillotine.

Suddenly, one of the demons holding his arm howls with pain, then releases it. Then Reign's head is released, allowing him to twist it and see what's going on. The two demons are writhing with pain, yet there's no one near them. Reign's confusion is quickly cleared when black smoke pours from their mouths and eyes and ears, then spears down like it's being sucked by a giant vacuum cleaner beneath the ground.

Reign's gaze finds Xeven again, relief coursing through him. Arielle's father is still kneeling, his mouth working fast as he recites the exorcism spell. He's saving Reign, Arielle, Renata and every one left in the village.

The demon kneeling on Reign's chest growls, her head twisting from side to side as she keeps her mouth tightly closed, fighting the spell. Reign uses his freed arm to swipe at her, but the demon rears back, swinging the knife wildly. It just misses Reign's throat as he flattens himself onto the ground, praying this spell hurries up.

Above him, the demon's eyes flash as if she just thought of something. She opens her mouth in a wide, wicked grin, now letting her demonic essence pour out of her willingly. It spears for the ground, just like the others', except it pours over Reign's face. He's instantly swallowed by black, moist smoke, blinding him. His already out of control pulse jackknifes up a gear as he waves his hands frantically. He needs to see!

The inky smoke clears enough for him to register the demon collapsing, eyes going dull, yet still grinning. She falls forward, no longer fighting her death. In fact, welcoming it. Because the demon's last act is to slam the knife into Reign's shoulder before slumping to the ground.

Pain like he's never experienced powers through him, inhaling him whole. Pain that's far out of proportion to a stab wound.

As agony steals his consciousness, Reign fights it, knowing one thing.

This is no ordinary injury.

DINAH

Dinah finds herself at the edge of a village that's defined by sand, tussocky grass, and rough-looking, square huts. A young girl is a few yards away, wearing a blue-gray dress and light-colored shawl over her head. She's carrying a large clay urn on her hip as she trudges away from the huts.

Suddenly, two guards in maroon robes and silver armor rush past her, heading for the village. They almost knock the girl over. "Get out of our way! We need to tell the priests!"

The girl stumbles off the path, barely keeping the urn from smashing to the ground, but the guards pay her no heed. She huffs, throwing the edge of her shawl back over her shoulder.

Dinah glances at Emma in askance. They're obviously still back in time.

"Jesus just resurrected," Emma explains. "The guards experienced the earthquake then witnessed an angel rolling back the stone door to the tomb."

"Pivotal time in history," Dinah observes laconically. "And?"

Emma arches a brow, either unimpressed with her casual acceptance, or acknowledging that Dinah knows there's more to this scene than just God's son doing the impossible. "When God resurrected Jesus, the barriers between Heaven, Hell and Earth thinned." She points to the girl. "It allowed Lucifer to throw the obsidian from Hell, even though he was trapped in the Cage."

The girl goes to pick up the urn again when she stops. She angles her head as if she just heard something. Turning, she walks away from the path, stepping around the dry tussocks of grass to stop a few feet away. She tilts her head as if she's listening again.

Dinah's eyes widen as she registers something the girl hasn't. Black fingers are pushing up from the soil, creating a circle around the girl. They continue to grow, the sand falling away to reveal gnarled, onyx hands. They twist and writhe, stretching over the ground in their attempt to get to her as she bends down, absorbed in what she's doing.

"The Sins," Emma explains. "Trying to get the obsidian so it can be returned to the darkness."

The girl's shawl falls away as she picks something up and straightens. Dinah doesn't need to look closely at what the girl has in her hand to know what it is, despite the distance. It's small, black.

And it's clearly speaking to her.

"Recognize her?" Emma asks.

Dinah blinks, registering the black hair now visible, the strong line of the jaw, the fine line of her nose. It can't be...

"Yes, she's your ancestor," Emma says even though Dinah didn't say anything. "She, too, thought she could control it."

Emma flicks her fingers and the sound of pages turning precede the scene dissolving and quickly being replaced by something that has Dinah taking an involuntary step back. The girl is standing over three dead men, a bloody dagger in her hands, a satisfied smile gracing her face. Another rustle of pages and the girl's standing inside a mud brick hut, throwing a lighted torch on a pile of bodies. The next scene she's in another hut, weapons stacked against a roughhewn wooden table—spears, sabers, swords. She's obviously planning a massacre.

Suddenly, several men burst into the hut and a fight ensues. The girl kills one but the others manage to pin her to the ground. The one holding her head starts muttering a spell and the girl's back arches in a scream.

"A secret organization found her and exorcized the obsidian," Emma explains, flipping the page, now showing an angel Dinah doesn't recognize holding the small, black stone. "Uriel then split it into seven pieces and hid them, transcribing the locations onto parchments which were entrusted with seven families."

Dinah turns away from the scene. She knows what happens next. The first part has been documented in Gabby's journals. The Grigori murdered the descendants of those seven families and the pieces of the obsidian were found. Gabby tried to hide it in a secret crypt but Arielle found it.

The second part Dinah's living. She took the obsidian from Arielle, thinking she could control it.

Except everything she's seen in the Book of Monsters tells her otherwise.

She was very, very wrong.

CHAPTER 12
ARIELLE

Renata runs frantically through the village, ignoring Arielle's cries for her to stop. Her shawl slips from her head and flaps behind her, catching on the edge of a hut as she weaves around it and tearing away. But Renata doesn't stop. She runs as if the hounds of Hell are on her heels, which they are.

She's an Innocent.

And the demons closing in on the village want her dead.

Renata's forced to stop when she reaches the other side of the village and all that stretches before her is parched desert and jagged rocks scattered at the foothills of the mountain range. She looks one way then the other, breathing hard, obviously deciding whether she'll continue.

"Renata!" Arielle cries as she closes the distance between them. "I can help you!"

She looks over her shoulder, her dark hair a mess and her eyes panicked, before darting left into the nearest hut. Arielle follows, skidding to a stop inside and panting as her eyes adjust to the gloom. Her gaze roams over the sparse furniture, the blackened fireplace, the sleeping mats against the wall. And finds Renata cowering in the corner.

Arielle's about to go to her when a sound has her spinning around. A demon is rushing at the hut, teeth flashing and claws extended. Arielle darts to the table, grabs the small knife that's sitting on it, turns and throws. The dagger lodges straight in the demon's throat.

He falls, gurgling and grunting, only to reveal another behind him. He storms into the hut, his wings smashing the edges of the doorway, sending dust and dirt into the hut. Arielle picks up the only chair in the room and smashes it over his head. It doesn't knock him out or over, but it stuns him enough that she can execute a spinning kick, shoving him back through the door he just entered. He lands on the ground in a spray of curses, but they're cut off as Arielle yanks the dagger out of the first demon and impales it in his chest.

She jumps to her feet, registering two things. Renata is still tucked in the corner of the hut, terrified. And more demons are pouring into the village, the sounds of the fight drawing them like a magnet.

Arielle raises her fists as she positions herself between the hut with the yawning hole where the door once was and the onslaught of demons. She's sure this is only a fraction of what Reign and her father are fighting. Her part is to keep these ones from reaching Renata.

She can't fail.

"Arielle!" screams Renata as three demons appear in the sky, spearing down toward the hut.

Feeling the most human she ever has, all Arielle can do is wait for them to reach her, attacking with their supernatural strength and inhuman speed. Tightening her fists and locking her muscles, she's about to execute her first kick when the closest of the demons twists midair and crashes at her feet. The other two scream as they do the same.

Arielle watches with horrified relief as black smoke pours from their mouths and eyes and shoots into the ground, leaving behind lifeless bodies. They've been exorcized! Renata's safe!

Not wasting any time, she rushes back into the hut. Renata is still in the corner, although she's now holding what looks like a walking stick. "Get ready! There could be more!"

Arielle opens her hands and tries to relax her posture. "They're gone. You're safe." For now, although she doesn't add that bit. Renata may not be terrified, but she still looks like her world has just come crashing down.

Her hands flex around the piece of wood, clearly not ready to let it go. "W—what's going on?"

"It's like we tried to tell you. Shell was right. She was an angel, so was Evelyn. And so are you. And demons want you dead."

Arielle almost winces at her bluntness, but the time for treading carefully is long gone. They need to get Renata out of here and back to the farmhouse.

The doctor slowly lowers her stick. "I can't be," she says, looking more confused than disbelieving. "I'm just human."

"Your powers and abilities are dormant, and have been for many generations. Most Innocents, as you're called, don't know who they are. Or that they're now being hunted."

Renata swallows. "This is a lot to take in."

Arielle nods in understanding. It definitely rocked her world, and she hasn't lived a life dedicated to hard science. "I wish I could explain it all to you now, but there's no time. We have to get you somewhere safe. I need you to come home with us."

To her relief, Renata agrees readily. Seems although she's

still trying to assimilate this, she's a practical woman, and recognizes she needs to trust them.

Arielle leads them out of the hut, stepping around the dead demons with an averted gaze. Their deaths are necessary, but she'll never relish in it. The day she doesn't have to take another life, possessed demon or not, will be a good one.

Renata pauses beside the one with the knife in its chest and Arielle hides her wince. Renata's job is to save lives, not take them.

The doctor looks up from the bloodied body, her gaze steady. "Shell would be proud."

Arielle blinks as the words spear straight to her heart. "She was a very special woman. I miss her." The guilt that she'd failed her slices through Arielle all over again. She can't let that happen with Renata too.

Renata steps closer, grasping Arielle's elbow. "I've lost a lot of patients during my time as a doctor. I still carry every loss with me. But I also had to learn to carry it lightly. I tell myself that every soul I fought to keep alive but lost knows I did everything I could. They wouldn't ask for more than that."

Arielle can almost hear Shell say the exact same words. "You tried, you fought, you gave it your everything, Ari. And that's enough."

She swallows, finding a hard ball of grief lodged in her throat. "Thank you." Then her lips twist wryly. "I'm supposed to be comforting you."

Renata grins back. "Sorry. Occupational habit." She squeezes Arielle's elbow before releasing it. "Although I'm glad I told you that. It's not something I've shared before."

Arielle nods in thanks, her throat even tighter as the determination to keep this Innocent alive also cements. "Come on, we need to get back." She needs to see Reign and make sure he's okay.

Arielle walks quickly through the village, seeing exactly how many demons had broken past Reign and her father, trying to get to Renata. Whoever did the exorcism spell was just in time. They reach the huts at the front of the village where the desert opens out and Renata gasps. The human bodies the demons possessed are scattered everywhere like rag dolls. Arielle scans them, not wanting to register the scale of the loss, looking for Reign. She's finding she needs him by the second more and more.

It's her father who she spots first, down on one knee beside a body.

Then it's Arielle's turn to gasp. It bursts from her chest like a bullet. "Reign!" She runs, leaping over still bodies as it's quicker than darting around them. "Reign!"

Her father doesn't look up as she approaches, his focus totally on Reign's still form. His hand on his chest as he frowns fiercely.

Arielle falls to her knees, gasping all over again when she sees the bloodied wound slicing through Reign's shoulder. "No," she moans.

Her father looks up, his frown impossibly deepening. "His demon power isn't healing him."

"What? How can that be?"

He turns back to Reign. "I don't know. I'm unable to heal him, either."

Panic grips Arielle's heart with tight claws. "No, you have to!"

Renata kneels on the other side, picking up Reign's wrist. "His pulse is weak. And his breathing is erratic." She examines the cut. "This is more than a stab wound."

Arielle's hands flutter over Reign's face, denial a deafening scream in her head. "Then what's happening?"

"I sense a poison," her father says gravely. He picks up a

nearby knife. Beneath the blood, the metal has a green sheen. "I think the weapon was laced."

Arielle shuffles closer, wanting to draw Reign into her arms but too scared to move him. "What do we do?" she asks desperately.

"He needs the antidote," says her father. "Without it he'll die."

The blunt words are like a battering ram to her chest. Arielle wraps her hands around Reign's, wincing when she registers how cold and clammy it is. "Then we find out what the poison is and we get the antidote," she says through gritted teeth.

It's the only outcome she's willing to consider.

Renata shoots to her feet. "I'll get my supplies. I'll do what I can to stabilize him."

Her father nods, then also stands. "I will clean this up," he says matter of factly, indicating toward the sea of bodies surrounding them.

Arielle suppresses a shudder. Her own father is speaking of destroying dozens of bodies like he's helping to clean up after a party. She pushes the thought away as she shuffles closer to Reign and holds on to his hand as if that alone will keep him alive.

"Fight this, Reign. Please."

RACHEL

Mercy City is in chaos.

Rachel ducks as she and Alexandra run from the safety of one building to another, ready to defend herself at any second. Laila squeals from somewhere behind them and Rachel grits her teeth. Laila and Seiko really don't understand the concept of stealth-mode.

They reach the protection of the awning over the entrance of a small upmarket cafe and stop. Like many of the places this close to the center of the city, the hotel has been ravaged. The large pots that held topiary citrus trees in them are smashed, the glass doors are shattered, and bullet holes riddle the stucco walls.

The city Rachel grew up in, the one she loves, is slowly being destroyed by the war between Heaven and Hell. Mercy City is now quarantined. No one leaves, no one enters. The kicker is that's not the worst of it. The obsidian and Eldritch are going to make angels and demons look like squabbling children. And the ripple effects will reach farther than one city.

A scream up above has Rachel peeking out from the shelter of the cement awning that would normally protect the rich from the weather as they climb out of their expensive cars. High in the air is the same show that's on repeat in every other corner of the city—demons and angels battling like fighter jets in a dogfight. If it wasn't for the sounds of them fighting, the area would almost be silent. Humans have either run, scared, or moved onto the next place to loot. Mercy City is gripped by greed, fury, and terror.

The angels and demons directly above them clash, an angel launching herself at a demon and grabbing him by the wings. She screams as she wrenches, tearing one from its back. The demon cries out then spirals to the ground. The angel doesn't even bother to watch, already preparing to hit replay on the nearest demon.

"Serves him right," Simon mutters with the same care-factor the angel showed.

Rachel spins to face him. "Demons aren't all bad," she says angrily. Simon knows exactly what Reign is and yet he's been making these statements the whole time they've been on this surveillance mission to find the Sins.

And kill them.

Simon snorts. "Maybe not, but they're also no leader of the Grail Keepers."

Rachel steps in close, glad to see his eyes widen slightly. Good, he knows a threat when he sees it. "See that up there?" she points in the direction of the battle in the air. "Reign was instrumental in killing the Sins up until now. Do you know how much worse things would be if it weren't for him?"

Simon's eyes nervously flicker to the side. He can't see up there because they're under the awning, but the sounds are inescapable. Grunts, thuds, abruptly cut-off cries. Hopefully he's also noticing the absence of sound in between. There are no humans here. They're either dead, furious and riddled with greed, or in hiding, terrified.

Someone moves in behind Rachel. "Reign and Arielle are central to winning this fight," Alexandra says. "I can feel it."

"Well, for what it's worth, I don't give a fig that Reign's a demon," says Bryn, jutting a hand on her hip and looking as if she hasn't been seriously wounded recently thanks to the healing. "This whole angel, demons thing is far from black and white."

Rachel steps back from Simon, noting the way Laila and Seiko's eyes are darting between everyone. Tariq is as silent as always, arms crossed as he also watches the altercation.

"Have you thought about what it would look like if you didn't have Reign," Rachel asks them. "He might be a demon, but he's also all you have."

Simon frowns then shoves his glasses up his nose when the action has them slipping down.

"Rachel," Alexandra says, her voice tight. She's turned to look down the street, her gaze focused on an imposing building halfway down the block. "I've found the place we're looking for."

The Sin's homebase. Greed and Wrath would have somewhere they retreat to as they continue to plan their chaos and destruction. And they need to find it.

Rachel studies the building, realizing it's the Luxuria Hotel, the finest in Mercy City. "Why do you think it's—"

She quickly realizes why Alexandra's so sure. It's the shiny chrome that glints under the strategically placed lights. The pretty garden beds. The sparkling, still-working fountain. The Luxuria Hotel is still intact. It doesn't look like it belongs in a war zone.

Of course that's where the bastards are. Living the high life, surrounded by opulence.

"We should check it out," Rachel growls.

Alexandra nods, that quiet intensity of hers slipping around her like armor. "Yes. We should."

"Ah, we should get back up," says Simon.

Rachel rolls her eyes but pulls out her cell, pressing the speed dial for Marlowe. He answers after the first ring. "Is everything okay?" he asks, even as the sounds of battle can be heard in the background. The nephilim and Knights Templar have been conducting sweeps of the city streets, helping any humans that need it.

"We think we've found the Sin's HQ."

"I won't be able to get there for a little while," Marlowe says, sounding like he's running.

And yet he still took a call from Rachel, wanting to make sure she's okay. Definitely deeply, madly in love with this guy. "I'm going to check it out, but I promise, I won't pick any fights."

There's a pause on the other end. "Tap out the word *hide* in morse code onto the screen of the watch I gave you. It triggers a spell I was given by a warlock. It only works for thirty minutes, but it has those around you believing you're supposed to be there."

Rachel glances at her watch, a little wide-eyed. "You just thought you'd tell me now?"

"I knew you'd be too tempted," he says, a smile in his voice. He doesn't sound like he's running anymore, and Rachel wonders if he's flown up somewhere with those magnificent wings of his. "And there will only be enough for two people."

"I love you," Rachel says, uncaring that there are others listening into this conversation. "Like, a lot."

Marlowe is trusting her to do this even though he'd much rather her wait till he was here. Not only that, he's giving her the means to do it with a lot less risk.

"You have my heart and soul, Rachel," he says, his voice warm and tender. "Forever."

Wishing she didn't have to hang up, Rachel does. Marlowe is off saving humans, and she now has a way to get into the Luxuria Hotel. She turns to the others. "Alexandra and I are going in with the help of some magic. You guys hide out in there and wait," she says to the Potentials.

Bryn frowns, possibly pouts, but doesn't argue. Simon looks relieved. Tariq turns and walks to the smashed doorway of the once-pretty cafe, a soldier who obviously follows his orders promptly. The other Potentials follow, leaving Rachel with Alexandra. "We'll be walking straight in," she tells her, indicating for Alexandra to move in closer.

Alexandra does and following Marlowe's instructions, Rachel taps on the phone screen—H, I, D, E. A small burst of light has them both blinking, and then a countdown timer starts on the screen. Their thirty minutes have started.

"Come on," says Rachel, stepping off the sidewalk and

crossing the road like she belongs here. "We have half an hour where the demons will believe we're one of them."

Alexandra falls into stride, not looking the least bit nervous. She either has total faith in this magic, or she's certain she can fight her way out if it fails. Rachel matches her footsteps, also realizing they need to look confident. Like they belong.

They approach the entrance of the Luxuria, noting that the front is beautiful as it is empty. It's only once they step through the revolving doors that Rachel discovers why. The foyer is swarming with demons, all prowling with barely contained energy. The sight has her pulse faltering and she has to make sure her feet don't do the same.

One or two glance in their direction as they enter, almost flatlining her heartbeat, but they look away, unconcerned by more of their kind joining them. The spell's working! Rachel and Alexandra walk to the lifts by silent agreement and step in. There, Rachel makes the executive decision they're going to the penthouse. It's exactly where Greed and Wrath will be.

The lift moves silently, whooshing up and leaving Rachel's stomach behind. A glance at her watch tells her five minutes have passed. Hopefully they can get some useful information in the time they have left.

The doors slide open with a soft *ding*, revealing another, smaller foyer. This one has glass tables on each side, large flower arrangements sitting on each of them. Their heels click on the marble floor as they step out, a mammoth-sized set of doors waiting for them across the room.

Rachel and Alexandra glance at each other. It's one thing to walk into a foyer full of demons thanks to some cloaking magic. But the den of two Sins is on the other side of those doors. Are lowly demons even allowed in there? Is there some sort of demon protocol when entering?

"The Sins are up to something," Alexandra mutters. "I can

feel it. They want more than just to kill Innocents and free more Sins."

"Then let's see what they've been up to," Rachel replies, making her way to the large doors.

Alexandra is instantly by her side, as wired and ready as she always is. Drawing in a breath, Rachel places her hands on the cool surface, not sure what they'll do if they find it locked. Demons breaking down the doors will certainly raise suspicion.

But they slide open seamlessly and noiselessly. Rachel's about to take a step when she stops, blinking.

She expected to see more opulence, more sleek gray lines, more I-just-stepped-into-Vogue decor. But what they find is far from that.

The entire room has been cleared out. Stripped and painted black.

Dozens of candles the color of midnight placed in the shape of seven-pointed stars are everywhere, throwing flickering light onto the ink-colored walls, hinting at the barely-legible symbols etched in black on black.

And on the swirling pool of energy in the center of the room.

Rachel takes a cautious step forward, Alexandra by her side as they try to understand what they're seeing. The onyx whirlpool swirls in an anti-clockwise direction, moving fast. Seamlessly. Hungrily.

Alexandra grips Rachel's arm and points up.

A gaping hole has been punched into the ceiling, revealing the sky above. A white light appears, shooting down through the hole as if it's being sucked in, spearing straight for the churning whirlpool.

"Angelic Grace," says Alexandra.

The moment it touches the surface, the light blinks out, turning a blazing black. It melds with the currents of the whirlpool, a flash of energy pulsing through the room.

"What the..." Rachel's not sure what she just watched, but she's pretty darned sure it wasn't good.

Another ball of shimmering white appears and it's quickly drawn into the whirlpool, once more turning from day to night the instant it's absorbed. But this time Rachel notices something else. The candles flicker, as if a breeze just tried to snuff them out. She draws in a sharp breath when she realizes they don't die out. No. The flames turn a disturbing, glowing color of death.

Once the angelic essence is swallowed, the flames return to their pale-yellow color. As if the impossible didn't just happen.

Black flames. What does that even mean?

Rachel's watch buzzes silently against her wrist, jolting her out of the shocked, and a little terrified, suspended animation. She glances down, registering they have five minutes before the cloaking spell ends. Alexandra must realize it too, because she turns away and strides to the lift, her face grim.

They don't speak once inside. They barely glance at the demons milling in the foyer on the ground floor. They walk as quickly as possible out of the Luxuria Hotel.

It's only once they've entered the cafe that Rachel lets out an explosive breath. "What the flamin' flamingos was that?"

"The Sins are conducting a spell," Alexandra says tightly. "Once I've heard of but never thought I'd see."

"What sort of spell," asks Simon, appearing from behind a door that must lead to the kitchen. "What did you see?"

"A whirlpool of death," Rachel says, realizing that's the best description for it. Even Grace, the pure light of angels, was destroyed in it. "Up in the penthouse."

Alexandra starts to pace, broken glass crunching beneath her boots. "It's well documented by the Greek Gods that there was once a dark fae priest conducting black magic. He sacrificed people at the altar of Gaia, creating a breach between this universe and the antimatter universe."

"He what?" Rachel demands, horrified.

Seiko frowns as she watches Alexandra stalk one way then the next. "The antimatter universe?"

"A mirror universe to ours," says Simon, surprising Rachel. "But while ours was forged from light, the antimatter-verse was forged from dark energy."

Bryn grins. "He reads *a lot*."

"Yep. None of that is in the Grail Keeper books," adds Seiko.

Alexandra nods, waving her hand as if that information isn't terribly important right now. "When the evil fae priest caused the breach, he released Eldritch onto the world. It created havoc until the Titans closed the breach, creating a key in the form of a Box."

"Pandora's Box," Rachel breathes.

"Yes. Zeus gave it to Pandora who then opened the Box. You all know what happened then. What many don't know is that what came out of the Box was used to make the obsidian and the Sins."

"What?" Laila gasps. "The obsidian and the Sins are connected to Eldritch."

Alexandra nods. "Yes, they are." She turns grave eyes to Rachel. "And now the Sins are trying to create the same breach."

Rachel's gut clenches. "The whirlpool."

"The Sins want to release Eldritch."

Alexandra's words hang in the dusty air for long seconds before Simon's arms throw out wide. "We can't let that happen!" he cries. "If the Eldritch comes into our world, nothing can defeat it. Once this universe is filled with antimatter, all life will cease to exist. The dark will devour it, destroying it then recreating a black, soulless home of darkness."

Rachel eyes Alexandra. "Then we stop the spell."

"It's not that simple," she says, shaking her head. "The spell is being fueled by the energy released when angels kill demons and vice versa. I suspect it's also being fueled by the death of the Innocents."

Rachel rubs her forehead, trying to understand how the stakes just multiplied exponentially. "We need to get back to the farmhouse and tell the others."

Just as she finishes, her cell rings and she's not surprised to find it's Marlowe. "Hey, we're just about to head back." She's about to tell him they need to talk when Marlowe speaks.

"Good," he says, his voice unusually tense. "You need to hurry."

Rachel does what she didn't think was possible right now, she tenses even more. Marlowe's rattled, and that doesn't happen. Ever. "What's happened?"

"Reign and Arielle are back. But Reign's injured."

"What?" Bryn hisses, revealing she's been listening in. "What's wrong with Reign?"

The other Potentials straighten, alarm flickering over their features.

"He's been poisoned," says Marlowe, almost as if he's answering Bryn's question. "And if we don't find the antidote..."

"We're on our way." Rachel spins on her heel and exits the cafe. "I'm driving," she tells the others curtly.

And she'll get them there in record time.

When she asked the Potentials if they'd considered it would look like if they didn't have Reign, the question had been rhetorical.

She has no intention that any of them find out the answer.

CHAPTER 13
REIGN

Reign had thought he'd experienced pain. The physical shredding of muscles and sinew. The emotional agony of loss. The inescapable torture of mental torment.

But the poison working through his veins is all that and more.

It eats at his flesh, corroding everything cell by cell. He wants to writhe. Scream. Tear at his skin to try and dig it out. But he can't move. If he wasn't being turned inside out by misery, he'd assume he's dead.

The only thing that stops him from wishing for that oblivion is knowing he has to get back.

To Arielle.

So Reign does what he's always done best. He fights. He focuses everything he has on lifting his lids, on finding a crack of light as darkness tries to devour him. Once he achieves that, he can master a finger, a twitch, a word. Any of those are one step closer to returning to Ari.

He almost gasps when his lashes flicker. Then his eyelids are lifting, even though they feel like boulders are sitting on them. Just a few more millimeters and he'll be able to see!

But the sight that greets him isn't Afghanistan or the farm-house or anywhere he expected to find himself. Reign jolts, quickly finding out he has control of the rest of his body as he spins one way then the other.

"Where am I?" he mutters aloud.

His surroundings echo the appearance of the hideout he lived in before he learned he's the Keeper of the Grail. The one he shared with Rico and Darnell. It's similar enough to be recognized, but different enough to have chills crawling over his skin. Everything is dark, as if it's been painted with shad-ows. And decomposing. The walls are peeling, the floors look as if they're rotting, and the sparse furniture is disintegrating.

"You're in Purgatory," says a voice behind him.

Reign turns, lifting his fists as he prepares to fight. The quick motion shoots pain straight to the tip of each nerve ending, where it erupts like lava. He gasps, working not to double over and failing. It's all he can do to angle his head up as he watches the tall man who spoke float closer.

"It's a pocket dimension between the universe and the anti-matter-verse," he explains. "A place where both the dark and light live."

"I'm dead?" Reign gasps.

"No," says the man. "More like in a holding pattern."

"Forever," adds a female voice from somewhere to his left. "Although dying would be a blessing, to be honest."

Reign drops to his knees as the growing pain steals his strength. "I don't understand," he groans. "What am I doing here?"

"Our numbers have been growing quickly recently."

Reign digs his fingers into the floor, dirt and decay crumb-ling into his hands. He can barely breathe, it hurts so much. Every muscle feels like it's seizing, impossibly holding the pain in even more. "What's happening to me?" He collapses on his side, panting and sweating.

"Oh, he's dying," the female says matter of factly. "Lucky duck."

"No!" Reign isn't sure if the word is shouted or whispered or whether it just ricochets through his mind, but it captures everything he's feeling right now.

He can't die.

He can't leave Arielle.

He can't fail everyone.

His eyes close against his will, dropping a blanket of black over him. Consciousness slips from his grasp, no matter how hard he tries to hold on.

No...

Reign sits up with a gasp, the pain roaring through him anew. He works to open his eyes all over again, once more finding himself in the dark echo of the hideout. The tall man is squatting in front of him. "You're back?"

Reign glares at him, wishing any of this made sense. "It appears so."

"You're an immortal soul," the man says excitedly, glancing over his shoulder. "He's an immortal soul!"

Reign's about to deny it when he remembers the brand on his arm. The Mark! The immortality it grants is why Aclima transferred the thing to Reign in the first place, all because she was unwilling to lose the gift of endless life.

But if he's been poisoned...and he's in Purgatory, does that mean he's going to die a painful death and keep returning? He's going to relive this, over and over?

Suddenly, more people appear around him, their animated faces closing in. Some women wear bonnets, some men wear top hats, others have weird-ass ruffles around their neck while some have piercings in every inch of their skin. Spirits of every age and era are now looking at him like he's their Jesus.

"You can save us!" someone cries.

"Let me touch him!"

"No, I've been here longer," shouts the female voice he'd heard earlier. "I'll be the one holding on when he's returned to his body."

There's a muted thud and Reign looks down, seeing a mermaid crawling toward him. Her impressive tail is a dull army green and her long hair hangs like rats tails over her shoulders. The desperation on her face is unmistakable.

Reign stands, hiding the grimace at the pain, and takes a step back. "No one is going to touch me." Right now, a feather would fell him.

"You think we're going to let our only ticket out just walk away?" the mermaid demands. The other spirits murmur an affirmation, contracting as they move closer.

"Especially when the reapers have stopped coming because angels and demons are too busy fighting?"

"You're the only one who can save us," calls a young voice. "Please! Evil is rising!"

The desperation in the voice is echoed in every face surrounding Reign. "What kind of evil?" he asks. It's clear something isn't right here.

"The First Spirit of Purgatory," the man says in a hushed voice, his lashes lowering.

"A dark fae priest," adds the mermaid. "He's been terrorizing us."

The crowd instantly sobers, pulling back as they curl into themselves. They go from desperate to terrified in a blink.

"He used to offer sacrifices to the Titans," says the mermaid. "But he became power hungry. He created a breach between our universe and the anti-verse. He's the reason Atlantis drowned." Her tail flops listlessly, obviously hurting at the mention of her ancient city.

"The fae priest was put to sleep," says the man, picking up the story as a black tear trickles down the mermaid's face. "But something woke him."

Reign jolts as he realizes it was probably Arielle touching the obsidian. The dark energy of that moment has had ripple effects far deeper than they could ever have imagined.

Suddenly, the spirits disappear. One second Reign has a crowd frantic to be freed, the next second they're gone. Gritting his teeth, he holds still as his eyes dart around. Something scared them away. Pain throbs, knitting through his joints and wrapping around his bones, but he does his best to ignore it. Who knows what's coming in this world that straddles the line between light and dark.

"Ooh, fresh meat," purrs a voice behind him.

Reign turns slowly, having learned that fast movements are likely to cripple him as his body objects. A tall man is standing a few feet away, wearing black robes covered in intricate dark blue armor. His black hair reaches far beyond his shoulders, while his piercing blue eyes regard Reign hungrily.

Reign holds very still, trying not to give away that agony is sucking his lifeforce all over again. "I'm not staying."

The man throws his head back and laughs, the hollow sound quickly absorbed by the shadows. "My name is Orion. I'm sure the spirits have already told you about me." His lip curls up. "And that nobody leaves."

"I'm pretty sure that's not how Purgatory works," Reign grinds out.

"Everyone who dies goes to Purgatory," Orion says, his gaze traveling hungrily over Reign as if he's a centerfold model. "Of course, then the reapers come to take them to Heaven or Hell, but they don't want to do that right now. Not with angels and demons having their little spat." Orion extends his arms out wide, the length of his sleeves almost touching the ground. "Leaving all that wonderful spirit energy for me."

"To do what?" asks Reign, his eyes narrowing.

"To be ready for when the Sins create the breach between worlds, of course," Orion says as if he's an imbecile. "When they succeed, antimatter will rush into the world, bringing Eldritch with it."

Reign's knees feel like they're going to give out, there's so much pain compounding in his body, but he locks them along with every other joint. "The Sins will be stopped," he grinds out through his clenched jaw. "So don't go getting too excited."

Orion's eyes flash with a strange black fire. "Oh, you're one of the fools who think they'll stop it, are you?"

Reign sees the intent to move flash across the dark fae's face a second before it happens. He tries to run, but the moment he unlocks his limbs, he crumbles. His face hits the decaying floor with a thud that feels like a nuclear bomb in his head. He rolls over, scratching at the black dust as he tries to get back up.

Except he's shoved with a boot. He screams as he lands on his side, too twisted with pain to know whether he should arch his back or curl up into a ball.

Something clicks around one wrist, then the other. "You're not going anywhere," Orion sneers close to his ear.

Reign has no choice but to admit Orion's right. He's dying. The poison has reached his heart once more and it's seizing it in its merciless claws.

Just so he can come back to life, and do this all again.

DINAH

When Dinah opens her eyes next, she's in a pale world of... vellum. All that stretches out is textured cream, as if the whole world is just one sheet of parchment.

"This is the last page of the book, isn't it?" she asks Emma.

The young woman nods. "Yes, you've seen how the obsidian was born, and why it wants to reunite with the Eldritch. Which is exactly what it will seek to do if the breach is opened again."

Dinah remembers the insidious voice that was a constant hiss in her mind. All it wanted was more power. More evil. It wanted Eldritch. "And the breach was first opened by the fae priest's spell."

Emma nods again. "And Archangel Michael used the darkness that escaped to create the obsidian and the Sins. For thousands of years they've been seeking to reunite. To replicate the spell."

"But they haven't succeeded," Dinah points out, realizing she's starting to sound like Arielle. She's actually being optimistic.

"Lucifer threw the obsidian out of Hell before the Sins could get their hands on it."

Dinah remembers the sight of the dark hands breaking through the soil, trying to reach the obsidian as her ancestor picked it up. "But they failed."

"That time they did," Emma acknowledges. "So the Sins wrought evil and destruction throughout Hell. Lucifer appointed three demons to fight them—Belphegor, Asmodeus and Beelzebub—the Kings of Hell. Belphegor had one fierce warrior loyal to him who used a powerful spell to put the Sins in a deep slumber."

Dinah's eyebrows shoot up. "Colt."

"Yes, Colt. But the Sins woke up when the Tear was created.

The energy from that spell not only released the Grigori but also the Sins. They started to influence demons once again." Emma levels her gaze on Dinah. "Now that the Sins are above, they'll be doing everything they can to replicate the spell. Once the breach is created, Pandora's Box is the final obstacle to releasing Eldritch. And the obsidian will do everything it can to make sure that happens."

Dinah holds still even though her heart is thundering. She holds the obsidian. It demands she do its bidding.

She's finally found out she needs to control it more than ever, even as she's learned that may be impossible.

She lifts her chin. She's always liked a challenge. "Then I'll have to make sure the Sins are stopped."

Emma nods soberly. "Yes, you will."

"One more question," Dinah asks, angling her head. She should've asked this when she first arrived in the Book of Monsters.

Emma looks at Dinah in askance.

"Who are you?"

Emma's response is to smile the biggest one so far. Before Dinah can tell her that's not an acceptable answer, there's a rushing pull.

There's no rustling of pages. Just a yank that starts somewhere deep in her core.

And then she's standing back in Veritas, the scent of leather and magic lacing the silence.

We will unite, the obsidian hisses, the insidious sound jolting Dinah. She hadn't realized how peaceful her mind had been without it. *You cannot stop us.*

Dinah closes her eyes and takes a deep breath. "I'll die before I let that happen."

CHAPTER 14

ARIELLE

"It's happening again," Arielle gasps, hands fluttering over Reign's twitching body but not knowing where to touch. "Renata, please."

The doctor moves in, her stethoscope already in her ears as she presses it to Reign's chest. Her face tightens. "Yes, it's happening again."

Arielle bites back the agonized moan that climbs up her throat. "But last time..."

Reign, to all intents and purposes, died. His heart stopped. His breath became extinct. Only for his body to jolt as it drew air in a few terrified seconds later. She's never felt such relief!

But now, the jerking has started again. The arching of his back that has the tendons of his neck standing out in stark relief. His eyelashes fluttering in a frenzy. Surely Reign can't survive this a second time.

"Blood pressure is spiking again," Renata mutters. "And his pulse is weakening."

Arielle clutches Reign's hand, gritting her teeth when she finds the skin cold. "We have to do something. He's in so much pain."

Every muscle in Reign's body is taut with agony, almost calcified with it. His back is a bow, his jaw clamped so tightly Arielle can hear his teeth grind. His fingers are claws. And all Arielle can do is sit here and watch as the pain steals him away.

Renata shakes her head. "I gave him what analgesics I have, but they're not making a difference."

Suddenly, Reign's body gives out, going from arched to collapsed. "No!" Arielle cries, grasping at his shirt. Her hands climb to his face to cradle it. "No!"

But Reign doesn't move. Doesn't breathe.

"Step back," Renata orders. "I'll commence chest compressions."

But before Renata can move, the sound of a harsh breath being yanked into starved lungs punches the air. Reign's breathing again. Renata presses the stethoscope to his chest again, shaking her head, but this time in wonder. "He's alive. His pulse is erratic, but he's definitely alive."

Arielle sinks onto the edge of the bed as her knees turn watery. "Thank God," she breathes.

Her father steps forward, having hung back and watched this all unfold again. "It's his immortality," he says. "The poison reaches his heart and kills him, but the Mark brings him back."

Arielle blinks, trying to separate the horror at what Reign must be experiencing and the relief that she won't lose him to this. "We have to do something."

Xeven's blue eyes flit over Reign's form, now breathing evenly. "I believe the poison is the demonic equivalent to witch's nightshade. The symptoms are identical."

Arielle shoots to her feet. "So we can treat it?"

"Any cure to the nightshade poison would work on the demonic one," he says, his frown sinking into his scars. "Although the antidote needs to be infused with demon blood."

Rachel strides into Reign's bedroom, Marlowe close behind

her. "You try to take demon blood from one and you'll have an army of them raining down on you." She stops and frowns when she sees Reign. "You said he was injured. Not...this."

Arielle wraps her arms around herself, rubbing away at the goosebumps pebbling her skin. "He's been poisoned. Xeven was just saying the antidote will need to be infused with demon blood."

Rachel's frown deepens as she glances at Marlowe. "That'll take some serious fighting power to get."

He nods. "Demon blood is powerful and can be used against them in potions. We'd need to take a contingent, kill one and then get the sample without any others noticing."

And demons always run in packs.

Rachel shrugs. "We don't have a choice. We have to save Reign."

Arielle moves closer to him, the gravity of what this will involve settling on her chest. Using angels and nephilim to do this means less protection for Renata and the Potentials. Wrath and Greed are going to be looking for an opening to attack. Arielle sits on the bed and takes Reign's hand, relieved to find it's warmer. "We have to," she says, repeating Rachel's words.

Reign's in pain. He's going to die over and over until he gets the antidote.

The thought makes her ill and her heart crack.

"There's another way."

Arielle whirls around at Xeven's voice. "What?"

"There's a warlock in Mercy City who will probably have what you're looking for. He collects demon artifacts."

Arielle's once more on her feet. "Take me to him."

"I cannot go," he says, shaking his head. "Cain and the warlock have history. I would not be welcome there."

"Then give me the address and I'll go," Arielle says, already making her way to the door. There's no time to waste.

"I'll come with you," Rachel offers.

"No, you need to stay here with Renata and the Potentials." Arielle glances between her and Marlowe. "They need to be protected."

Rachel and Marlowe exchange a look, and Arielle can tell they know she's right. "I'll see if I can get the demon blood and then return. If anything happens, I'll call."

Rachel's mouth twists. "Fine, but only because I know the chick who taught you to fight, and she's pretty awesome."

Arielle finds a smile hovering on her lips. Those days in Rachel's father's dojo feel like a lifetime ago. "She really is."

"Agree," adds Marlowe, moving to clasp Rachel's hand with his. His blue eyes turn serious. "We'll take care of the Potentials. And make sure Renata is safe, too."

"Thanks," Arielle says, meaning it. She'd be falling apart right now if it wasn't for this team.

Xeven moves, catching her attention, and he opens his mouth as if he's going to say something. But then he closes it again, giving her a curt nod that Arielle has no idea what to make of.

Turning away, she looks at Reign one last time, Renata hovering over him. *I'll get the demon blood*, she promises silently. *No matter what.*

THE MAN who opens the apartment door even before Arielle finishes knocking isn't what she expected. He's short, stout, and bald. He pushes his rounded glasses up as he somehow manages to peer down his nose even though he's a foot shorter than her. "Yes?"

Arielle glances at the door number, confirming it's the

address her father texted her, then turns back to the man. "Fabian?" she confirms.

His nose twitches. "Yeah. Who's asking?"

"My name's Arielle." She drops her voice. "I believe you have something I want. Something...of demonic origin."

Fabian's nostrils flare as his chest inflates. He takes a step back. "Welcome, Arielle."

She enters, finding herself straight in a living room that she has to suppress her reaction to. The furniture and color scheme are largely unremarkable with their gray tones and simple lines —it's everything else that has her eyes widening. Three paintings of Captain America in different poses take up most of the wall above the couch. The rug beneath her feet is a recreation of his shield. Red, white and blue color everything else—the lamps, the coffee table, and the overstuffed chair that Fabian takes a seat in.

"How can I help?" he asks smoothly.

Arielle takes a few steps, then hovers, standing on the tip of the large white star in the center of the rug. "I need some demon blood," she says, deciding to get straight to the point. How many times will Reign go through the pain, die, and come back in the period she's gone?

Fabian's eyebrows shoot up with such speed that his glasses slip down. He pushes them back up. "Demon blood. Decided to go straight for the good stuff, huh?"

"Do you have some?"

"Of course, I have some," he snaps, sounding offended. His gaze narrows behind his round glasses. "But it doesn't come cheap."

Arielle remains where she is, still and waiting. She's not going to tell Fabian no matter what the price is, she'll pay it.

He steeples his fingers as he rests his elbows on the arms of his Captain America-colored chair. "There's an amulet I want. It was stolen from me a long time ago and I want it back."

"What sort of amulet?" Arielle asks, already knowing she'll get it for him.

"It's rumored to have belonged to the Egyptian Goddess, Imentet, Goddess of the Afterlife." Fabian smiles, looking a little like a gleeful child. "This amulet protects one from evil."

Arielle watches him closely. Just because she's going to do this, doesn't mean she's not interested in knowing what she's getting caught up in. "Got yourself some enemies, do you, Fabian?"

He snorts. "We're all going to need protection soon." Arielle assumes he's talking about the Gates of Hell, which means she's surprised with what he says next. "There's an ancient evil on the move in Purgatory. If Orion escapes, no one on Earth will be safe."

Arielle nods, even though Purgatory and some evil entity trying to rise sound like small potatoes compared to what she's dealing with right now. "Do you know where the amulet is?"

"I do," Fabian says, his eyes turning to flint in his rounded face. "It's in City Hall."

Arielle keeps her neutral expression even as she recognizes that the Mayor must have the amulet. "Fine. I'll be back with the amulet."

She spins on her heel and leaves the apartment, intending on going straight to City Hall. Maybe the Mayor will give her the amulet once she realizes Reign's life is at stake. Gabby has always said Virginia was on their side.

Arielle's just climbing into her car when her cell rings, Marlowe's name appearing on the screen. She answers, then tucks the phone between her ear and her shoulder as she prepares to maneuver into traffic. "Yes, I'm still alive," she says jokingly. "And I know how to get the demon blood."

"That may have to wait," Marlowe says, his voice wound so tight Arielle almost drops the phone.

"What? Why?"

"It's Renata. We were transporting her to a safe house as we knew the Sins would try the farmhouse first when we were attacked."

"And?" Arielle asks, her limbs feeling numb. She already knows the answer.

"I'm so sorry, Ari, but the demons attacked and took her."

"I'm on my way," she says, hanging up before Marlowe hears the tightness in her own voice. Tears are crowding her throat, caught behind a solid stone of grief.

She sits in her car for long seconds, head resting on the steering wheel, even as she knows she needs to get going. Time is even more precious than it was when she arrived. But Arielle finds herself frozen. The world is crashing down around her.

Not only is Renata gone.

But she now has to choose between saving the Innocent or saving Reign.

CHAPTER 15
REIGN

Reign opens his eyes even though it feels like his eyelids have sandbags stacked on top of them. His bones feel hollowed out, his muscles feel as if they've peeled away, leaving him disjointed and broken.

But he's alive.

And if he's alive, he can get back to Arielle.

"Finally," a female voice whispers. "Wake up!"

The mermaid's face comes into focus, hovering above him. Reign groans, rolling over as he realizes he's on the old mattress he used to sleep on in the hideout. Except it's a gray, decaying version of the mattress, just like the house is. Colorless. Lifeless.

"Shh," the mermaid hisses. "You need to get up and get us out of here."

"That's the plan," he mutters, trying to get his aching body to comply.

"Quick, he's—"

The mermaid's words are cut off as she's flung across the room, her cry quickly swallowed by the airless atmosphere of Purgatory. Her body hits the wall with a dull *thud* before dropping to the ground. She cries out again, her tail flapping and fluttering. Then she's sailing through the air once more and hitting the opposite wall, this cry of pain laced with fear. She hasn't hit the ground before she's flung to the other side, like some sick game of tennis.

"Stop!" Reign roars. He staggers to his feet, discovering the handcuffs around his wrists.

Orion chuckles from where he's standing in the doorway. "You can't stop me," he sneers, enjoying the power. "Those handcuffs were forged by the Titans to hold faeries. They're unbreakable. You certainly won't be stopping me." He takes a step into the room. "No one can."

Reign stays on his feet through sheer force of will. He considers pointing out he just did, seeing as Orion's now distracted and no longer battering the mermaid, but decides against it. The mermaid is lying against the wall, panting as she watches this with terrified eyes. "You think you're pretty powerful, don't you?" he says, deciding to keep Orion's focus on him.

"I know I am," he spits. "And so do they," he adds, waving a hand toward the mermaid and making her flinch.

Reign staggers forward, lurching as he steps off the mattress, but it draws Orion's attention back to him. "You certainly rule the roost." Which makes him a great big coc—

"I certainly do," Orion boasts, cutting off Reign's thought. "And they don't even thank me for picking up that mantle."

Reign notices in his periphery that the mermaid pushes up onto her hands, so he takes another step toward Orion. "Gratitude may be pushing it," he says dryly.

"Do you know what it's like for the spirits who have been stuck here?" Orion demands, entering the room more fully. "Time loses meaning in a world with no color or life. They lose hope. They lose their sense of self. I have given them something."

"It's called fear," Reign snaps back, then instantly regrets it. He's trying to distract this megalomaniac, not piss him off.

But Orion simply grins. "It's very effective," he purrs. "And once I gift them with untold power, they'll certainly be grateful."

That has Reign's attention. He narrows his eyes on Orion, ignoring the pain that's swelling through him again. "How do you intend to do that?"

"Why, with Eldritch, of course. Once the spirits are strong enough to reclaim their bodies, Eldritch will reward them for their service by making them immortal."

"And your servants."

"We will all be Eldritch's servants," Orion snaps. "Because it will be our god."

"You're fucking crazy," Reign says, partially shocked, partially disgusted.

Orion takes another step closer. "No, I'm the only one with vision. Once Eldritch is released, it will remake the universe in its dark image. And I'm the one who served it from the beginning. I'm the one who it will reward."

The mermaid shuffles backward but Orion's too inflated with his twisted vision—as he calls it—to notice. Reign shakes his head. "You know old age can lead to senility, don't you?"

Orion's lip curls. "It was faeries who once ruled the Earth, long before anyone or anything else. But we were banished when God created humans." He spits the last word. "Humans who went on to destroy the very Earth they were gifted with."

"Fair point," Reign says mildly, wanting to keep Orion talking. Not only is the mermaid slipping out the door, but he's curious to hear what this crazed faerie has planned.

"And when Eldritch claims this universe as its own, faeries will once again be free to return to Earth and rule this world."

He smiles a cold, hard smile. "And I will rule the fae with my army of immortal spirits."

"If you weren't a power hungry asshole, I have to admit that's a solid plan."

"I'm an unstoppable asshole," Orion says, his grin growing. "And you'd best remember that."

Reign's retort is cut off by a wave of pain that seems to start in his marrow and explode through him. He bites down on the gasp, tasting blood but almost welcoming anything that registers on his senses that isn't agony. Instinctively, he curls in, then hisses when the handcuffs on his left wrist brush against the Mark on the opposite arm.

The flash of fire leaves his nerve endings sizzling and his joints liquified. He drops to his knees, even as he hates the vulnerable, submissive pose it leaves him in.

Orion stalks closer, then squats down, peering at Reign's arm. "You carry the Mark," he hisses. "This is why the spirits are so interested in you."

"I'm pretty sure it's my hot bod," Reign grinds out through gritted teeth.

Orion sniffs the air above Reign's head. "And you've been poisoned," he says, sounding pleased. "That's why you keep dying and returning. You're immortal."

"Or I keep returning so I can kick your ass the moment these things are off," Reign snarls, yanking at the handcuffs then losing the ability to breathe thanks to the painful price the movement costs him.

Orion's hollow laugh fills the dead air. He's clearly enjoying Reign's pain. He pushes to his feet, lifts a booted foot, and daintily places it in the center of Reign's chest. All it takes is a twitch and Reign tumbles backward, a cry wrenched from his soul as the pain swallows him once again.

Somewhere beyond his tightly clenched eyes, Reign hears Orion speak.

"You aren't going anywhere," the fae promises. "Especially now that I know how useful you are."

DINAH

Dinah stands in the clearing of the secluded forest that borders Mercy City. She glares at the object sitting on the ground in front of her, chunks of shattered boulder scattered around it.

You cannot destroy it, the obsidian hisses with glee. *It's only a matter of time before it's opened.*

And so will the breach between worlds.

"Not freaking happening," she mutters, glaring even more intensely at Pandora's Box.

Dinah knew at the time not to give the Mayor the true Box. She knew there was something about it that was important, that it contained more than just untold horrors.

Turns out it's a key. All that stands between this universe and the anti-verse.

And she can't freaking destroy it.

Drawing in a determined breath, she raises it into the air with her mind, narrowing her eyes as it hovers higher and higher. She's tried crushing it, incinerating it, attacking it with every spell she can think of. But nothing's worked.

Pandora's Box still glints in the sunlight, silver and proud. Silently gloating.

Dinah lifts it higher, deciding to hit it with everything she has. She brings her arms out wide as heat builds in her palms. She feeds it, enjoying the burn. The fireball she's going to throw at the Box will be the most powerful she's ever created. Enough energy to raze a country pulses up and down her arms.

Pandora's Box has just reached the height of the treetops—enough distance that she won't be harmed by any shrapnel—when there's an additional surge of power. She draws in a sharp breath at the unexpected boon. She's a living, pulsing mass of energy.

Nothing can stop her now.

Dinah focuses her attention on the hovering silver box, feeling exhilarated and invincible.

Yes. It feels good, doesn't it?

This time the obsidian doesn't whisper, it shouts. Reverberates through her every cell.

"Never," she mouths.

Now you will see what we're capable of.

Dinah cries out when her arms lower to the level of her shoulders and her palms point out as if she's communicating no.

Except that's the opposite of what the obsidian is planning.

Her hands heat. The power peaks, making her feel like a nuclear reactor.

"No!" Dinah screams, terrified of what she's capable of.

This forest will cease to exist, along with every life in it.

It takes every shred of Dinah's strength to curl her fingers in and make two fists. They're loose ones, violently shaking ones, but a frail, flimsy barrier between the obsidian intent on destruction and the rest of the world.

You are nothing against me.

Dinah finds she's panting. Her heart is frozen and thundering all at once.

Because she knows the obsidian is telling the truth.

There's a flicker of movement in her peripheral vision.

A demon swoops down, snatches the hovering Box, and powers away.

"No!" Dinah screeches, although she's not sure what she's denying. She uses the distraction to tighten her fists. To contain the volcanic eruption of evil she was about to become.

And to watch the hell spawn tucks its wings in and dive for the protection of the canopy. It disappears, no doubt weaving its way through the trees as fast as it can.

"Shit!" Dinah screams.

She's lost Pandora's Box.

And the obsidian almost won.

CHAPTER 16

ARIELLE

A rielle stands beside Reign's bed, her eyes tracing the familiar lines of his handsome face. Dark hair brushing his forehead, strong eyebrows, chiseled lips. Yet his face is relaxed and vulnerable in ways she's rarely seen.

He's not in pain. At the moment...

It's only a matter of time before the heart-breaking cycle starts all over again. The tension pulling his features tight. His back arching. His breath hissing through gritted teeth.

And all she can do is watch. Helpless as his agony echoes through her heart.

"There's nothing you can do until we find the antidote," Xeven says quietly.

Arielle snaps her head to look at him as he stands at the end of the bed. "If that was you lying there, and my mom standing here, she'd be torn, too."

He blinks. "I see."

But she's pretty sure he doesn't. The Ryder who loved her mom is buried too deep. Or lost...

Arielle turns away, not able to think of that right now.

Renata has been abducted by the Sins. And Reign is in a perpetual loop of painfully dying and coming back to life. And she has to choose.

"If that were me lying there, I'd want your mother to fight the evil threatening thousands of lives rather than just mine," Xeven says. He glances at Reign. "Would Reign want that, too?"

Arielle presses her lips together. Could the ghost of Ryder still be alive in Xeven? Because he makes a good point. Fighting the Sins is exactly what Reign would want her to do. He'd know how important it is that they get the Innocent back.

Arielle's shoulders sag. "Even if I could, I don't know where the Sins are, nor do I have a weapon to kill either Greed or Wrath."

Xeven reaches behind him and beneath his t-shirt, pulling something out. His hand returns, holding a knife. One Arielle recognizes.

It's a weapon that can kill a Sin.

"I told you that Cain collected artifacts. This blade can kill Greed."

She hesitates. "And you're giving it to me?"

He nods, looking perplexed. "I told you I would." He glances at Reign. "And I'm bound by the Mark."

Arielle takes the knife, testing its weight in her palm, wondering which reason is more compelling to her father, even as she knows she doesn't have time to dwell on it. "Now, we just need to locate the Sin."

The door to Reign's bedroom opens before she finishes her sentence. Marlowe enters, his face somber. "We've found a location with a high level of demonic activity. We think one or both of the Sins are there."

Seems Fate is trying to tell them something.

Arielle tucks the blade into the back of her jeans. "As coincidence would have it, I have the knife to kill Greed."

Rachel appears behind Marlowe, a grim smile climbing up her face. "It's time to party."

Arielle glances at Reign, registering that his features are beginning to tighten. The cycle is about to start once more. The thought of leaving fractures her heart.

But killing Greed is a goal that's actually in reach right now.

MARLOWE GLANCES at his watch as the nephilim warriors who accompanied them spread out around the palatial two-story house. "This place is a gambling den for the rich." His mouth twists. "And a brothel."

Arielle shifts her weight from one foot to the other, restlessness pumping through her muscles. Time is running out, she can feel it. Images of an obelisk are hovering in her periphery. "But at least one of the Sins is here?"

He looks up, eyes narrowed as he scans the white stucco. "Either that, or it's a demon conference. There's a significant amount of dark energy coming off the place."

Rachel nods where she's standing beside him. "The Innocent might even be here."

Xeven lifts his chin as if he's scenting the air. "Yes, I believe Renata may be here."

Marlowe holds his finger to his ear as he listens to the small piece in there. "The Knights are in position. Do we storm the place, or try for the element of surprise?"

Arielle breaks into a run, answering the question for him. She's going in. Now.

"Ari!" Rachel calls.

She's pretty sure she hears Marlowe curse.

But Arielle doesn't stop. She needs to know if Greed's here so she can end him. Then she's getting back to Reign.

A flying kick taught to her by Alexandra has the double door at the entry caving inward. Arielle lands in a large foyer. Black and white tiles stretch out over the large expanse, a small chandelier dangling high above. Large white pots with lush tropical plants stand on either side of the wide staircase leading to the second floor.

Arielle dismisses the opulent decor as she spins around, fists raised. She barely even notices the demons pouring out of arched doorways or leaping from the balcony that skirts the floor above. It's Greed stalking down the stairs that holds her complete attention.

The Sin is almost as broad as he is round, thick gold chains around his neck, arms, resting on his inflated chest. His lip curls up as he prepares to say something. Arielle's response is to run. Leap. And brandish the blade that will end the Sin before it's too late. A feeling has lodged deep in her gut.

The time of the sacrifice is drawing near.

The demons roar, closing in the moment she moves, and Arielle prepares herself to fight her way to her target. Her hand tightens on the knife. She'll do as much damage as necessary to reach Greed.

Except cries drown out the roar as the Knights pour in from every direction. Behind her, Arielle hears Rachel's shout, then Marlowe's grunt. Quickly followed by a demon's scream of pain. It's just the distraction Arielle needs. Rather than attack the demons coming at her, she dodges and weaves. She slips under black wings, slashes the knife at anyone who tries to get too close, and steadily makes her way toward Greed.

The Sin extends his wings as he sees her approach, the flames of Hell flashing in his pale green eyes. He launches into the air and soars over the stairs, his gaze zeroed on Arielle.

Which is just what she wants.

With a cry of her own, Arielle leaps the moment Greed is

within reach. She spins. Tucks. Executes a move in just the way Alexandra taught her. The knife that she'd tucked along her arm snaps out, already aiming for the throat. Greed dives, fists extended like battering rams, but she anticipates the move and twists the other way. Holding the blade so hard her tendons stand out, she slashes.

Greed ducks and the edge of the knife glances off one of his countless gold chains, following through with a strike of his own. It connects with Arielle's temple, snapping her head to the side, one of the jeweled rings on his fingers splitting her skin. He roars in delight as blood trickles down the side of her face.

Arielle doesn't even bother to wipe it away before she's striking again. Greed parries, responding with a kick of his own, but she leaps before it can connect with her ribs. As the sounds of battle rage around them, they don't take their focus off each other. Both looking for a vulnerability. A way to end this.

And Greed uses every one of his advantages. His ability to leap higher thanks to his wings, his ability to move faster, thanks to his demon strength. Arielle gets close over and over, but the blade never connects with his skin. Greed's blood doesn't start flowing like hers does. The wound at her temple throbs, but soon her lip is bleeding, as is a cut on her cheek. She pants as she circles the Sin, realizing something.

She may want this, but so does Greed. And he has evil powering his hunger for victory. Blood. Death.

And the only way she's going to win is to give it to him.

Arielle feints left, then strikes right. Greed smiles as if he was expecting it, then whips out a meaty fist toward her face—his preferred bullseye. The blow smashes into her jaw and this time, she allows the pain to show. She cries out, the sound cut off by a punch to her gut. Then her chest. And another to her face.

"Arielle!" Rachel cries out.

Stumbling back, Arielle tries to glance over her shoulder to tell her friend to stay back, but the break in eye contact only feeds Greed's bottomless appetite for violence. He kicks her and Arielle goes sailing back, smashing into the stone stairs. She groans, but it's not because it feels like her body just shattered, too. The images of the obelisk are getting stronger. More dominant.

If they don't save Renata, another Gate of Hell will be opened.

"No!" Rachel screams.

Arielle stumbles as she tries to stand, extending her hand toward Rachel. She could ruin everything and all this pain would've been for nothing. One look and she sees her friend running toward her, fury etched across her features. Suddenly Xeven appears, wrapping his arms around Rachel and hauling her against him. She struggles and screams, but he doesn't release her. In fact, he nods at Arielle.

He's letting her do what must be done.

Greed's next strike almost has Arielle losing consciousness. She focuses on her grip on the blade, holding it even tighter as she pushes away the pain and encroaching darkness. She can't afford to fail.

Greed stalks forward, his arched wings blocking out the battling demons and Knights. "This is going to be so satisfying," he growls, breathing heavily but not from exertion. He's excited. Hungry for more.

Arielle realizes she never would've won an outright fight with this Sin. He wants this no matter what. And then he'll want more. And more. Whatever death and destruction he wreaks, it will never be enough.

She moves fast. Possibly the fastest she ever has. She pushes away the images of hideous cracks splicing through the obelisk, she ignores the agony crackling through her bones, and she strikes. She sees the flash of surprise on Greed's face a split-second before she impales the blade in his fleshy stomach.

He lets out a garbled scream as blood gushes out, splattering on the black and white tiles. Arielle yanks her hand back, but not before the sticky, crimson fluid coats her skin. Greed takes a single step back, stumbles, and falls to his knee. He looks up at Arielle, and grins. "You were too late."

With a cry of denial, she spins and runs up the stairs, not bothering to watch the Sin die by her hand. Somehow, the higher she climbs the stairs, the stronger the tug is to the Innocent. Arielle follows the instinct blindly as she reaches the second floor, thick black carpet muffling her frantic footsteps as she makes her way to a large mahogany door. She pushes it open. Stops.

"No."

Arielle whispers the word even as her heart screams it.

Renata is lying on a large, ornate table. Her arms and legs dangle off the sides, limp and pale. Blood runs in thin rivulets from her chest and down to her wrists, still fresh enough to be dripping silently onto the carpet.

They're too late.

Another Innocent is dead.

Arielle falls to her knees and buries her head in her hands as grief overwhelms her. Images of the obelisk breaking try to crowd into her consciousness, but she pushes them away. She doesn't need to see it. She was hoping she'd never have to see it again.

She doesn't even look up when she hears footsteps enter the room. Rachel gasps. Marlowe curses as he slams a fist into a wall.

"Wrath may still be in here," he says.

Arielle doesn't move. Her body is too heavy. Her heart is hurting too much. They can't have lost.

Again.

A hand lands on her shoulder. "We'll take care of him, Ari."

She nods, her head still in her hands. She doesn't want to face the world beyond the darkness she's created. Reign is trapped and in pain. And now Renata is dead.

The sound of running feet fade down the corridor, followed by doors being barged open. Arielle still doesn't move. She feels like if she does, she might fall apart.

She startles when a hand once again falls on her shoulder. Instinctively, she leaps to her feet and spins around, ready to fight, only to find Xeven standing there.

His eyes narrow in his scarred face. "Do not lose hope, Arielle."

She scoffs out a laugh. "I know you don't really feel things the way I do, so I'm not going to try and explain exactly how crap things are looking right now."

"I know another Innocent has been killed. It means another Sin has been released."

Arielle lifts a hand. "I don't need it spelled out to me." She steps to the side. She can't be here right now, doing this. "I'm going to go see Reign."

He's her hope. He always has been.

But Xeven also side steps, blocking the way to the door behind him. "You've been doing it all wrong. The Innocents aren't the key to stopping the apocalypse."

Arielle's gaze flies to his misshapen face. "What are you talking about?"

"There's a way to end this." Xeven extends his arms wide. "All of this."

Crossing her arms, Arielle shakes her head. "I can't do this right now. I need to see Reign."

"Yes, you do. You'll need him to help you. He must be healed of the demon poison."

Arielle shakes her head again. "I don't understand what you're trying to tell me."

Xeven takes a step forward, his pale blue eyes blazing with conviction. "The Grail is the cure. It can close all of the Gates of Hell. Forever."

Arielle blinks. Then blinks again. "No one has been able to find the Grail," she points out.

"Then find it, daughter. Along with the Keeper of the Grail."

The words are said simply. As if it's possible.

And yet, in that moment, she knows he's right. They have to find the Grail.

A short, sharp nod is all she gives Xeven as she strides past him. As Arielle rushes down the stairs and to the line of vehicles they arrived in, she finds he's right beside her. She glances at his profile as they silently climb in her car.

Of all the people to give her hope right now, it was her father.

RACHEL

Rachel leans against Marlowe as they watch the last of the Knights Templar drive away. "So freaking annoying that Wrath wasn't here, too."

He presses a kiss to her temple, his arm tightening around her waist. "We'll find him. Then we'll end him."

Rachel turns so she's facing him, then tucks herself into his chest. She thinks of how Arielle looked when they'd discovered Renata dead. Images of Reign, tortured and still in his bed, quickly follow. "I don't think I could do this without you."

Marlowe's arms are a band of strength as he pulls her in close. "You're stronger than you know, Rachel."

She presses up on her toes so their lips are level. "I need you, Marlowe," she says, the words tight with truth. "I *need* you."

He's her strength.

Her hope.

Her heart.

His breath exhales, caressing her lips. "I know. I need you, too." His hands come up to cup her face. "I love you with everything I have, Rachel. Always know that."

She smiles, feeling the sensation deep in her heart. "I don't have a great memory. You'll have to remind me every day."

His echoing smile takes her breath away. "I look forward to it."

Suddenly, Marlowe's eyes widen. His mouth goes slack as his breath whooshes out.

"Marlowe?" Rachel asks, knowing something's wrong. Very, very wrong. "What's—"

He collapses in her arms and she catches him, but doesn't have the strength to keep them upright. She crumples, bringing him with her, trying to understand what's happening. "Marlowe!" He doesn't respond and Rachel gasps when she finds crimson blooming across his chest. "No!"

A cackling laugh has her head snapping up. Wrath steps back, holding a bloodied blade, his smile as cold as Rachel's heart just became. "That's for killing Greed." He lurches forward. "And this will be just because I want to."

He raises the knife high above his head, his eyes burning with fires of Hell and hatred. Rachel curls around Marlowe's still body, tears stinging her eyes. She can't tell if he's breathing or not. That means she's not sure if she wants to live or not.

Wrath swings the blade down and Rachel braces herself. A scream fills the air, the screeching sound quickly cut short. Rachel looks up to find Wrath dissolving into black smoke. The knife drops to the ground, clattering beside her as the Sin spears into the sky, twisting furiously.

Dinah steps forward and lowers her hand. The crackling energy that had been sparking between her fingers dissipates. "He's banished. Well, for now, anyway."

Rachel nods her thanks, her throat too tight to speak. She returns her focus to Marlowe, trembling fingers running over his face, then his chest. He's as still as the air in her lungs. "Please," she whispers. She can't lose him, too.

Relief is a waterfall when she sees his chest rise. He's breathing!

"Marlowe!" Rachel gasps. "We'll get you help."

He doesn't respond.

But he's far beyond her reach.

CHAPTER 17
REIGN

The still air feels too heavy. It rests against Reign's skin like a dead weight, making it hard to breathe. It takes effort to open his eyes, but now that the latest near-death experience has passed, he needs to find a way out of here.

Back to Arielle.

Glad his throat is too raw to groan, Reign rolls over, already panting from the exertion. Every time the poison wracks him with pain and brings him to the point of death, he becomes weaker. Focusing on being alive, even if it's agonizing, he sits up. Blinking away the nausea—it's not like his stomach has anything to throw up—Reign looks around the gray room he's stuck in. The door looks a universe away.

His handcuffs clink as he tries to stand.

"You won't make it to the next thought, let alone the door."

Reign curls his lip, not bothering to look in the direction Cain's voice came from. "If I can have a hallucination as awful as you, I can get to the door."

Cain appears in front of him. "I'm not a hallucination," he says smugly. "I'm stuck in Purgatory, just like you are."

That has Reign pausing. So does the fact the room is spinning. "You're a spirit?"

"Abel killed me." Cain extends his arms. "So here I am."

"Karma really did a number on you, huh?" Cain killed Abel. Then Abel killed Cain.

Cain smirks. "On both of us, descendant-of-mine." His gaze rakes over Reign as he sways despite himself. "Although I'm certainly not a proud grandpappy."

"I'm not exactly loving the family tree, either," Reign growls, thinking of his demonic heritage. "Now, get out of my way."

Cain crosses his arms as he arches an eyebrow. "Or what? You'll sway on me?"

"Move."

"Sorry. But I'm planning on returning, just like you are." He takes a step closer. "In fact, you're my ticket out here, son."

If Reign could spit, he would. "I'm not helping you cause more chaos on Earth."

"I don't intend to." Cain's face tightens. "I've spent centuries hating my family, in part because the Mark twisted my mind." His gaze flashes down to Reign's arm and then back again. "It's time to make it right. It's time to heal the rift between my siblings."

Pain is climbing back up Reign's nerves, prickly and sharp. The cycle is starting again. He wanted to be at least by the door before that. "Sounds noble," he scoffs. "But I'm still not helping you get out of here."

To his surprise, Cain smiles. "You need me, Reign. Just as much as I need you." He grabs Reign's arm and twists it so the Mark is visible. "You're going to need help controlling its influence. Especially if you want to be with your beloved Arielle."

White dots dance in front of Reign's eyes as his breath stutters through the pain the sharp movement caused. "I don't... need...your help," he grits out through clenched teeth.

One moment Cain's there, holding his arm, the next he disappears. Reign stumbles as if a support beam was just torn away from him. He quickly rights himself, closing his eyes for a moment as he tries to find his feet beyond the wall of pain closing in around his mind. He doesn't care why Cain just disappeared. Only that he's out of his way.

Reign opens his eyes just in time to see Orion place his fingertips in the middle of his chest, smile coldly, and flick. Reign goes sailing through the air and he slams his eyes shut once more, this time scrunching them as tightly as every other muscle he just tensed.

He's bracing himself for when he hits the ground.

He tries to be ready. Tries to prepare himself for the inevitable shredding of his mind.

But he's not even close.

The moment Reign's body connects with the floor, he cries out. His whole body is a grenade that just detonated. Fractured. And disintegrated. His back arches so hard his head jams into the hard ground, every sinew and tendon are being stretched as his body tries to escape the pain. It slowly abates, dissipating until he collapses, gasping as the contact of his spine on the floor reverberates straight to his skull.

Orion appears above him. "Now that you've finished, I have something to show you."

He holds aloft a book, turning it one way then the other. "The Book of the Dead. It's how I'll survive the onslaught of the Eldritch."

Reign works on steadying his shallow breathing. Even in his pain-riddled brain, he knows what Orion's about to tell him is significant. He can't black out yet.

Orion opens the book, stepping back a little as he flicks a

glance of contempt at Reign on the floor. "You see, there's an amulet that once belonged to the Egyptian goddess, Imentet. It's capable of warding any evil, no matter how powerful it is."

"Good for you," Reign grinds out.

Orion ignores him and Reign suspects the fae is doing this more for his own ego than educating Reign. He wants to talk about his great plans. To glory in them.

"I have a warlock acquiring the amulet for me," he continues. "And once he sends it to me here, in Purgatory, then I'll use you to escape to the outside world."

"Get in line," Reign mutters.

Orion snaps the book shut, the sound a small explosion in Reign's head. "It'll be amusing watching the angels and demons wreak havoc, clueless that the apocalypse will be something bigger. Far darker." He smiles delightedly. "That I will be the one destined to rule them all."

This time, Reign doesn't respond. The pain is becoming overwhelming. The poison is once more reaching his heart.

"Which reminds me," Orion says, looking as if he forgot to put something on his grocery list. "I'm going to need the key to release Eldritch." He spins around and strides to the door, his black robes fluttering behind him. "Which means I need to go see a certain witch about Pandora's Box."

He exits, not bothering to glance over his shoulder at Reign, uncaring that he's about to die again.

Reign closes his eyes, giving himself over to the inevitable. Even though he wants to run after Orion and stop him. Stop him from finding that certain witch they should never have trusted.

As blackness claims him, Reign fights the despair that hitchhikes with it.

Dinah has Pandora's Box. Possibly because she was working with Orion all along.

CHAPTER 18
ARIELLE

Arielle strides straight into Mayor Virginia Goodstone's office, the secretary she passed spluttering behind her. "You can't go in there! You don't have an appointment!"

Arielle ignores her, glad to find Virginia sitting behind her large mahogany desk. "I need to talk to you." She lowers her voice. "Aclima."

The only sign the Mayor heard her is the slightest pause as she puts down her pen. "It's fine, Mr. Bailey," she says to the portly man practically hopping from one foot to the other. "I'll see Arielle."

Grumbling under his breath about the need to respect a schedule, Mr. Bailey leaves the room and closes the door with a sharp click.

Arielle strides over the remaining feet to lean her hands on the desk. "Yes, I know you're Cain's sister, and that you're the one who transferred the Mark to Reign." Her father told her everything.

Virginia laces her fingers together and smiles as if she was just given a compliment. "I started researching Reign when I learned that Cain couldn't strike him without causing himself pain. It took a while, but I learned that Reign has a connection to Cain's bloodline." Her smile warms with satisfaction. "It was just what I needed to transfer the Mark so I could kill Cain. He paid for what he did to Abel."

Arielle grits her teeth, not wanting to rehash what a centuries old sibling feud has meant. "Reign's been poisoned. He's in a lot of pain, but the Mark is keeping him alive."

"You're welcome," Virginia interjects.

Arielle glares at her. "I need demon blood for the antidote. And I need the amulet you have to trade for the demon blood."

Virginia slowly comes to her feet, leaning forward with her hands on the desk, mirroring Arielle. "No." The word is said slowly. Emphatically. "I will not give you the amulet."

The thought of Reign cycling through pain and death has Arielle pressing her fingers into the mahogany until they turn white. "Give it to me, Aclima. You owe us after everything you've put Reign through."

"The amulet is dangerous. It's why I hid it in the first place." Virginia's face looks like it's carved from marble. "I will not give it to you."

Arielle's about to argue when Virginia presses a button on her phone, never once breaking eye contact. "Mr. Bailey. Please see Arielle out."

She considers fighting this, either verbally or physically, but the stony look on the Mayor's face tells Arielle it wouldn't be time well spent. Mr. Bailey walks toward her, the material of his pants swishing between his thighs, a scowl on his face. Arielle steps around and straight past him, her head held high. "I can see myself out," she snaps.

She continues down the corridor and toward the exit to City

Hall in the same determined strides she entered with. She walks straight to the parking lot and slips into the passenger side of her car. She has no doubt Virginia and her security team are watching to make sure she leaves.

"Did you get it?" she asks the young woman sitting in the driver's seat.

Alexandra smiles as she turns the ignition and accelerates. "Of course I did."

"Good." Arielle finally allows herself to relax, sagging into the seat. That was actually easier than she thought it would be.

Alexandra navigates her way onto the main road leading away from City Hall. "It took me a little while to find it in that room—so many cupboards. But I focused on the smaller ones first."

"Good thinking." Arielle rests her head back. She can picture Alexandra stealthily breaking into the secret rooms in City Hall hidden behind the panel with the obsidian symbol on it, then quickly and systematically checking every cupboard. "Thanks. I knew Virginia wouldn't let the amulet go willingly."

Alexandra's brow contracts as she executes a turn at a set of lights. "Did she say why?"

"Only that it's dangerous. Not that it matters. We need it to save Reign."

"I know of the amulet," Alexandra says, sounding thoughtful. "It's powerful. Very powerful. I wonder what the warlock wants it for."

Arielle glances at Alexandra, hoping she's not having second thoughts. "He seems to know what's coming. Protecting himself is smart."

Alexandra's eyebrows sink a little lower. "He may have other plans for it."

"Trading the amulet is the only way we can get the demon blood, Alexandra. We have to do this."

She doesn't answer, seeming to focus on the road, but the downturn of her lips says it all. Arielle clasps her hands in her lap, conscious of how tightly she's gripping. She knows this is risky. That there are too many unknowns. But Reign's life depends on it. There's no other choice.

Fabian answers the door so fast, Arielle suspects he already knew they were coming. "Did you get it?" he demands.

Alexandra pushes past him and Arielle follows, not wanting to have this conversation in the corridor either.

The warlock shuts the door with a huff. "Well, did you?"

"You're being very impatient," Alexandra observes, her eyes narrowed.

Fabian shoves his glasses up his nose, clearly irritated. "And you're hedging. You either have the amulet, meaning we have a deal, or you don't."

Alexandra's lip curls, but she withdraws the amulet out of her pocket. The circular pendant is made of sterling silver, hieroglyphics etched into the border. A single eye rests in the center, a perfect jade jewel as the iris.

Fabian draws in a sharp breath. "Yes," he hisses. "That's it."

Alexandra curls her hand around it, cutting it off from view. "What do you want it for?"

"The answer to that question isn't part of the agreement," Fabian snaps. He walks over to a bureau that proudly displays framed images of Captain America. He pulls open a drawer, removes something and turns around. "While these are."

He holds up two vials, dark red blood within. Demon blood.

"Give him the amulet," Arielle tells Alexandra. The cure for Reign is only a few feet away.

Alexandra's lips are once more a thin line as she walks to Fabian and exchanges the amulet for the vials.

Fabian tucks the amulet away immediately, shoving it into his jacket pocket. "Pleasure doing business with you, ladies." He strides to the door and opens it. "Have a wonderful day."

Alexandra stalks out, her back ramrod straight, and Arielle follows. The door's just been sharply closed behind them when she lets out her breath. "Wow, we did it."

Tucking the vials into her pocket, Alexandra frowns. "Yes, but at what cost?"

"There's no price too high for Reign's life," Arielle says. "I'm more than willing to pay it."

Alexandra nods, looking thoughtful. "I admire your dedication to him. You clearly love him."

"But?" Arielle asks, knowing there's one.

"It's not your intentions that I'm questioning." Alexandra looks at the door behind them. "It's who wants to take advantage of them."

Arielle glances down the corridor, now anxious to get back to Reign. Who knows how many cycles of painful death and resurrection he's gone through while she's been gone. "We'll deal with that if we have to. Come on, let's go."

She's taken one step away when Alexandra spins so fast her hair flies out and the foot she flicks out smashes the doorknob of the warlock's door.

"Alexandra!" Arielle gasps.

But she's already bursting into Fabian's apartment. Arielle quickly follows, stopping just in time to see what Alexandra is.

Fabian is standing over a Captain America shield coffee table, the amulet sitting in the center. His arms are outstretched, his mouth almost as wide as he smiles with his eyes closed.

The amulet explodes with light like a small sun going supernova.

Then disappears.

"What have you done?" Alexandra roars.

Fabian's eyes fly open, but his grin doesn't die. "I sent it where it's supposed to go." He chuckles, the sound breathless as if he just exerted himself. "To Purgatory."

Then he disappears as completely as the amulet does.

Arielle rushes over to where he was standing, even though she knows it's too late. "He sent it to Purgatory!"

Alexandra's lips are pressed in a grim line. "The dark priest might already have it." Her gaze falls on Arielle. "You need to get it back."

"What?" Arielle takes an instinctive step back, her calves coming up against the couch. "How would I even do that?"

And what about Reign? How can she leave him again?

"As a demigod, I cannot go. It has to be you, Arielle. You need to make this right."

Because she was so desperate to help Reign that she handed over the amulet without asking too many questions.

Arielle's shoulders sag as her heart thuds heavily against her ribs. "Yeah, I do. How do I get to Purgatory?"

Alexandra draws out a small dagger. "I have to kill you."

"What?" Arielle asks, her hand flying to her throat.

"Not actually kill you, but stab you. You'll fall so deeply unconscious you'll essentially be dead. Enough to enter Purgatory."

Arielle swallows, finding her mouth dry. "How will I get back?"

"You can use the energy of the amulet. Use it to breathe life back into your body and you'll wake up again." Alexandra takes a step closer. "Ready? We cannot afford to wait."

A denial is the first thing that leaps to Arielle's lips. Yet she knows she can't speak it. Not when countless people could pay for her mistake.

I'm so sorry, Reign, she silently whimpers.

"Yes," she says, trying to sound stoic. "Will it hurt—"

Alexandra moves fast. She leaps over the coffee table, bringing the blade down in a swift arc. It slams into Arielle's shoulder and buries deep. A second later Alexandra yanks it out.

Hot pain slices through Arielle as her knees give out. She crumples to the couch, shocked to find the room is already going dark.

Then, there's nothing.

CHAPTER 19
REIGN

"Wake up."

If his bones didn't feel like they'd break the second he moved, Reign would blindly hit out at the annoying voice. It sounds close. Too close for comfort.

"Wake up!"

The whispered voice is growing in urgency. And the louder it is, the more Reign's yanked from the bliss of oblivion. He cracks his eyes open, even the gray hues of Purgatory feeling too bright for his aching eyes.

The mermaid's face pushes in closer. "Hurry up! We need to get out of here."

Reign almost laughs. He's not going anywhere. Even without the chains around his wrists, he's unable to move. His entire body is one twitch away from shattering. Just so it can loosely knit itself together and do it all again.

Something he's deeply grateful for.

"Come on! We're running out of time!" The mermaid shuffles along the floor of the room they're in, and even that muted sound draws a groan up Reign. "That's it," she urges.

"Look—"

The gasp that shoots from the mermaid is soft. But terrified.

Reign's eyes bolt all the way open, knowing there's only one thing that scares every spirit here in Purgatory so completely.

Orion.

The colorless room is empty, the walls nothing more than shades of hopelessness. The mermaid's gone, which means there's someone coming. Clenching his throat closed to trap the scream that will want to erupt the moment he moves, Reign drags himself into a sitting position. His joints grind, his muscles feel wasted and withered.

Yet he not only sits, but drags his drained body to a stand. If Orion's coming, Reign refuses to face him at any more of a disadvantage than he's already at. The room spins sickeningly, the shades of melancholy looking like a spiral of gray. And through it, Reign hears footsteps up the stairs. Then in the hall.

Only a few feet from the door.

He tries to raise his fists, but the metal clamped around his wrists is too heavy. Heck, the air feels like it's made from stone.

When a body appears in the doorway, Reign blinks. Then blinks again.

Then one more time, just to make sure.

Yep. His mind has finally snapped. The endless cycle of pain, death, then waking to endure it once more has finally taken its toll. Although it's not surprising that when the inevitable happened, he'd see Arielle. She's the one reason he's been holding on. She's the reason he's been glad to wake up, even if it hurts.

"Reign?" she asks, clearly shocked.

He frowns. If this is a delusion, she would've been looking for him. She'd be here to rescue him.

He can't even get a hallucination right.

Although she looks...like Heaven. Even in the soul-sucking

drabness of Purgatory, she's a vision. A beacon. A light he's undeniably drawn to.

Reign finds himself stumbling forward, uncaring this is a mirage in a desert of pain. Arielle breaks into a run, just like he knew she would. His delusion is finally getting it right.

It's when their bodies collide, jolting another rush of pain through him, that he gasps. "Ari?" he whispers, incredulous. His hands roam over her hair, down her throat, coming back to cup her face.

He can feel her. Touch her. Almost hold her if it weren't for the damned cuffs.

She smiles, tears shimmering in her blue eyes. "I didn't know...." Her gaze roams over his face, so much love and joy in there it takes Reign's breath away. "You're in Purgatory?"

"Because of the Mark. The poison is killing me, but I can't die." He drops his hands, hating the cuffs more than ever.

Arielle must notice them for the first time, because she gasps. "Who did this to you?

Reign frowns, for the first time finally registering something beyond Ari being here. She wasn't looking for him. Which means she's here for some other reason. "What are you doing here, Ari?"

She clasps his hands, her brow furrowing as she studies the metal handcuffs. "I needed demon blood for your antidote, and the only way to do that was trade with a warlock." Her fingers flutter over his wrists, the first touch that's actually soothed. "So I retrieved the amulet he wanted and exchanged it."

"An amulet?" Reign asks, dread turning his insides to stone.

She glances up. "Yeah. The warlock didn't waste any time in sending it Purgatory. We don't know what for, but it's powerful. I had to get it back."

Orion's words are like a rush of ice through Reign's mind.

I have a warlock acquiring the amulet for me. And once he sends it to me here, in Purgatory, then I'll use you to escape to the outside world.

"I know why," he says. "Orion's going to use it to not only escape, but to protect himself. So he can rule once he releases Eldritch."

Arielle's gaze shoots to his, her eyes widening. "He's here?"

"Not for long. Now that he has the amulet, he doesn't need to use me to get out of here."

Arielle pales, then quickly reinstates her frown. "Even if he does get his hands on the amulet, we'll stop him." She looks back down at the chains. "Which means I need to get these off you."

Reign studies the strands of her blonde hair as she bends over to focus on his wrists. They're a pale gray here in Purgatory, yet the warm, cornsilk color is forever emblazoned in his mind. As is its clean scent. The way it feels wound around his fingers, or brushing across his skin. And just like the girl it belongs to, it may look fragile and fine, it's strong. No matter what, Arielle's never given up.

Just like she gave up on him.

She looks up, smiling triumphantly. "Got it." She holds up the cuffs, then throws them onto the mattress where they land soundlessly. "Come on, we need to get out of here."

She takes his hand and tugs him toward the door. Reign's about to tell her it wasn't the cuffs holding him, but the endless cycle of pain that he can feel progressively building again, when they both stop.

They're no longer the only people in the room.

Cain smiles as he stands in the doorway, not seeming surprised to find Arielle here with Reign. "Thinking of leaving, were you?" He leans against the doorjamb. "Without accepting my offer?"

Arielle narrows her eyes. "Whatever it is, it's a no."

Cain crosses his arms, not looking the least discouraged. "It's one worth considering."

Arielle turns to Reign. "Aunt Shell is dead because of him, just like all the other Innocents. He's the one who started this, all to get rid of the Mark."

The brand on Reign's arm flares with heat. With the endless cycles of agony, he'd almost forgotten about it.

Cain's face tenses. "For centuries, it's all I wanted. Because it twisted my mind..." His gaze flickers to Reign's arm. "But it also gifts great power. Power that needs to be harnessed and controlled, or you'll end up like me."

"Not. Happening," Reign growls.

"I thought I was strong enough, too. But the darkness is insidious. Never-ending. Always there."

Reign clamps his mouth shut. He's had a taste of endless torture. And the knowledge that it would break him eventually.

Cain nods even though Reign didn't speak. "All I ask is for you to take me with you when you leave. So I can make this right."

Arielle shakes her head. "We can't trust you."

Cain opens his mouth to speak, only for his eyes to widen in shock. A blink later, he's sailing through the air and crashing into the opposite wall. He slides to the floor, unmoving.

Orion stalks into the room, his lip curled. "You're not going anywhere." He grins, his expression changing faster than Cain's impromptu flight. "Well, not without me. Especially now that I have this."

He holds up a small silver amulet, hieroglyphics surrounding a perfect jade eye.

Arielle stiffens beside Reign. Anger churns in his gut at the unfairness of it all. Arielle was trying to save him, and yet now she'll feel responsible if Orion succeeds with his evil plans.

Orion throws the amulet up in the air, then catches it.

"Everything is going fabulously to plan. The Sins will release Eldritch. I'll be the one who can reap the benefits of the new world Eldritch will forge."

He stalks forward, his gaze squarely on Reign. His ticket out of here.

Reign braces himself as he tries to tuck Arielle behind him, but he doesn't even have the strength to do that. She slips around his arm and returns to his side, planting her feet into the ground as she prepares to fight.

She has no idea how powerful Orion is.

Or how much he wants to rule a black, sick world.

Reign lifts his curled fists, drawing in a sharp breath at the pain the movement causes. It's happening again. And each cycle is getting faster. He doesn't have long before he's riddled with so much pain he can barely think.

Orion's dark eyes flare as if he just realized exactly how weak Reign is. That he'll crumple the moment he's touched.

"Run, Ari," Reign chokes, even though he knows it's useless. She'd leave him behind as much as he would leave her behind.

Orion leaps before she can answer. Before Reign can tell her he loves her. That they'll somehow make this okay.

Orion's just left the ground when a voice slices from behind him. "I don't think so."

Unsure exactly who else could be joining this shitstorm, Reign's eyes widen when he sees Gabby standing just inside the door, her white wings extended. She lifts an arm, then throws what looks like a block of steel.

Orion turns just in time to see it slam into his face.

His shocked cry is cut off as he disintegrates.

DINAH

Dinah pushes up from her knees, avoiding Rachel's pleading gaze. "I can't wake him," she admits.

Rachel moans a denial, then crumples over Marlowe's still body. "There has to be a way!"

Dinah glances around the parking lot, telling herself this is why she's never let anyone get close. She learned from her mother how much loving someone can hurt. All the more reason to push Oliver away. "We need to get him to the farmhouse."

They're sitting ducks out here. Vulnerable ones. The demons would've sensed that Greed has been killed. They'll want revenge.

Rachel looks up at her, tears tracking down her cheeks. "Is he..." She swallows, her face twisting with pain. "Please tell me he'll live."

"His nephilim blood is keeping him alive," Dinah assures her, relieved she can at least give her that. "But I have no idea what the nature of the curse he's been put under is."

"Is it like Reign? Is there demon poison?" Hope flares in Rachel's eyes. "Ari's gone to get the antidote for that."

Dinah shakes her head. "It's not demonic in origin." She frowns, realizing why she couldn't trace the essence she sensed. It's not of this world. "It's faerie."

"Faerie?" Rachel looks down at Marlowe, blinking. "What does that mean?"

Dinah suppresses a sigh. The good news quickly came to an end. "It means only a faerie can reverse it."

Rachel's hands curl into Marlowe's shirt. "I didn't even know they were a thing."

Dinah tenses, bracing herself for what she has to say next. "That's because they're little more than legend."

Rachel's face crumples. Then her body does. She curves over Marlowe, her sobs as broken as her body looks. "Marlowe," she gasps. "I need you!"

Gravel crunches under Dinah's shoe as she turns and strides to her car, trying to escape the agonized words.

You're right, the obsidian hisses. *Emotion is for fools. Look at her. She can't function without him.*

Dinah reaches her car and climbs in, pretending the contemptuous voice isn't in her head. She drives over and parks beside Rachel and Marlowe, allowing a sliver of the sadness and regret she's been denying to touch her as she notes Rachel's shoulders are shaking hard.

Fool. They'll never trust you. All you're doing is making yourself vulnerable.

Dinah winces despite herself. She climbs out and squats beside Rachel. "Let's get him safe and comfortable," she offers softly.

Rachel nods, wiping away her tears. "Thanks, Dinah."

The flush of warmth is so unexpected, it takes Dinah by surprise. She nods, and together, they lift the comatose Marlowe into the backseat. Rachel climbs in with him, tenderly putting his head in her lap.

Dinah moves around back to the driver's seat. She's doing the right thing. She can feel it.

I'll wait, the obsidian growls. *Once they reject you, I'll be here. Then it will be time to use this power for what it was supposed to.*

To release Eldritch. To unite them.

And she's the only thing standing in its way.

CHAPTER 20

ARIELLE

rielle looks from the space where Orion was a second ago, to her cousin, and back again, trying to process what just happened.

The moment she does, she launches herself at Gabby. "Your timing is amazing!"

Gabby giggles as she clasps her back. "Good to see you too, Ari."

Arielle pulls back, conscious that Colt is moving past them to stand over an unconscious Cain. "How did you know?"

Gabby glances around the gray room. "I didn't. But all the research we've been doing in Rome pointed to one thing—the obsidian is part of a greater power."

"Yeah," Arielle says heavily. "Eldritch."

Gabby nods. "And that Orion was working hard to help it." She shrugs. "So I popped into Purgatory to take care of him."

"Is he...is he dead?"

"Unfortunately, he's just out of commission for a little while. Orion can't be killed."

Arielle's frown starts somewhere deep in her chest. She should never have brought the amulet here—

Reign's groan has her spinning back to find him crumpling onto the thin mattress, his face a pale shade of ash. "Reign," she gasps, running to him.

He grimaces the moment her hand brushes his shoulder, so she yanks it back, the familiar helplessness of seeing him this way taking hold all over again. But Reign reaches out a shaking hand and takes hers. "No, please, I need to feel you."

Arielle's heart feels like it's gripped in a vice as she carefully, gently wraps her fingers around his. Reign's face contorts, even that faint hold clearly causing him pain. Yet he grips her with strength he couldn't possibly have after enduring these agonizing cycles.

Gabby comes to stand beside her, glancing over at Colt who hasn't moved from his guard over Cain. "Stopping Orion was only a temporary measure. We need to end this. Once and for all."

Arielle's gaze falls on Reign and she's not even sure he can see her anymore, his eyes are so filled with agony. "I know, Gabby," she whispers. Since the moment she found out the truth about the supernatural, that's what she's been fighting for. "I'm so sorry I've failed with the Innocents."

"You haven't given up, and that's what counts," Gabby says fiercely. "And we now know there's a way to close the Gates of Hell completely."

Arielle closes her eyes, wondering when the tidal wave of overwhelm will stop. "I know. But we have no idea where to start looking."

"Sierra and Mac believe they've solved part of the riddle. That's the other reason I came back. To tell you we're closing in on the Grail."

Arielle nods, unable to take her gaze off Reign even though that's the best news she's heard in a while. "I can't do it without him."

To Arielle's surprise, Gabby rests a hand on her shoulder. "I know. I get it."

When Arielle looks up, Gabby's not looking at her, but at Colt. And he's staring back, the stable, steadfast love in his gaze unmistakable. Their connection is solid. Their foundation.

Just like Arielle and Reign.

Gabby looks down at her. "You have to get back. And fast. The longer you remain here, the more the pain will weaken Reign."

Arielle has to resist the urge to tighten her grip on him. The thought of leaving him again tears at her heart.

Colt grunts, nudging a lifeless Cain with his boot. "He's out of it. Now's the time to do it." He walks over to Gabby. "And we need to go."

Gabby nods, even though she looks pained. "We do. Orion's taken care of, for now. We need to focus on the Grail." She turns back to Arielle. "I wish we could stay."

Arielle smiles faintly, wanting to reassure her cousin. "You saved us. That's more than I can even thank you for."

Gabby presses a quick kiss to Arielle's cheek, and although the sensation is muted here in Purgatory, it still brings tears to her eyes. She would've liked to talk a little more. Maybe asked them to look over Reign until she can return him to her side. But what she said is true—Gabby and Colt have already helped more than they could ever know.

With a regretful wave from Gabby, they exit through the door, although there's no sound of footsteps going down the stairs. They're gone. Off to continue helping in ways no one can predict.

"You need to go, too," Reign croaks.

Arielle's head spins back to him, shocked to discover he heard everything. "But—"

"Now, Ari," he gasps, his eyes fluttering shut. His breathing is short and choppy. "Go."

If leaving didn't mean the chance for him to be free of pain, Arielle's not sure she could do it. But it does, so she presses a faint kiss on his forehead, wincing internally when Reign grimaces. "I'll get you out of here. I promise."

He nods once then falls unconscious, the poison robbing his body of life.

Choking back a sob, Arielle stumbles to where Orion last was and picks up the amulet. Cain is a few feet away, but she ignores him. An unconscious Cain is the type of Cain she likes. Not entirely sure how this works, she grips the amulet in her palm. Alexandra said to focus on returning breath to her body, except Purgatory is so...airless. It doesn't even feel like her lungs are working.

Arielle expands her chest, frowning when she doesn't feel anything. She deflates it again, noting the absence of sensation in her throat. She's alive. But also dead. Determined, she repeats the process, acting as if there's air to breathe, and a body to nourish. In. Out.

In.

Out.

She closes her eyes, focusing as hard as she can. In. Out.

"I saw her hand move!"

Arielle's eyes fly open, finding Alexandra leaning over her.

"She's woken up!" Alexandra looks over her shoulder. "I told you she would."

Arielle struggles to a sitting position, discovering she's on the couch at the farmhouse. "How long have I been out?" she asks, suddenly worried. No doubt time works differently in Purgatory.

Alexandra steps back. "A few hours," she says, glancing over her shoulder again. "Long enough for us to get you back here."

It's then that Arielle realizes who else is in the room.

Dinah regards her steadily. "Good to have you back."

Arielle swings her feet onto the ground. "We don't need you here."

"Actually, we do," Alexandra says. "Dinah's the one who's created the antidote with the demon's blood."

Alarm shoots through Arielle. "What? You know we can't trust her!"

"You did, once," Dinah points out.

"That's when I was far more naive," Arielle snaps back. "And this is Reign's life we're talking about."

Alexandra shakes her head. "We have no choice, Arielle. Dinah's the only witch powerful enough to have created the antidote. The alternative is to wait until we find someone else."

Arielle was about to stride toward the stairs, the need to be with Reign screaming through her veins, when she stops. Surely this isn't the decision she's now being faced with.

"You can trust me," Dinah says, her voice low and level.

Arielle lifts her chin. "Do you still have the obsidian inside you?"

Dinah's lashes flicker. "Yes."

Arielle remembers the power of that dark force. The relentlessness of the evil.

And now they know the obsidian wants to reunite with Eldritch.

Yet Dinah's the only one who can help Reign right now...as long as she's telling the truth. That the antidote will cure him.

And not kill him.

Arielle almost curses aloud. "Fine. Give him the antidote. And if he doesn't wake..." She doesn't finish the sentence, hoping even a hint of the fury she'll unleash is conveyed in her words.

Dinah shrugs. "He will."

She spins around and stalks for the stairs, but Arielle quickly overtakes her. She runs up to Reign's room, bursting in and rushing to his side. He looks like he did in Purgatory, yet somehow, in a world of color he appears in even worse shape. Pink should be on his cheeks, but it's not. The dark circles under his eyes are a startling contrast to the white of his skin. He looks like he's leeched of color, right down to his bones.

Dinah steps around her. "Give me some room."

Arielle ignores her, falling to her knees and taking Reign's cold hand. "Hurry up."

Dinah sighs, but pulls out the vial of demon blood from her pocket. She holds it up as she murmurs a few words, and the contents go from red-black to total midnight. Pulling off the stopper, she leans down, angling the vial over Reign's mouth.

Arielle's hand shoots out to stop her. "If you hurt him, I'll make sure you regret it."

"I already do," Dinah responds.

Before Arielle can ask her what that means, Dinah pours the onyx contents into Reign's mouth. The fluid spreads over his lips, painting them in a ghastly black, then disappears.

Arielle finds she's holding her breath. Even her heart feels like it's holding still. Waiting.

For Reign.

Yet he doesn't move. His barely-there breathing doesn't change.

He doesn't wake.

Arielle gives it another few excruciating moments, waiting, hoping, for the antidote to work.

Nothing.

Dinah pulls back, looking satisfied. It's all the signal Arielle needs. She shoots to her feet and shoves the witch back. "Did you kill him? Or just leave him to die painfully, over and over?" she shouts.

Anger flashes across Dinah's face. "Don't push me, Arielle." She hasn't finished the warning before, for the barest of seconds, her eyes turn black.

The obsidian.

Arielle steps closer. "I'm about to do more than that."

The thought that if it wasn't for Gabby she would've unleashed Orion in the world for this, and she failed Reign anyway, has rage churning in her chest. Not only that, she foolishly trusted Dinah all over again.

"As much as I'd like to see you take it to Dinah, I think I'd prefer you in my arms, Ari."

She spins around, the sound of Reign's voice like joy just exploded through her veins. "You're awake!"

He grins, looking exhausted and pale, and opens his arms. Arielle rushes toward them, a sob escaping her lips. She works hard to slow her momentum as she barrels over the short distance, conscious Reign's still weak, but the moment she's close enough to reach, he yanks her to him.

Arielle tumbles into his lap, her arms clasping around him like a band. Their lips clamp together, relief and joy and love and more relief sealing their kiss.

Reign pulls back, resting his forehead against hers. "You feel good."

She smiles. "Actually, I feel better than I have since Afghanistan."

He grins back. "Me too." He frowns as if he just thought of something. "How did you get me out?"

Arielle stills, slipping off Reign's lap as she turns to face the witch standing silently on the other side of the room. "Once I had the final ingredient for the antidote, Dinah used her magic to create it."

Reign's frown deepens. "Thanks," he says gruffly.

Arielle expects Dinah to respond with one of her usual

snarky comments, but she just shrugs. "No big deal."

"It kind of is," Arielle says. "You brought Reign back to me."

Dinah's dark gaze doesn't waver. "I wasn't able to do the same for Marlowe."

"What?" Reign shoots to his feet, sways, then quickly rights himself. "What's happened to Marlowe?"

Before Dinah can answer, the sound of a door slamming downstairs rockets through the house.

"Marlowe!" booms the General. "Where is my son?"

RACHEL

Rachel's not surprised when the General storms into Marlowe's room. She doesn't know how he found out about Marlowe, but nephilim are mysterious, ancient beings, so who knows what's possible.

The stocky man whose presence has always been bigger than his size stops when he sees Marlowe lying on the bed. Pale. Motionless. Unreachable.

"What happened," he whispers, the first time Rachel's ever heard him speak quieter than a drill sergeant.

She wipes at her cheeks, even though there are no tears there. In fact, she feels parched. Desiccated. Like the grief has sucked her dry. All she knows is that the sadness is soul deep. An agonizing weight inside of her.

"Wrath stabbed him," she says through lips she can barely feel. "He's been like this ever since."

"I'll kill him!" the General roars, his face turning a ruddy red.

"I banished him," Dinah says calmly as she enters. "It's the most we can do without the blade to end him."

Arielle and Reign are right behind her, looking pale and shocked. "Dinah just told us," Arielle says. "I'm so sorry."

Reign looks drawn and a little haggard, but he strides straight to Rachel. "We'll do whatever it takes," he promises.

Rachel launches into his arms, her eyes stinging with the first prickles of tears. "He won't wake up," she whispers brokenly into his chest.

The General stalks to stand beside his son's bed, a ferocious scowl on his face. "Who do we need to see to fix this?" His fists clench. "I'll talk to the angels if I have to."

Dinah shakes her head. "The magic is fae."

The General finally goes still. The color drains from his face. "Fae?"

He realizes what that means. Rachel forces herself to say it so Arielle and Reign understand exactly how desperate things are. "Only fae can reverse the curse," she tells them.

Reign frowns. "Fae? As in faeries? I've only read about them in passing the Grail Keeper books."

"That's because they're ancient," Dinah says. "Like, before angels and demons ancient. No one has seen one in centuries."

Reign's mouth goes grim. "Where's the fun if it's not a challenge, huh?"

Except there are the Sins. And the Gates of Hell.

And now Eldritch.

Rachel tries not to let hopelessness drag her down, but she realizes she's gripping Reign's arms so tight her nails are digging in. She eases her hold, even as she wonders if she'll stay standing if she completely lets go.

And if she falls, will she want to get up?

Life will be empty without Marlowe. It's not a reality she wants to be part of.

The General huffs, bends down and scoops his son up.

Panic punches through Rachel. "What are you doing?"

Adjusting Marlowe so he's effortlessly carrying him even though his son is taller than him, the General levels his gaze on her. "There's a rumor," he says, clearing his throat when his voice cracks. "About a small town hidden deep in a valley somewhere in the Himalayas. A magical spell protects it, but there are those that believe it's where some of the faeries still live."

Rachel draws in a sharp breath. "They could save Marlowe?"

"Assuming it exists," Dinah points out.

The General snaps his gaze to the witch. "It's all we have right now, and I will do whatever it takes to heal my son."

He waves his hand and a portal opens on the wall, bright light on the other side.

Rachel rushes to him, her heart jammed in her throat. "Wait! How...how long will he—you be gone?"

To this mysterious town in Tibet, hidden by magic.

The General grunts. "As long as it takes."

She reaches out to touch Marlowe's face, feeling as if her chest is cracking. Surely, this can't be it. They weren't meant to say goodbye.

A hand lands on her shoulder. "You should go with him," Reign says.

Arielle appears by his side, nodding. "It's where you belong."

This time, the tears prickle, then overflow, blurring Rachel's vision. "But..."

Reign's mouth twists into a smile. "Face it, you'll be useless here without him."

He's right. The moment the General leaves, he'll take her heart with him. And a world without Marlowe isn't one she has the will to fight for.

Rachel throws her arms around Reign, yanking Arielle into

the embrace. "Thank you," she whispers hoarsely. "For everything."

"It you we should be thanking," Arielle says, squeezing tight. "We wouldn't have found the last few Innocents without you."

Rachel pulls back, glad she can at least leave them with something. "Speaking of that. I think I found another. I printed the information right before we had to rush off to fight Greed and Wrath."

"It's time," the General says curtly. "Marlowe's only getting weaker."

Another quick round of hugs and Rachel moves to the General's side. She looks away from the friends she's leaving, to the man she would lose everything for.

She follows the General through the portal, not knowing what's on the other side, or what's going to happen.

Yet knowing with so much surety that she's doing the right thing.

She'll be with Marlowe.

And that's all that matters.

CHAPTER 21
REIGN

R eign can't stop touching things. The glossy timber of the banister. The serrated edge of a leaf of a pot plant. The slightly rough texture of a wall.

After spending what feels like a handful of lifetimes in Purgatory, everything is new. Fascinating. No longer taken for granted.

But there's one thing he touches the most. Can't stop brushing his fingers over. Misses even before he's drawn his hand away.

Arielle.

They've been inseparable since he woke up, and he's made the most of their need to be close. He's made it his personal mission to find all the places she's soft. All the places she's smooth. And all the places that make her sigh.

Which turns out to be everywhere.

Admittedly, his own breaths stutter or stop or are sharply drawn in every time she touches him. The echoes of the countless cycles of pain, death, and waking up still pulse through his marrow, yet it's Arielle's touch that heals him in a way nothing else could.

Even now, as they sit on the couch reading over Rachel's print out, Arielle's on his lap. She's tucked into his chest, pressed as close as possible, and all he wants to do is pull her in until an atom couldn't squeeze between the two of them.

"Jilian Beck," she reads. "And she's in Mercy City."

Reign presses his lips to the crown of her hair, breathing deeply. "Of course Rachel's being amazing, without even being here."

Arielle nods, burrowing in a little more as she stares at the sheet of paper. "I hope they can help Marlowe."

First, because Marlowe is one heck of a guy.

Second, because the devastation on Rachel's face when she thought she wouldn't be able to see him wasn't something a heart can endure for too long.

"Between the General and Rach, the fae won't stand a chance." He gives her a quick squeeze. "Just like whatever Sin is now roaming the city."

Arielle looks up at him, blue eyes softly smiling. "Even though we don't know which one it is?"

"Minor detail."

"Or that we don't have the weapon to kill it?"

"Also a minor detail," Reign instantly responds.

Arielle's smile grows, but then she sobers. Her hand comes up to cup his cheek. "I love you, Reign."

The aching honesty in her gaze constricts and fills his heart all at once. "I love you too." He rests his forehead on hers. "Which is why I'm not going anywhere."

The Mark on his arm flares, as if reminding him exactly how true that is. Right now, he's immortal.

Reign pushes away the thought, not wanting to muddy this moment. It's another minor detail, he tells himself as he brings his mouth down onto Arielle's. Their lips brush, graze, then melt. They both temper this kiss, knowing there's no time for the passion that's always a breath away to gain life. They simply reaffirm that what they have is real. True. And binding.

Arielle pulls away with a sigh. "We have an Innocent to save."

Before the Sins find her.

Sighing himself, Reign pushes to his feet, keeping Arielle close to him as she lowers her legs to the floor. "I'm thinking the most efficient way will be the hessian bag over the head, bring her here, then see if she's willing to listen."

Arielle's eyes twinkle. "So, kidnapping?"

He grins. "Hey, I said it's quick, not legal."

They turn to leave, hands clasped, when the front door swings open. Although they're surrounded by wards, Knights Templar, and even some nephilim warriors the General left behind, Reign tenses. They live in a world when unbreakable rules keep getting broken.

Alexandra strides in, her gaze instantly finding them even though they haven't moved. "I have news."

At times like these, Reign appreciates the demigod's no-nonsense, warrior manner. Time isn't something they have right now. Although he also notes she didn't state what kind of news she's about to offload. "Good or bad?" he asks.

"Both," Alexandra says, closing the door behind her and approaching them. "Which would you like first?"

"The good," Arielle responds.

Reign squeezes her hand. "Saving the best for last, huh?"

"An old witch visited me while I was at the demigod camp," Alexandra says, still all-business. "She said her name was Trivia."

"And that's significant?" Arielle asks.

"It is. Trivia is the name of the Goddess of Witchcraft. Also known to us as Hecate."

"Sounds powerful," Reign says.

"She is. But not only that, she's one of the few gods who prefer to roam Earth. She's very rarely seen in Olympus. Yet she sought me out as she had a message."

Reign can feel the tension winding through Arielle. "What sort of message?" she asks.

"She said the Mark will lead to the Light."

Now it's Reign who's wound as tight as a coil. "The Mark?"

Alexandra glances at his forearm. "Yes, the Mark you bear. Hecate said that because the Mark was forged by Lucifer, it was created from a spell that channeled Primordial Light." She looks at him steadily. "The same Light the Grail is forged from."

Reign lifts his arm to gaze at the brand he never wanted. "You're saying the Mark could lead us to the Grail?"

"Hecate believes that may be possible."

Arielle blinks. "Wow."

While Reign wonders if it's too good to be true. Cain said the Mark would corrupt him. That it would mess with his demonic blood. Yet, if they can use it for good...

"Did Hecate say anything about the Grail itself," Arielle asks.

Alexandra shakes her head. "She said the Grail is shrouded in mystery, but she'd heard a rumor that the archangels bound it to something."

Arielle nods, mulling this over. "Thanks, Alexandra. This could be really helpful."

"Hecate also said she received a vision of an obelisk breaking and another Gate of Hell opening," Alexandra says. "She said Sloth has now been released."

Reign glances at Arielle. "One minor detail now known. Sloth is the Sin we'll be hunting."

She rolls her eyes. "The other minor detail of the weapon that can kill Sloth is still outstanding."

"Another reason I'm here," Alexandra says, stepping

forward as she pulls something out of a scabbard strapped to her belt. "Hecate gave me the knife to kill Sloth."

It's Reign's turn to blink. "Minor detail number two, check."

Arielle takes the blade, looking stunned herself. "Thank you. This is just what we needed."

Alexandra nods, but doesn't respond. There's something in her stoic face that has Reign tensing again. "And the bad news?"

The demigod's shoulders contract. "Hecate also said Eldritch is just as much a threat to Olympus as it is to Earth. She said it's in danger."

And there it is. The moment-killer.

"What are you saying, Alexandra?" Arielle asks.

"Olympus must be protected, just like Earth." She lifts her chin, looking every part the demigod daughter of Athena. "It's my duty to be there."

Reign nods, even as he can't believe they're losing another member of their team so soon, although he understands Alexandra's decision.

"Thank you for everything you've done," Arielle says solemnly.

"Your support and kick-ass skills have been invaluable," Reign adds.

There are no hugs, no tears glittering along eyelids with Alexandra. He almost expects her to salute them. Instead, she nods once. Sharply. Efficiently. Yet with a world of meaning.

This war will be fought on multiple fronts.

And they all have their part to play.

Alexandra strides out the door, although the bittersweet moment doesn't end when she shuts the door. They've gained valuable information, the weapon to kill Sloth.

And just lost another ally to the spreading evil.

JILIAN'S HOUSE is more of a small cottage in a cute suburban alcove. Right down to the petunias in the window boxes and the cute little front gate that's small enough to step over. Reign's done just that and Arielle is shaking her head as she opens it to step through when another car pulls up on the street.

They both tense, Arielle's hand going to the knife tucked in the back of her jeans, but it's Xeven who unfolds his tall body from the vehicle. He strides toward them, his scarred face as impassive as always. "I've come to help."

Arielle looks like she's trying not to frown. "How did you find us?"

Xeven glances at Reign. "I am tied to the Mark," he says simply.

Reign grits his teeth, unsure how he feels about Arielle's mentally-absent-yet-here father being so powerfully connected to him.

Xeven glances at the cottage. "You've found the next Innocent."

Arielle turns to look at it, too. "Yeah. And we need to get her to the farmhouse before Sloth or Wrath finds her."

"I can carry her if necessary."

Reign likes it even less that Xeven just suggested the same thing he did. His only consolation is that he was joking, yet Xeven clearly isn't.

Arielle steps through the gate. "Let's hope it doesn't come to that," she says, her look suggesting she's not sure how much she can trust him.

Xeven nods curtly, then steps over the low fence to stand beside her. The three of them approach the whitewashed door and Ari knocks.

The door opens on silent hinges.

They break into a run, dread that they're too late injecting through Reign's gut. Not again!

The frantic sprint is almost instantly cut short as they find themselves in a cute little living room, a woman standing in the center as she stares at a wall above a flower-print couch. She's frozen and pale, her hands pressed over her chest.

The Infinity symbol etched in enough blood that the edges bleed and trickle in thin beads is probably doing that.

Jilian spins around, her mouth open to scream although nothing comes out. Impossibly, she goes even more pale. "Are you...here to kill me?"

"No," Arielle assures. "We're here to help. I promise."

"We did not leave that symbol on your wall." Xeven says, sounding almost indignant. "We are not part of the cultus infit-intialis."

Jilian frowns. "The who?"

"The Infinity symbol was always used when a cult within the organization called The Tenth Legion murdered anyone they thought may possess the Holy Grail," Xeven explains. He returns his gaze to Jilian. "This symbol suggests she's their next victim."

Arielle draws in a sharp breath. "Why would they think Jilian possesses the Grail?"

Reign watches the woman closely, noting her neatly pressed slacks, perfectly symmetrical cardigan and carefully styled hair. The color that was returning to her cheeks drains away. Her hands flutter back to her chest. "Sweet lord, they know," she says.

Reign takes a step forward, his lungs frozen. "Know what?"

Jilian sinks to the couch, sitting primly on the edge as she clasps her hands in her lap. She raises her gaze, her eyes heavy with truth. "I'm an archaeologist. I've traveled the world." She sighs. "Hunting for the Grail started off as wanting to one-up Sierra."

Arielle moves to the nearest overstuffed chair and sits heavily. "Sierra's my mother."

Reign quickly steps to stand beside her. "And you knew her," he says to Jilian.

The woman pats her hair, even though there's not a strand out of place. "We studied together." She sniffs. "She was the only one to get better marks than me."

Reign has to stop his eyebrows from shooting up. Jilian was threatened by Sierra?

"So when I learned Sierra was absolutely obsessed with finding the Holy Grail, I decided I'd be the one to find it first." Jilian sniffs again. "When I found a lead that led me to Jerusalem, I followed it and found an ancient lair beneath a temple."

Reign decides Arielle was smart to sit down. This is the closest they've come to learning more about the Grail.

"And?" he asks. "What did you find?"

Jilian purses her lips as she looks at them in thought, and right now, he's not sure if Arielle being her archnemesis's daughter is a good thing or not.

Jilian pushes to her feet, obviously reaching a decision. She walks to a bland watercolor painting on the opposite wall and removes it, revealing a safe behind it. Reign watches with wide eyes as she enters a code he learned to break when he was thirteen. She reaches in, pulls something out, and turns around.

Arielle gasps.

Xeven lets out a strangled sound.

Reign's knees go weak.

Jilian holds out the silver goblet, the light catching softly on the rim.

Arielle leans forward. "Surely it's not..."

If Reign could speak, he'd agree.

Surely the Grail can't have been in the hands of an Innocent all along.

In Mercy City.

His breath hisses through his teeth when the Mark flares to life. He looks down, registering that the red is blazing bright. His shocked gaze travels to Arielle, who's looking at it, too.

"It must be," she breathes.

Hecate said the Mark would lead them to the Grail.

A sound behind them has Reign spinning around.

A man with olive skin, hooded eyes, and slicked back hair smiles at them as black wings spring out behind him.

"An Innocent, a Grail Keeper, a thorn in our side, a demon's lackey, *and* the Holy Grail, all in one room," he purrs lazily. "Even for the Sin of Sloth, this is a little too easy."

CHAPTER 22

ARIELLE

Arielle leaps into action in the same moment Reign and Xeven do. As Jilian screams and scurries to the corner of the room, they run at Sloth.

Adrenaline punches through Arielle as she pulls out the blade she was only just given. The need to bury it deep in Sloth's chest thunders through her veins.

A slow smile climbs up Sloth's face as he takes a sauntering step forward and raises his arms. Demons pour past him, red eyes gleaming and teeth bared.

"We'll cover you," Reign shouts. His red wings explode from his back and his feet leave the ground as he shoots forward, a battering ram that instantly mows down three demons.

Xeven's face is a cold mask as he yanks out two blades from his boots and throws them. Two demons explode into black smoke.

Arielle keeps running, her focus on Sloth. If they don't succeed in killing him, Jilian is dead. A demon leaps over Reign, sidesteps her father, and launches at her, snarling. One spinning kick and he's sent sailing through the air, slamming into the Infinity symbol on the wall and smearing it as he slides down.

Ahead, Reign jumps, wraps his legs around the shoulders of a demon and snaps his neck. Xeven picks up an antique side table, smashes it and uses the sharp legs to impale another. They're exterminating the demons faster than they can enter the cottage. A window smashes and Jilian screams as another onslaught of demons pour through, surrounding them.

And far closer to Jilian.

"I'll protect her," Xeven shouts, spinning and plowing into the newest opponents.

Knowing she has no choice but to trust him, Arielle turns back to the entrance, gasping when Sloth is no longer there. She looks around frantically, terrified that the coward's retreated. She tucks the blade into the back of her jeans, deciding to keep it safe until she has the opportunity to use it. And use it she will. They can't lose their chance to end him!

A demon rushes at her, but one swipe of Reign's magnificent red wing and she's slammed into a bureau, splintering it. She goes to rise but another demon attacks Reign before he can finish her. Arielle moves, prepared to do it herself, when a body materializes in front of her.

Victory flashes in Sloth's pale eyes a second before he grabs her neck, shoots forward, and pins her to the wall. Any attempt at crying out is abruptly cut off by the sharp claws wrapped around her throat.

"Ari!" Reign shouts.

"One move and I'll snap her neck," Slot drawls, not even bothering to raise his voice.

But the panic that shoots across Reign's face tells Arielle that he heard it. That his hands were just tied.

Sloth leans in close, his smooth face and slicked back hair dominating her vision. "I usually like to slow things down so I can enjoy it, but that won't be happening. We've had enough of you."

Pain shoots through Arielle as Sloth's hand tightens. She desperately wishes she could get one last glance at Reign.

"Kill her and I kill the Innocent!"

Sloth spins around, his hold loosening enough for Arielle to see her father holding Jilian to his chest, a knife at her throat.

"She dies now, and you'll have to find her reincarnated soul to sacrifice," Xeven warns.

Sloth's lip curls. He stands where he is, one arm keeping Arielle pinned to the wall, glaring at Xeven as he considers his options.

Xeven jerks Jilian closer and a bead of blood trickles from where the blade is touching her skin. Her eyes and mouth are wide open, terror bleeding from them.

Arielle's frozen. Surely her father wouldn't kill an Innocent to save her? His feelings didn't seem to run that deep. He's nothing but a slave to the Mark and Mask.

Yet his gaze is unflinching in his scarred face as he glares at Sloth. His hand tightens around the hilt of the knife.

The knife!

Her father is creating a distraction so she can use her own blade!

Arielle moves fast. She arches her back enough to reach the knife, yank it out, and slam it into Sloth's chest.

The Sin spins to face her, clearly shocked. His hand falls away from her throat as he glances down at the hilt protruding from his sternum. "You—"

Sloth's head snaps back as black smoke pours from his mouth. The inky mass twists and writhes as it shoots to the floor, then disappears. The remaining demons scream and roar their denial, then retreat out the door and broken window, disappearing into the sky.

Arielle sags against the wall, breathing hard. Reign appears before her. "Are you okay?"

She looks up at him, a little stunned. "We did it."

His delicious grin is all the proof she needs that they have. "Sloth is dead."

"Get away from me!" Jilian's indignant screech has them both turning to face her. "Asshole!"

Xeven steps away, looking unruffled. He strides toward a nearby corridor. "I'll check the rest of the house to ensure there are no surprises."

Arielle returns her focus to Reign, a smile exploding across her face. His expression mirrors hers. They leap into each other's arms, squeezing tight and laughing with relief.

Sloth barely had a chance to have an impact on Earth before they exterminated him. And Jilian is still alive.

Reign lifts Arielle and swings her around as he presses a kiss of celebration on her lips. They smile, gazing into each other's eyes. This is what victory feels like. Full of hope.

She blinks just as Reign stops. Can it be real? Have they finally found the—

"I had a feeling you'd cope just fine without me."

Arielle spins toward the doorway and the voice that just carried through the room. "Mom?" she gasps in shock.

Which is exactly who's standing there, smiling.

Arielle's running before her mother replies. They grasp each other, laughing, and joy dances through her all over again.

She steps back, still holding her mother's hands. "What...I didn't know you were coming back!"

"It was a last minute decision. I went to the farmhouse, but you weren't there."

Arielle's about to ask how she knew to find her here, when Reign speaks first.

"Surely you're not connected to the Mark, too?" he asks incredulously.

Sierra looks at him, confused. "No, I found the piece of paper with Jilian's address at the farmhouse."

He nods, his cheeks pinking. "Oh yeah. That makes more sense."

"What are you doing here, Mom?" Arielle asks, still a little stunned. Her mother looks so achingly familiar—just a little more tanned—that tears sting her eyes.

"We think we've cracked a few lines in the riddle for the Grail," she says excitedly.

Reign approaches them, smiling as he stuffs his hands in his pocket. "And seeing Ari in person was the only way to tell her?"

Arielle's mother grins. "Obviously." Her smile softens. "You look good, Reign."

Arielle shifts to slip her arm through his. "He does, doesn't he?"

"You both do," her mother replies, warmth twinkling in her eyes. "And you're going to be so excited to hear what I've learned."

Arielle and Reign glance at each other. Her mother has searched for the Grail her whole life. A quest Arielle has also devoted herself to.

And they may have found it.

Before they can respond, Jilian steps forward, tucking her cardigan across her front. "Hello, Sierra."

Arielle's mother stiffens. "Jilian." She looks around the demolished room. "This is your place?"

"Yes." A small smile slips over Jilian's face. "I've discovered what lengths some dark individuals will go to when searching for the Grail."

"I beg your pardon?"

Jilian's response is cut off by a strangled sound to her left.

Everyone turns to see Xeven standing frozen in the hallway entrance, his wide-eyed gaze zeroed on Arielle's mother.

Who's also lost the ability to move.

Arielle's heart clenches painfully as she realizes her parents are seeing each other for the first time since before she was born.

And so much has happened in that time.

SIERRA

"Ryder," Sierra whispers, the name of the man she's loved for almost two decades bittersweet on her lips.

Even though his face is twisted and scarred, she could recognize him anywhere. It's there in his strong shoulders. The angle of his chin. The thick hair she used to run her fingers through.

He flinches. "That hasn't been my name for a very long time."

Sierra walks toward him feeling as if she's in a daze. "It's always been your name, Ryder."

His hand twitches at his side. His face tightens. Both movements are so subtle, if her entire universe wasn't focused on him right now, she would've missed them.

Sierra stops in front of him, her heart thudding in a way she hasn't felt in a very long time. "Where have you been?"

His eyes scan her face, hungrily, but also curiously. "I knew you before, didn't I?"

A thread of alarm filters through the haze of the moment. Through the joy of having Ryder close enough she can touch. "Do you...do you remember me?"

"I remember..." He frowns, looking like it's an effort. "I

remember the desert with the trees. I remember a fight." He shakes his head. "Then darkness."

Sierra swallows. "Do you remember what we had?"

The love that refused to be denied.

The combustible chemistry that means they now have a beautiful, amazing daughter.

The knowledge this feeling was forever, no matter what.

When Ryder shakes his head, Sierra's knees buckle. She reaches out to the wall for support, noting the way his hand twitches again. But doesn't come up to touch her.

"I'm...I'm sorry," Ryder says, looking pained.

"Cain placed him under a spell," Arielle says softly. "Xeven wears one of the Hell Masks. It's...changed him."

"His name is Ryder," Sierra says, steel in her voice.

"Everything before that moment at the seven trees is shrouded in darkness," he says, sounding almost hollow. "It's like I didn't exist before that moment."

Sierra's hands become hot fists. "You most certainly did."

"I remember nothing," he continues, his tone hardening. "And I feel even less."

And yet that strangled sound when he first saw her suggests otherwise. As does the fact he hasn't moved. Her Ryder is in there. Their connection hasn't been severed.

Sierra drags her gaze away to glance at Reign, then Arielle. "A Hell Mask, you say? Well, I'm going to get the thing off."

"I tried," Ryder says, sounding as if he's hoping to let her down gently. "Many times, but the pain... Then Cain told me removing it would kill me."

Ryder tried to remove the Mask. That also gives Sierra a shred of hope. "Then I'll talk to Cain," she says, fury starting to burn in her gut. "And he won't be able to say no."

"Sierra," Reign says, regret making his voice heavy. "Cain's dead."

"No, he's not," Ryder says. "He's very much alive."

"Impossible. I saw his spirit in Purgatory. Abel killed him."

Ryder shakes his head. "I sensed him, my guess is the moment you returned, Reign. Seems Cain hitched a ride when you left. That's what I came to the farmhouse to tell you."

"Son of a bitch," Reign mutters. "He got what he wanted."

Sierra turns back to Ryder. "I love you. I always have, and always will. And I'm going to get that thing off."

She's going to get her man back.

Ryder blinks. Nods.

Then glances at Jilian. "We should really focus on the fact we may have found the Holy Grail."

CHAPTER 23

REIGN

There are a lot of people in the living room of the farmhouse, yet no one's really moving. They're certainly not talking.

Their focus is on the silver goblet sitting calmly, probably proudly, in the middle of the coffee table. Plain, even a little tarnished, it feels surreal to think this is what Reign was destined to find and protect.

Yet it's almost anticlimactic.

Not that the Potentials seem to think so. They're crowded together, eyes wide with awe. It's the quietest Reign's seen Simon since he met him. Bryn, too. Laila and Seiko are gripping each other's hands, looking like they've forgotten how to blink. Tariq's blinking more than Reign's ever seen. The significance of this moment for them is undeniable.

Blaise stands beside Nim, her hand on her shoulder as they stare at the cup intensely. Sierra doesn't seem to have stopped frowning since Xeven announced they believe they've found the Holy Grail. Jilian's wrapped her cardigan around her like it's an emperor's robe, fully aware she's the one who found something generations have failed to do. Xeven—Ryder, as she insists on calling him—stands apart from everyone else, the only one to be far more focused on something else.

Sierra.

He keeps glancing at her, the emotions difficult to identify beneath the ravages of the Mask. He looks confused. Watchful. Possibly hopeful...

Joseph moves into Reign's line of vision, appearing for the first time in a long while. Although Reign's not sure why he's surprised. Of course Joseph of Arimathea, the first Keeper of the Grail, would be here to see this.

Reign also notes the people who aren't here. Rachel and Marlowe's absence tugs at his chest. As does Alexandra's. They were part of this. They should've been here to celebrate the moment. All he can do is hope they'll be successful in their own quests. Considering the alternatives has a shudder rippling down his spine.

Arielle glances up at him, concern in her blue eyes. He squeezes her hand, not wanting to take away from this moment. Especially when he can see how curious she is about the cup. No one's been more fascinated and drawn to it than Arielle. Which is odd, because as the Grail Keeper, shouldn't it be him? Yet he'd prefer to stay by her side rather than touch it...

Reign indicates with his chin, figuring it's his own cautious tendencies, and wanting to encourage Ari to do what he can see she wants.

Plus, someone has to break the thrall the room is in.

Her eyebrows furrowing, Arielle releases her hold on his hand and takes a step closer to the coffee table. The whole room not only stills, but everyone seems to hold their breath.

Arielle kneels down beside the table, and carefully, unflinchingly, reaches out and picks up the goblet.

Her eyes widen. "I feel something!"

Blaise takes a cautious step closer. "There's definitely an

aura to it," she says thoughtfully. She glances at Arielle. "It's connected to you somehow."

"You think..." Reign clears his throat. He's spent a life struggling to trust, so it's not an easy habit to break. "You think it's *it*?"

The Holy Grail.

Arielle stands and holds the silver cup out. "Here. You take it."

He approaches cautiously, his heart struggling to beat in his too-tight chest. He hears Bryn draw in an excited breath. Reign stops before Arielle and the goblet she's offering him.

He reaches out a hand, glad to see it's not shaking even though there's a strange quivering deep in his gut. The instant his finger brushes the silver, he gasps.

Yanks his hand back.

And grips the Mark as it burns the hottest yet. It feels like the brand is searing him right to the bone.

Reign's wide eyes climb up to meet Arielle's. She murmurs the same words ricocheting through his mind. "The Mark will lead to the Light."

"I knew it!" Bryn crows. "The Grail is in da house, peoples!"

A ripple moves through the room, a new energy electrifying the air. Reign glances at the Potentials, seeing the new way they're regarding him.

Like he was right all along.

And yet...

He still can't bring himself to believe it.

"How will we know?" He clears his throat, finding his voice husky. "How will we know it's the Grail?"

"The riddle, of course," Jilian says, sniffing in that way of hers that's fast becoming annoying. "It's what I followed all along."

Sierra winces. "So did I."

"It was very cryptic," Jilian offers condescendingly. "It took me a long time to decipher it."

Reign knows the riddle. So would the Potentials. And Blaise and Nim, as Archivists, would too. He suspects Xeven does, as well. It's the same riddle that had Gabby and Colt going to Rome, along with Sierra and Mac. They were so sure they were cracking it.

Sierra quietly murmurs it, as if she's barely aware she's doing it. Joseph steps closer, his lips mirroring hers.

"Born of light, made to fight,
Conquering shadows and gathering dark.
Residing in humanity, it transcends immortality,
Resting in red and mortal spread.
A guard that protects, an aura it ejects,
When evil looms, it can close the doors of doom."

"The first two lines clearly refer to Eldritch," Nim says.

Blaise nods. "It's certainly gathering."

"The same with the doors of doom," adds Bryn.

"The Gates of Hell," Sierra says soberly.

Jilian tucks an invisible strand of hair that would never dream of being out of place. "It was the resting in red that drew me. Especially when I was in Jerusalem and found red tunnels underneath a temple. The tunnels wove for miles in the ochre-stained dirt."

Resting in red. A labyrinth created by humans—a mortal spread.

It all fits.

"I found the cup in an ancient grave," Jilian continues. "One I believe belongs to Joseph of Arimathea."

Although the Grail wasn't residing in humanity, it was certainly beside it. And it's most definitely transcended immortality.

No wonder Jilian's so confident.

Reign glances toward the old man, surprised to find his face inscrutable beneath his gray beard. Shouldn't he be rejoicing?

Yet Joseph is looking at Arielle, as if it's her expression that he wants to see. As if it's the one that counts.

"Well done, Jilian." The words come from Sierra as she grips her hands so tight her knuckles are white. "You figured it out."

The victory that flares in Jilian's eyes is so bright that Reign wonders if this moment is the real win for her, not finding the legendary Grail itself.

Even Xeven frowns, glancing at Jilian as if he doesn't like her, but he isn't sure why.

Reign does.

Jilian may be an Innocent, but she's also a bitch.

Sierra shrugs, the most almost self-conscious. "The best I found in Rome was another book. And we didn't even need it, as it turns out."

Reign steps closer to her. "What book?" he asks, a strange sense of protectiveness overcoming him. He thought he'd be angry at Sierra for the rest of his life for giving him up, but he finds that feeling's little more than a memory.

Sierra lost just as much as he did in the quest for the Grail. And now that it's here, it's time to focus on what they've gained. By working together.

She glances at him, warmth pooling in her eyes. "I'm not sure it's even relevant. It was a book on English churches, most of which would be ancient by now. I couldn't figure out why it was hidden so deep in that crypt we scoured for hours in Rome."

"I'd like to see it," he tells her, angling his back toward Jilian. "We've found valuable information where we least expected it."

Unlike Jilian's claims, nothing's been obvious or straightforward in the search for the Grail.

Sierra's eyes crinkle as she steps past him. "I would've been proud to have called you my son," she murmurs quietly as she passes.

Reign's breath whooshes out, which is a good thing. His heart needs the space as it swells, fed by those beautiful words. A glance over his shoulder reveals Ari looking at them both, her hands clasped to her chest. He grins crookedly, unsure what he's supposed to do or say now.

Sierra picks up an old book not much larger than a novel from a side table. "Here," she says, passing it to Reign as if the moment they had was nothing out of the ordinary. "The drawings are exquisite, if nothing else."

He takes it, glad for the opportunity to get his emotions under control. He opens the book, leafing through the thick, vellum pages. Arielle moves closer so she can see too, and Reign acknowledges that Sierra's right—the drawings are impressive. Although they're small, the detail capturing churches that may not even exist anymore is exquisite. The artist's almost photo-like portrayals must be superb, because even Joseph appears, carefully looking at the images over Reign's other shoulder.

Simon clears his throat. "Shouldn't we be trying to figure out how to use the Grail, now that we have it?"

"He's right," says Blaise, even if she looks like she doesn't like it. "We need to know to close the Gates of Hell and stop Eldritch."

Feeling a little disappointed that he didn't find anything, Reign's about to close the book when the next picture catches his attention. Although it's not the imposing church that has him peering closer.

"That tree..." he murmurs.

Arielle looks from the picture to him. "What about it?"

The large tree is almost as tall as the cathedral-size church itself, its boughs stretching out wide to shade the two-story entrance. There's nothing exceptional about it apart from its size. In fact, it almost obstructs the view of the church itself.

"I've seen it before," Reign says, trying to place it. Then it comes to him. "I'll be right back," he tells the room of confused faces.

He races to the basement, impressed with himself when he finds the tome he was looking for straight away. Maybe all that time spent reading to the Potentials wasn't a total waste. Taking the stairs two at a time, he returns to the living room, opening the book to one of the first pages.

Sitting in the center is the drawing of a tree.

The exact same one as the one in the book Sierra found.

"Wow," Arielle breathes, bringing the two books side by side. "They're identical."

For the first time since they congregated around the Grail, Joseph smiles. He even leans back, looking satisfied.

Reign returns his focus to the book, reading the two lines beneath it. "Here lies the curse of Joseph of Arimathea." He frowns, looking back up at the old man. "What curse?"

Joseph clamps his mouth shut, then promptly disappears.

Jilian frowns at Reign. "Who are you talking to?"

"Apparently, no one," he growls in frustration.

Arielle taps the books Sierra found. "It says here the tree is outside the Temple of Solomon, on the outskirts of London."

"It still exists," offers Nim. "The church is a historic landmark."

Reign snaps his book shut. "We need to visit it."

"What?" Simon gasps. "Now that the Grail's here, you decide to leave?"

Reign ignores him, focusing on Sierra, then Arielle. "I'll use the Travel Stone. It won't take long. But this book was hidden for a reason and it's linked to the first Grail Keeper." The same one that just disappeared for some mysterious reason. "We may even find out exactly how we use the Grail to close the Gates of Hell."

Arielle doesn't hesitate. "We won't be long," she promises.

Simon scowls. The other Potentials look a little confused. Blaise and Nim, like the true Archivists they are, simply nod, possibly relating to the need to leave no stone unturned. Jilian looks like she just sucked on a sour grape.

And Joseph doesn't reappear.

Reign's gaze settles on Arielle, touched by the unquestioning trust he sees there.

Maybe he's stalling.

Maybe he's being driven by his loyalty to Sierra and wanting to show that although she didn't find the Grail, she's found something of importance.

Maybe he's onto the final piece of the puzzle—how to tap into the power of the innocuous-looking goblet sitting on the coffee table.

But this feels right.

They're going to pop over and visit England and the Temple of Solomon.

CHAPTER 24

ARIELLE

Arielle watches her mother leave the farmhouse, conscious Xeven is doing the same. Does he realize she's off to see what she can do about the Hell Mask he wears?

That by being with him, but unable to *be* with him, her heart is breaking all over again?

Her mother throws Arielle a quick smile over her shoulder, her gaze drifting to where Xeven's standing in the entrance to the kitchen. Pain flashes. But so does determination. She closes the front door with a soft click, and Xeven frowns before turning away and disappearing, too.

Arielle remains where she is in the living room, unsure how to feel about all of this. Images of what it could look like if her mother's successful are never far away. They'd be the family she's never had, but not only that, she'd never catch her mother staring off into space again, her hand over her heart as if it hurts. But those idyllic images are quickly followed by what it will look like if the Mask can't be removed from her father.

It will break Arielle's mother.

Possibly permanently.

Reign appears by her side, a backpack slung over his shoulder. "I think that's everything." He frowns. "Has something happened?"

Arielle slips her arms around his waist and nestles her face into his chest, breathing deeply. "My mom just left to see what she can learn about the Hell Masks."

Reign's arms wrap around her and the tightness unwinds in her chest. "Your mom will stop at nothing for those she loves." He tips Arielle's chin so he can see her face. "I just hope she's not too disappointed to find Ryder's aged under that mask."

A smile bursts across her face. Just when she thought she couldn't fall in love with this guy any deeper, he goes and says things like that. "Somehow, I don't think she cares."

Reign's about to lean down and kiss her, but the sound of firm steps down the stairs has them pulling apart.

Jilian strides toward them, clutching her cardigan. "I don't think you should go," she announces. "It's a waste of time."

Arielle feels Reign tense and she can't blame him. She doesn't like Jilian, either.

"We won't be gone long," Arielle assures her. "But we need to follow every lead we have before making a move."

Jilian rolls her eyes. "I would've thought you'd realized by now that you're doing it all wrong."

"I beg your pardon?" Reign growls.

But Jilian seems unaware of the warning in his tone. "If I was the leader, I'd take the cup—the Grail—and lead us straight toward the demons."

"Two words, Jilian," Reign barks. "Reckless. Suicidal."

Arielle can't help but agree. "The demons are only getting stronger. It's far too dangerous when we don't know how to utilize the Grail."

If the Sins get hold of it, then the world ends. Including every life on it.

Jilian waves a dismissive hand. "I say bring on the demons. That will ensure more angels arriving, neutralizing them."

Reign's frown is one of the deepest Arielle's seen so far. "You think angels are the good guys?" he asks incredulously. "You think a war between Heaven and Hell will solve this?"

"Well, your Indiana Jones methods haven't exactly worked, have they?" Jilian spits back.

Reign goes to take a step forward, his body vibrating with anger, but Arielle places a hand on his arm. "We'll be back as soon as we can. Until then, remain in the farmhouse, Jilian. This is the only place we can ensure you're safe."

Jilian sniffs, and the action only seems to inflame Reign more, but he turns away in disgust. "Come on, Ari. Some minds are too full of their own importance to be able to fit anything else in, like someone else's view."

Arielle takes his hand. "I'm really proud my mother's not like that," she murmurs.

Jilian gasps as Reign snorts a chuckle. He draws Arielle a few steps away, his other hand wrapped in a fist, no doubt holding the Travel Stone. He throws a warning glance in Jilian's direction. "Don't leave, please. It's for your own safety."

Jilian opens her mouth to reply, but the farmhouse disappears with such suddenness, that Arielle clamps herself around Reign's arm. As the world blurs she squeezes her eyes shut, feeling like her stomach's been left behind.

"We're here," Reign says gently.

Arielle pops one eye open, then then next. They're standing on a country road verged by hedges, more emerald grass stretched around them than she's ever seen. "Wow," she breathes.

The air smells of green. It's now afternoon, when it was mid-morning only a second ago. And a sheep bleats somewhere in the distance.

They're in England.

Reign pulls out a map from a pocket in his backpack. "Nim said the church is only open on weekends for services and guided tours. So it should be empty."

Arielle blinks, amazed that they've just morphed halfway across the world. "Great. Let's see if we can find this book on..." She frowns, momentarily forgetting why they're here. Maybe her brain got left behind, too.

"The curse of Joseph of Arimathea," Reign finishes for her, grinning.

Arielle nudges him with her shoulder. "Some of us haven't been living the jet setting lifestyle."

Reign takes her hand and starts walking down the road. "I prefer to call it the Travel Stone lifestyle," he jokes back.

They round a bend, stopping when they find the Temple of Solomon is only a few feet to their right. It looks just like the drawing in the book Arielle's mother found, as if it was only drawn recently.

"That's some impressive maintenance," Reign comments.

"It really is," Arielle agrees. "The place looks like Joseph could wander outside any moment."

Reign snorts. "I'm not sure Joseph has ever wandered anywhere. Plus, he just floats everywhere now."

Arielle registers the fondness in Reign's voice and it makes her smile. Joseph may have been dead for centuries, but he's very real for Reign. The fact no one else can see him is the one, undeniable link that he's the Keeper of the Grail, and for that, she's glad.

"There's the tree," Reign says, now a little subdued.

Just like the image, the large tree stretches out on the left side of the church, its boughs shading the entrance.

"It seems like an odd place to plant it," Arielle muses. "It's practically in the way."

"Visitors, Nancy!" comes a gravelly, very British voice.

An elderly man in a wheelchair being pushed by what looks like a maid trundles over the gravel driveway. He waves a hand and the maid stops. "Welcome," he pants, sounding like those three words have left him out of breath.

"Huh," Reign says under his breath. "Nim didn't mention there's a caretaker."

"I'm no...caretaker," wheezes the man. "I'm a...professor of... ancient history."

"A professor with impressive hearing," Reign mutters.

Reign continues to make his way to the old man and Arielle follows. They'll need to see if this professor will let them have a look around the church, otherwise they'll have to come back after dark.

The closer they get, the older he looks. Every inch of skin is wrinkles on wrinkles, from the folds surrounding his sunken but intelligent eyes, to the weather-beaten leather hanging off his hooked frame.

Arielle smiles. "Hello, Professor..."

"Breckenridge," he supplies. He indicates the woman dressed in a white uniform behind him. Not a maid, but a nurse. "This...is...Nancy."

"Lovely to meet you Professor Breckenridge," Arielle says warmly. "We're sorry to disturb you, it's just that we heard about the Temple of Solomon and were so intrigued by its history."

"It's...certainly...fascinating," he wheezes, then coughs, looking as if the motion could snap his fragile skeleton.

Nancy leans down, placing a gentle hand on his shoulder. "You don't want to overdo it, Professor."

But he waves a bony hand. "I'm...fine."

Reign glances at the tree, then back at the Professor, probably wondering if they should just come back after dark.

"We're particularly interested in the Curse of Joseph of Arimathea."

The Professor's sparse eyebrows shoot up his bald head. "A rare legend...indeed." He indicates to Nancy to wheel him to the cottage. "Come."

Arielle and Reign glance at each other. It's the church they really want to see and search, and this sounds like it's going to be slow and painful. But maybe amongst those breaths and gasps they'll learn something useful.

They follow as Nancy pushes the Professor over the gravel and onto a path that leads to the front door of the cottage. A man steps out from behind a shrub, holding a large set of garden shears. "Professor," he says respectfully.

"Good work..." the Professor pants, not even bothering to finish the sentence.

The gardener goes back to his pruning, not paying much attention to the visitors. The cottage is small and packed full of books. Nancy has to carefully navigate through as she wheels the Professor into a living room and parks him beside an open hearth. The Professor pats her hand, and she nods, leaving.

The room fills with the soft, irregular sounds of the Professor's wheezy breaths. Arielle wonders if he even has any energy left to speak.

"The...legend...of—"

"Yes, the curse of Joseph of Arimathea," Reign finishes for him. "If you have any books, we're happy to read them."

For the first time, the Professor frowns. "Listening isn't a strength of yours, is it?"

Arielle blinks. That was the longest and most complete sentence the Professor has spoken so far. Her eyes widen, her eyelids forgetting to function, when the Professor pushes up from his wheelchair and steps away.

Reign instantly moves closer to her. "Did your meds just kick in or something?"

The Professor sends him a dry look as he walks to the fireplace and picks up a bound sheaf of papers from the mantlepiece. "My dissertation was on the curse of Joseph," he says, his voice strong and clear. "What would you like to know?"

"What tablet you just popped, to start with," Reign says, clearly suspicious.

The Professor chuckles, moving until he's facing the hearth and the mirror above it. Arielle watches in fascination as the years melt away from his face. His skin tightens and fills out. A thick mane of brown hair frames his face. He goes from stooped and aged to tall and youthful.

Reign moves until his body is angled in front of Arielle. "Who the hell are you?"

"I told you," the Professor says, turning to face them. "Professor Breckenridge. I just haven't looked like this in a very long time."

"How long," Arielle asks, unsure what they're dealing with here.

The Professor waves a hand dismissively. "Somewhere in the thousands. I've lost count." He strides back to the door of the cottage. "Now, did you want to see the church and learn about the curse?"

CHAPTER 25
REIGN

Reign didn't realize it until now, but he just learned that he doesn't trust guys who go from Yoda-level-ancient to dude-in-his-prime in the space of a breath.

Yet, the Professor is offering them answers.

Reign rubs his brow, not quite believing he's about to say this. "Sure, we'd love to."

The Professor grins. "Excellent."

Spinning on his heel, he exits the cottage, waving at the gardener as he passes. "Lovely afternoon, Boris."

The gardener looks up and tips his hat. "Yes, sir. Is the professor asleep?"

"My grandfather's just having a nap," the Professor replies, his feet crunching on the gravel that ten minutes ago, he didn't have the strength to wheel over. He glances at Reign and Arielle. "I followed in the footsteps of my grandfather. We're both Professor Breckenridges, now."

Reign takes Arielle's hand, waiting until they're out of earshot before asking the question they should've started with. "Who are you?"

"And how have you lived for so long?" Arielle adds.

The Professor slows until they're walking beside him. "Do you believe I'm a threat?" he asks Reign.

Reign frowns. "No," he says, realizing it's the truth. Although he's yet to trust the Professor, he's strangely not on guard. "But I also don't assume I'm right."

"I suspect that's part of the problem," the Professor replies. He turns to Arielle before Reign can ask what he means by that. "In answer to your question, I was cursed a long time ago," he says. "I will walk this Earth until it is broken."

They reach the tree and Reign stops beside it. "Speaking of curses," he says, deciding to focus on what they need to know, rather than another mystery. "What do you know about this tree?"

The Professor stops beside it, patting a hand on it like it's an old friend. "Some believe Joseph of Arimathea placed it here, himself."

Every cell in Reign's body stands at attention. "Who does?"

"Those who built the church," the Professor replies. "Legend has it that Joseph traveled here with the Holy Grail. He was desperate to protect it after hearing that a darkness was corrupting the world following the Resurrection."

"The obsidian," Arielle breathes.

The Professor looks up at the canopy shading them from the afternoon sun, not seeming to hear her. Or ignoring her statement. "It's rumored that Mary Magdalene came with him. And had a daughter in this very church."

Reign raises a brow. "How very *DaVinci Code* of them."

"Were you there, son?" the Professor asks archly.

"Were you?" Reign shoots back. Just because the Professor is old, doesn't mean he was present at every pivotal moment in history.

Humor, maybe a little respect, twinkle in the Professor's

eye. He returns his focus to the tree. "It's also said this tree grew from Joseph's staff. He planted it here. As a message."

Reign stills. "What message?"

The professor steps away from the tree and toward the church door. "*Now* you're assuming I was there?" he says over his shoulder.

Reign frowns, feeling like they're going in circles. He slips the backpack off his shoulders, reaches in, and pulls something out. "What can you tell us about this, then?" he challenges, hiding the grimace of pain as the Mark burns.

Arielle gasps. "You brought the Grail?"

He passes it to her, grinning to cover the fact the pain is growing. "I figured as Keeper of said Grail, I should have it with me at all times."

"Or you don't trust Jilian," Arielle points out.

He shrugs, trying to keep his voice light. "Or I wanted to piss her off a little bit if she went looking for it."

Arielle's rueful headshake is cut short by the Professor appearing beside her. "You've found the Holy Cup?" he asks, sounding awed. "That chalice was used by Jesus during the Last Supper. Joseph of Arimathea also used it to catch Christ's blood at the Crucifixion."

"We believe it might be the Holy Grail," Arielle tells him, holding it up. "We were hoping to discover some link to Joseph, the first Grail Keeper, which would help us know for sure."

The Professor chuckles. "He's definitely the one person who could tell you."

And yet he didn't. He was practically underwhelmed by the sight of it. And then he promptly disappeared.

Reign takes a small step back as a bead of sweat zigzags down his temple as the Mark continues to fester with heat. He clears his throat. "Could we have a look in the church?"

"Of course," the Professor says. "Although I've been here for centuries. There's nothing left to find."

"We believe there's a book on the curse of Joseph of Arimathea," Arielle volunteers. "And that it's here."

"I heard that, too. It's why I came here." The Professor smiles sadly, stopping before the church doors. "I felt a certain affinity with him."

Reign realizes he does, too. The Mark certainly feels like a curse right about now. His whole arm is on fire.

Arielle leans forward. "And? What did you find?"

"Nothing," the Professor says flatly. "The curse has barely been spoken of, let alone written about." He indicates toward the tree. "More has been recorded about it, truth be told."

Reign grits his teeth, taking another step backward even though the distance doesn't seem to help. The Mark is burning hotter and hotter. "We'd like to have a look, anyway, if that's alright."

Arielle frowns. "Is everything okay, Reign?"

He throws her a crooked smile. "Seems I'm allergic to the cup."

Of course he is.

A Grail Keeper who's allergic to the Grail.

Her frown deepening, Arielle quickly pulls off his backpack and jams the goblet back in. Then she cups his face, her hands cool against his cheeks. "Just breathe."

Except the moment she touches him, he no longer needs to. The pain washes away. The fire is doused. It's as if the Mark is nothing more than a tattoo he got when he was drunk and deeply regrets.

Reign lets out a huffing breath. "I'm fine." Because Arielle is here.

Their connection is powerful enough that she heals him with a touch.

"Are you sure?" she asks, concerned. "It looked...painful."

"Hey, it's further proof the cup is the real deal," Reign says, trying to lighten the situation. "Why else would the Mark react to it so strongly?"

The Professor snorts. "Asking the right questions will give you the answers you're looking for," he mutters. Reign and Arielle turn to him, and he straightens, trying to pretend he didn't just say that. "So, you wanted to see the church, even though it's a waste of precious time?"

Reign angles his head to the side. The Professor wants them to ask the right questions, huh? "You haven't asked who we are," he observes. "Why is that?"

In fact, he's practically welcomed them, barely asking a question himself. That's the oddest part of this whole visit.

The glint returns to the Professor's eyes. But then they widen as he focuses past Reign and Arielle. And fill with alarm.

Reign spins around, the sight that greets him immediately launching his heart into his throat. Adrenaline into his muscles.

And the powerful drive to protect Arielle, no matter the cost.

The hellhound running toward them is massive. Monstrous. Red eyes glow with infernal power, teeth as long as a knives glisten with the beast's slavering excitement. It's paws shoot out clods of dirt behind it as it vaults over the green landscape.

They may be halfway across the globe, but they've been found. Reign's wings explode from his back as he breaks into a run.

Evil is trying to get hold of the Grail.

Yet all he thinks about is protecting Arielle.

DINAH

Dinah stands in the same spot she fought the obsidian as she'd tried to destroy Pandora's Box, the forest unusually silent.

She almost lost the battle.

And most definitely lost the key to open a breach between their world and one harboring untold horrors.

She closes her eyes again, focusing her entire being on trying to trace the demon who stole the Box.

You won't find it. You never will.

I won't let you.

Dinah growls with frustration, unable to get past the black barrier the obsidian throws up every time she tries. She's being sabotaged from within.

Yet, if she doesn't find the box...

"I can help you, Dinah."

She spins around, hands already engulfed in flames as she faces the young man who somehow snuck up behind her.

Kill him!

Resisting the urge is hard, and for a split-second, Dinah worries she won't be able to. The flames dance higher around her hand, hungry for flesh, but she doesn't let it get any further. In fact, she lowers her hands, the fire licking up her arms.

The young man smiles from beneath his mop of blond waves, blue eyes gentle and friendly. "You're trying to trace the demon who stole the Box," he says. "I can help you with that."

"Who are you?" she grinds out, panting with the strain of keeping control of the obsidian. "And how do you know who I am?" Let alone what she's trying to do.

He takes a step forward, seemingly oblivious to the danger she poses. "My name's Oliver. And like I said, I can trace the demon."

"I don't trust you."

231

"I didn't expect you would," he says, unruffled. "So the question is, how much do you want to track down Pandora's Box?"

End him. He's a threat.

Dinah was going to refuse Oliver until the obsidian spoke. If it thinks Oliver is dangerous, then she's willing to find out who or what he is. And why he's here, pretending to help her.

She lifts her chin. "Prove it. Take me to the demon."

Oliver smiles broadly. "I'd love to."

Dinah leads him to her car parked in a nearby parking lot, conscious of his every move. Yet Oliver looks as if he's just a guy, walking in the forest and enjoying the scenery. He even pauses to listen to a particularly annoying bird.

She stops with her hand on the door. "You try anything, and I end you."

He nods. "Of course." Then smiles again. "I'm a friend, Dinah, you have nothing to fear."

She lets out a harsh bark. "I have no friends." Before, she refused to be that vulnerable. Now, she's carrying a slice of Eldritch inside her. She can't afford to let anyone get close, even if she wanted to.

Oliver climbs into the passenger side seat, smoothly folding his tall form into her little car. "You'll want to head back to Mercy City," he says. "I'll direct you from there."

Frowning, Dinah slips into the driver's seat. Starting the car, she leaves the forest, conscious she's getting desperate to be sitting in such close confines with a complete stranger. Yet, she follows each of Oliver's instructions as he leads her through Mercy City, ignoring the way he smiles at her if she happens to glance his way.

In fact, she stops doing that all together. Oliver's calm friendliness unnerves her. He acts as if they're not only friends, but ones who have known each other for years. Apart from telling her to take a right at the next set of lights, or to go straight for three blocks, he doesn't say a word. He sits in his seat, relaxed and at ease, comfortable with the silence.

It's only when they come to some dingy bar in the seedier part of town that he leans forward, staring through the windscreen. "This is it. This is where the demon went."

Dinah's instantly out of the car and striding toward the door with the *closed* sign on it, energy sparking between her fingertips.

She has to get Pandora's Box back.

She's not surprised when Oliver appears by her side, but she is surprised when he doesn't try to stop her. In fact, he's thrumming with tension, looking like he's ready to back her up.

Dinah kicks the door in, ignoring the confusion his presence triggers and focusing on the fight ahead. Who knows how many demons are inside, protecting the Box. And who knows how much the obsidian is going to try and stop her.

The first thing that hits Dinah is silence. The kind of silence that settled into a room long ago.

The second thing is the scent of stale blood.

Then, it's the sight of a dozen dead bodies scattered around the bar.

They're too late. She doesn't need to search the place to know Pandora's Box isn't here. If it ever was at all...

Dinah rounds on Oliver, suddenly furious. "You lied to me!"

He deserves to die!

She leaps toward him, fury punching through her veins. "I've killed for far less."

Oliver studies her face in a way that strangely reminds her of how Reign looks at Arielle. "Is that you, or the obsidian speaking?"

Dinah reels back. "What did you say?"

"I was going to wait until you told me—"

"I would never trust a stranger with that information," she snarls.

"Except I'm not a stranger," Oliver says softly. "I've known you for a very long time."

She retreats another step, knowing she doesn't want to hear this.

Then kill him. It's the only way you can ensure silence.

"I've been watching over you since you were a child, Dinah." He smiles. "When you played with your sister, Lydia." The smile fades. "When your mother, Samara, would torment you both."

Dinah's struck dumb. She didn't think there was anyone left alive who knew any of that.

"Then when your mother died, I watched as you made one destructive choice after another, ultimately joining the Tenth Legion." Oliver takes a small step forward. "So I reached out to Aclima and had her propose a deal to come and work with her, before the Legion fully corrupted you."

Oliver is some sort of guardian angel.

Her guardian angel?

The idea is so preposterous that it snaps Dinah out of her shocked stupor. She moves away, reclaiming the distance between them. "Stay. Away. From. Me," she grinds out. "The Legion is far from finished," Oliver continues. "You want to find out what you can on something called the cultus infinitialis."

"Are you listening?" Dinah shouts. "Never, ever come near me again."

Oliver's disappointed face is the last thing she sees before she breaks into a run, trying to get as far away as possible from him.

She would never let someone in and make herself vulnerable.

And now that she has the obsidian, it's far too dangerous.

CHAPTER 26

ARIELLE

"Reign!" Arielle calls out, about to run after him when the Professor's hand reaches out to stop her.

"He's protecting the Grail," the Professor says. "It's his duty."

Arielle tears her gaze from the man she loves as he spears straight toward a hellhound the size of a horse. The Professor looks at her, his gaze heavy with meaning.

One she has no chance of understanding.

The hellhound lets out a violent roar and she turns back in time to see it dig its massive claws in the soil and leap.

Reign cries out as he does the same, his crimson wings pumping as he launches high.

The hellhound opens its monstrous jaws a second before they clash midair, shooting Arielle's heart into her throat. Reign seamlessly changes angle and flips over the beast, twisting until he lands on his back. He wraps his arms around its thick throat and clamps on.

The hellhound's jaws snap shut as it goes from attacker to being strangled. Reign tightens his arms, his face twisting with the effort as his hands barely reach the other. The hellhound lands, savagely shaking its entire body. Trying to dislodge Reign.

Arielle takes an instinctive step forward, discovering that the Professor is no longer holding her. Her entire being focuses on willing Reign to remain on the hellhound.

A rasping growl ejects a spray of white spittle as the beast tries to roar its fury. Then it convulses when it can't draw a breath back in.

Reign's doing it! He's winning!

The hellhound tries once more to shake him off, crouching so the ripple works right up its muscle-bound body, but Reign holds on. His face is red and contacted with the effort, but he doesn't let go.

The hellhound crouches again even though its losing strength as it starves of oxygen, only to leap high in the air.

Twist.

And land on its back, crushing Reign.

"No!" Arielle cries out.

The hellhound scrabbles to its feet, roaring so loud it makes the air shake. It leaps, pinning Reign to the ground by his shoulders. It stands over him, the low snarl far more terrifying than the savage blast of a second ago.

Reign's hands shoot up to stop the monster bearing down on him, his arms barely longer than the massive skull of the infernal beast. He turns his head as teeth snap an inch from his face, frothy foam collecting along the rows of blade-like teeth.

"Arielle," Reign cries. "Get out of here!"

She shakes her head, even though he can't see her. Although she knows that trying to help will be suicide, that Reign just wants to protect her, she can't stand here and watch him be torn to shreds. She'd rather die.

"The Grail can save him."

The Professor's words stop her just as she's about to launch forward. She spins to face him, registering his calm face.

And knows he's telling the truth.

The Grail is Light. The hellhound was forged from the evil tainting Hell.

Wrenching the goblet out of the backpack, Arielle breaks into a run. She lifts the cup high as she sprints toward where Reign is trapped. She can see the strain on his face. Practically feel his frantic heartbeats as he knows he can't hold the beast away forever. The moment his arms give out, he's dead.

"Begone!" Arielle screams, holding the goblet aloft. "By the power of the Light, begone!"

The hellhound's head shoots up and it pins her with its red eyes, snarling.

But she doesn't stop running.

She can feel it.

She can feel the power of the Grail.

It courses through her, alive and warm and beautiful. Bright light explodes outward, swallowing her surroundings with blazing white. For a breathless second, it obliterates everything, seems to freeze time. Arielle can no longer feel her heart beating, her blood pumping, her lifeforce ceases to exist.

In an endless moment, anything is possible.

And then it all returns in a rush.

She gasps.

She blinks.

And sees Reign lying on the ground, the hellhound gone.

Arielle drops to her knees, astounded at what just happened. Reign rolls onto his side with a groan, squinting as if the world is too bright. Because for a moment, it was.

He stumbles to his feet, his wings disappearing as he lurches to the side, rights himself, then staggers toward her. He falls to his knees, cupping her face. "Ari..."

She focuses on the sensation of his hands on her skin. On the sweet relief that's echoed in his eyes. Reign's alive.

He glances down at the silver goblet she's still holding. "So, I think we have our answer."

Arielle nods mutely.

They have the Holy Grail.

Reign pushes to his feet then reaches out a hand to haul her up. She's glad to see her legs keep her upright, despite feeling boneless. She's never experienced anything like those moments where the world was pure white. There's no doubt in her mind the Grail can end this. It has the power to close the Gates of Hell.

To fight the evil of Eldritch.

"Let's get back to the farmhouse," Reign says. "We don't need the book on Joseph's curse. We learned what he wanted to do."

The Professor appears beside them. "I'd like to come too."

Reign's brows shoot up in surprise. "I don't think so."

"And not see the Holy Grail in action?" the Professor says. "I've lived far too long to miss such an opportunity." He even takes a step closer and clamps his hand on Reign's shoulder.

Reign hesitates, but Arielle can already see he's made his decision. They don't have time to fight this. Nor does Reign have the heart to do something like knock the guy out, which is probably the only way they'll get away without him.

He sighs. "Fine. We need all the help we can get."

The Professor nods sagely. "Yes, you will."

The foreboding words dampen the strange mix of empowered and shaky still gripping Arielle, but she tries to ignore all three.

The need to keep moving forward.

Especially now that they have the Grail.

SIERRA

It's been a long time since Sierra's returned to Sinclair Mansion. Everything that transpired since she discovered something as fantastical as the Holy Grail is real feels like a lifetime ago.

And yet, the memories are so fresh, they've never lost their impact.

She may have failed in finding the Grail, but she did find love.

And that love gifted her Arielle.

Now, there's only one thing she wishes for as deeply and as totally as she did the Grail.

To have Ryder back.

Which is why she's back here, in the library, hoping this will work.

"Cain," she calls out, slowly turning in the circular room. "I need to speak to you."

Sierra has no idea if the bastard can hear her, but she has to try. Cain was the one who stole Ryder from her and enslaved him with the Hell Mask. He's the one who can take it off.

"Yes?" comes a mildly annoyed voice from behind her.

Sierra spins so fast her hair flies out, then whips her in the face. She flicks it away impatiently, trying not to frown when she sees Cain standing beside a desk. Fury is the first emotion that slams through her.

Then rage.

Then lifelong grief.

She pushes her shoulder back, knowing none of those are going to be helpful right now. "I want you to take the Mask off Xeven," she says, her voice firm. "I want my Ryder back."

Cain shakes his head. "I can't do that."

Sierra takes a step forward, trying to clamp down on the storm of feelings gaining momentum in her gut. "You don't want to," she says through gritted teeth.

"What I want is irrelevant," he snaps. "I'm telling you the truth. I cannot remove the Mask. Doing so is likely to kill Ryder."

Sierra shakes her head, refusing to believe there's no way forward. That Ryder is here, yet will never be hers again. "You're just saying that because you want to punish me for what I did to you all those years ago when you tried to raise Abel from the dead."

Cain arches a brow as he comes a step closer. "And you don't think I've punished you enough by placing that Mask on Ryder because he chose you?"

Sierra flinches despite herself. Every day has been bitter-sweet hell as she's watched their daughter grow into the amazing young woman she is, without Ryder by her side. "Do you have no regrets at all?" He's even more heartless than she thought.

"I've lived too long to carry the weight of something like regret," Cain says, his voice hardening. "All I can do is keep moving forward."

"Which would be to free Ryder," Sierra snaps, the fury worming its way back into her heart.

A muscle ticks in Cain's cheek. "I can't," he grinds out. "Those Masks were forged in Hell by channeling the power of darkness. They are infernal and evil. And they affect humans in ways even I didn't expect."

Sierra stalks forward, stabbing a finger into Cain's chest. "There has to be a way!" she shouts in his face. "I will not lose the man I love!"

Not again.

Cain's eyebrows twitch up ever so slightly. "Ryder may not even exist under that Mask anymore."

The deflection is all Sierra needed to hear. "Tell me," she says, the words like smoldering coals.

He studies her for long seconds before sighing. "If the Masks were forged from the power of darkness, then the only thing that can oppose that is the power of light."

"What are you saying?" Sierra asks, finding her voice is a whisper.

She already suspects she knows the answer.

"The Grail, Sierra," Cain says. "It's forged from Primordial Light. It's the only thing that can break the hold the Mask has on Ryder."

CHAPTER 27

REIGN

Reign stands in the living room of the farmhouse once more. Just like earlier, the team is here.

And so is the Grail.

It sits on the coffee table in the middle of the room, acting like it didn't just obliterate a hellhound into non-existence.

"I told you," Jilian says, her nose twitching in a pre-sniff. "I knew exactly what the riddle meant. That is the Holy Grail."

Reign's a little relieved Sierra isn't here right now. Hopefully Jilian can get through most of her gloating before Arielle's mother returns. Then he won't be tempted to put duct tape over the woman's mouth. And that superior nose of hers.

"Unless you're wrong."

Everyone's head snaps in the direction of the Professor and Reign almost facepalms. He didn't think he'd regret allowing the guy to come with them so soon.

Bryn's hands jam on her hips. "I don't care who you are, you don't get to come in here and throw words like that around. You heard what Reign and Arielle just told us."

It was mostly Arielle who told the story of what happened

in England. Of how she used the cup to save Reign from the hellhound.

And he didn't correct her. Even though it's not entirely the truth.

The Mark flashes with heat at the memory of those moments when the hellhound was bearing down on him, teeth snapping viciously. Things had almost gone very, very wrong.

The Professor shrugs, unrepentant. "I'm a man of research. I'd hate for you to jump to conclusions."

Reign frowns. "That cup most definitely saved me." In more ways than one.

"Did it?" the Professor asks, his voice dropping. "Did you know there are legends that Mary Magdalene herself was tasked with carrying the Grail by Joseph of Arimathea?"

"Fascinating," Bryn says, sounding anything but. "None of that really matters when we have the Grail itself right here, with us now."

"I felt it," Arielle interjects softly. "I felt the power of the Light."

The Professor's gaze falls on her, glinting with intensity. His eyes bore into Arielle with such ferocity that Reign steps into his line of vision, flashing the Professor a look of warning. "We're here to decide our next steps, not debate this."

"Especially when we know that goblet is the Grail," Jilian says, this time most definitely sniffing, a sound that is fast getting on Reign's nerves.

Bryn is almost doing a highland jig. "So, what now? Are we gonna go kick some serious Sin butt?"

Reign shakes his head. "Not without the weapon to kill Wrath. We don't know if the blade is an essential part of killing him."

The Professor grunts. "Wise move."

Reign ignores him as he looks around the room at Blaise,

Nim, and the Potentials. "Dinah is still trying to retrieve Pandora's Box." The same one she lost. "And we still need to find a way to stop the spell the Sins are working on to open the breach."

Arielle nods. "In the meantime, we protect Jilian."

As much as Reign doesn't want to, he also nods agreement. Jilian may not be likable, but she's an Innocent. Her death would mean another Gate of Hell opening.

Jilian pats her perfect hair. "Although now that we have the Grail, that won't be an issue for long."

Blaise squeezes Nim's shoulder. "I think we could strengthen the wards around here a little more."

Nim rests her own hand on Blaise's. "Great idea."

They exit through the front door, already talking about which herbs they'll need.

Bryn turns to the Potentials. "Come one, let's go train with the Knights and nephilim," she says, still clearly pumped.

Simon groans, but they follow her to the kitchen and out to the backyard. Looking thoughtful, the Professor follows them.

Jilian quickly moves to pick up the goblet, springing Reign into action, only for him to stop. The memory of the burn each time he touches the cup flares through his nerve endings.

As does the knowledge of where that could end up.

Arielle smoothly swoops in and picks up the cup, smiling widely at Jilian. "I'll put it somewhere safe."

Jilian stiffens. "I could—"

"It's fine," Arielle assures her. "We have a safe. And this way, we'll have it nearby for when we need it."

Tucking her cardigan around her like armor, Jilian stalks out of the living room with her sniffy nose high in the air.

Reign lets out slow breath once she's gone. He never thought he'd actually be tempted to strangle an Innocent. Then again, he'd never met Jilian.

Arielle turns to him, and he tenses as the Grail comes close. "I'm going to give my mum a call," she says. "Let her know where things are at."

He nods, pressing a quick kiss to her forehead before stepping back. "Good idea. Tell her that if Jilian had a daughter, I could never have fallen in love with her."

Yet Arielle's answering smile is short lived. "Is everything okay, Reign?"

He sighs. "There's just...a lot to take in."

They may have found the Cup of Light. The one he was destined to protect.

But the darkness within him has never been closer to the surface.

Arielle nods, instinctively moving closer just as he would if she were troubled. Except she's holding the Grail.

And he has the Mark.

He takes another step back. "I might go join the training session." He smiles crookedly. "Facing a hellhound sure gets a whole lot of energy pumping through a guy's body."

"Okay," Arielle says, hesitating.

But Reign's already on his way to the kitchen. He knows he needs to tell Arielle what's going on.

He just has to figure out what that is, first.

The sound of fighting reaches him as he steps onto the back patio, yet Reign stops. He told Ari the truth that there's a whole lot of excess energy crackling through his veins. But the last thing he feels like is company right now.

Which is why he finds himself ducking left and circling the large farmhouse until he's making his way toward the garden shed tucked beneath a large tree. A few minutes of quiet is all he needs, he tells himself.

To get the darkness swirling within him under control.

"I used to do that, too. Hope that a little peace will help."

Reign spins, already swinging a fist, but Cain easily side-steps the blow.

"It didn't help, by the way."

"Fuck off, Cain," Reign growls. "I don't even want to know why you're here."

Cain leans against the side of the timber shed. "Why, to help, of course."

Reign snorts. "I need that as much as I needed a hellhound trying to rip my head off." He spins, deciding he'll be the one to leave if Cain isn't.

Except the next words having him stopping in his tracks.

"Ah, that's why I felt it."

Reign turns slowly, even as he hates himself for doing it. "Felt what?"

Cain's dark gaze glints knowingly. "The surge in dark power. Although I no longer have the Mark, it seems I'm still linked to it somehow. Like an echo in my bones."

Reign wants to get the hell out of here. To tell Cain to go suck a hellhound.

Yet he doesn't move.

Because he knows exactly what Cain's talking about.

Those moments when the monster of Hell was bearing down on him, the power of the Mark had surged, just like Cain says. It had filled him with strength that felt limitless. Bottomless.

The power to snap the beast's neck had been within reach. A choice away.

Yet he could also feel how dark it was. Evil. That one hellhound wouldn't be enough.

That he'd no longer be someone deserving of Arielle.

Cain pushes away from the wall of the shed. "I owe you, Reign. You helped me escape Purgatory."

"Not by choice," he points out.

"No descendant of mine would be stupid enough to do that by choice," Cain scoffs, not that Reign appreciates the round-about compliment. "I still owe you. Which means I'll do as I promised—I'll tell you how to control the Mark."

"No, thanks." Cain failed. The Mark drove him to kill count-less people.

Cain jams his hands in his pockets, the smug look on his face suggesting he hasn't finished. "And once you do that, you can channel it. The Mark is linked to Hell, just as the weapons to kill the Sins are."

Reign freezes. "Are you telling me I could channel the Mark to find them?"

"You could easily do that." Cain inclines his head. "Once you learn to control the Mark's dark influence. Doing so will leave you vulnerable to it."

Reign doesn't hesitate. They have the Grail. All they need is the blade to kill Wrath and they can attack. "Show me."

Cain moves closer, his dark eyes flaring with something that looks disturbingly like excitement. "The key is to balance the darkness with Light. In the same way the Grail is the cure for evil, Light keeps darkness at bay." His lips turn down at the edges. "Killing Abel twisted me. Made me vulnerable."

"Except I killed Lance," Reign says, his gut clenching, hating that he repeated history.

Cain's gaze is as still as it's sure. "But you have something I never did."

Love.

Arielle.

Something so precious, there's nothing he wouldn't do to keep it.

Cain must see that Reign's determination only cements. He moves until he's standing before Reign. "Close your eyes. Connect to the Mark. Find the link to Hell, then trace that energy signature." He smiles a little. "And remember why you're doing this."

Not to get even.

But to make things right.

Reign does as he's told and closes his eyes. He centers his focus on the Mark and the power surges immediately, as if it was waiting for this. The same feeling courses through him as when the hellhound attacked, thirsty to be free. To devour and destroy. The draw to it is strong.

The Mark wants him to embrace it. For him to give it control.

Yet Reign thinks of those seconds when Arielle was running toward him, holding the Grail high. When the world turned white. In that moment, the darkness couldn't exist. It was nothing but a memory.

And that's what Reign embraces. Invites into his mind.

Then allows himself to explore the Mark he's done nothing but deny. He becomes curious about its origins, about what it's connected to.

When Reign opens his eyes, Cain is gone. Yet he still says the next words aloud.

"I know where the weapon to kill Wrath is."

CHAPTER 28

ARIELLE

Mercy City Bank is a tall, imposing building, yet
Arielle doesn't crane her neck to take in the story
upon story of stone architecture. Not when Reign
saw the blade that can kill Wrath inside a vault.

And a quick bit of research revealed that the vault is below
ground.

The bank itself is closed, like most stores and services close
to the city's center. Although Greed is dead, the bank would've
been attacked with vengeance as people sought to quench their
insatiable need for more. And Wrath's influence still has hold of
Mercy City. Fury has wrought destruction everywhere Arielle
looks, making her heart ache. So much pain. So much loss.

And now they have a way to stop it.

Arielle adjusts her backpack. The weight of the Grail is a
comforting one. They just need to find out where and when to
use it.

The Knights Templar and nephilim warriors spread out,
some scaling the walls to the second story. The Potentials stand
with the handful of fighters still with Arielle and Reign, various

shades of pale except for Bryn. She has almost as many knives strapped to her as Alexandra would.

"Ready?" Reign asks Arielle.

She wishes she could kiss him, a reminder of what they're fighting for. Humanity. And Love.

Arielle nods. "Ready."

Then they're running together, the Potentials and warriors behind them, their sights on the large glass doors at the front of the Bank. Reign lifts his hands and shoots out a ball of fire at the same time as his wings appear. They curve around himself and Arielle, protecting them from the shattering glass.

When the red shields retract, the doors are nothing but frames. Reign leaps through first, followed closely by Arielle, then the others. Glass crunches underfoot as they barely break momentum and power into the expansive, marble-tiled foyer.

One filled with demons.

Arielle spins and strikes one demon, then another. Beside her, Reign is a flurry of movement, using each one of his weapons, his hands, feet, wings, to mow through the enemy. The Knights and nephilim pour in through every entrance, even dropping from the floor above, joining the battle. Cries and grunts and thuds fill the room, carrying high into the soaring ceiling.

"The door to the fire stairs is over there," Reign calls, pointing to the far wall, then turning his hand into a fist and powering it into a demon's throat.

Arielle ducks a savage strike from another, crouches, then leaps into a spinning kick. Her foot connects with the demon's jaw, sending him flying into two of his comrades. "We need to get to it," she grunts, hoping it won't take too long.

Reign glances around, seems to see what he was hoping for, because he vaults to Arielle, grabs her around the chest, and launches into the air. Arielle holds on tight as they fly over the battle, straight toward the door. A handful of demons also take to the air, trying to stop them, but between Reign's artful twisting and weaving, and a few well-aimed kicks from Arielle, they cover the distance within moments.

They've just landed when a cry rings out, making Reign spin around. "Simon!" he gasps.

The Potential is surrounded by four demons, blood trickling from his nose as he spins one way then the other, trying to defend himself. One demon slams a fist into his temple. Another plows a boot into his gut.

Reign takes a step toward him, then hesitates.

"Go," Arielle urges, knowing he's torn between his responsibilities and the need to protect her.

Reign leaps and flies over the distance, landing in the center of the circle just as one of the demons grabs Simon by the throat, clearly planning on snapping his neck. One twist as he cracks his wings out is all it takes for Reign to scatter the other three demons. Increasing the pace of his spin, he crouches low and sweeps the legs out from under the demon. He crashes to the ground with a cry, releasing Simon.

It's the last sound he makes as Reign slams the pointed tip of one red wing into the demon's throat.

Simon staggers to his feet as Bryn appears by their side, two Knights with her. "I've got this from here," she tells Reign, flinging a blade that impales in the eye of a demon who was running toward them.

One glance at Simon, then Bryn, and Reign vaults back to Arielle. He executes a back kick as a demon tries to attack them, then grabs her hand and rushes for the door. "Quick, before I'm tempted to punch the kid myself."

Arielle goes with him, even as she knows Reign would never do such a thing. He just saved Simon's life.

The stairwell is empty, but the thundering on the door

Reign just locked tells them it won't be for long. Arielle and Reign sprint down the stairs, their harsh breathing quickly filling the small space. They burst into the basement level of the bank, finding themselves in a large room with only one thing in it.

A massive metal door that leads to the vault.

They rush toward it and Reign runs his hands over the round, cool surface. "The blade is in there. I can feel it."

Arielle grips the thick handle, realizing two things. There's no way it's unlocked. And they have no idea how to get in.

Make that three.

Without Rachel or Marlowe, they have no way of opening without the use of force.

"My guess is the doors and walls are thick and reinforced," Reign says, probably realizing the same. "I don't suppose you brought a truckload of explosives with you?"

Arielle takes a step back, wondering if even that would be enough. How are they going to get inside the vault? Before they're overrun by blood-thirsty demons...

Suddenly, a voice sounds from the bottom of the stairs. "I'm going to carve that thing like butter."

Arielle and Reign spin around, shocked. It was a female voice. One they haven't heard in a very long time.

Mac grins at them as she steps forward and lifts her hands, palm out, black wings stretched out behind her. Red balls of fire appear, blazing hotter and hotter with each passing second.

"You might want to step back," she says, the same fire glinting deep in her eyes.

Arielle and Reign do as they're told, and Mac unleashes the two cannonball-sized rounds. They converge into one as they shoot toward the vault door. Arielle braces herself in the same moment that Reign places himself in front of her.

But there's no outward explosion.

The ball hits the metal door and detonates out, liquid flames engulfing most of the circular surface, then instantly pushing forward. The metal screeches, melts, and fractures all at once.

Leaving a large hole where inches of steel used to be. Inside is a single table, a knife with a red gem in the center of the hilt sitting on it.

Reign spins back to look at his best friend. "Mac!"

She grins. "Yeah, I missed you, too."

Their hug is short but fierce, and Arielle's throat clogs with emotion. Reign and Mac's joy at being reunited seems to light the whole room.

They pull back, grinning at each other. "We should totally catch up some time," Mac says.

Reign yanks her in for another quick squeeze. "Pencil in a block of time, *a lot* has happened."

He turns toward Arielle, then the vault. And the blade sitting in its center. They approach it simultaneously, stepping through the hole Mac created, then standing around the table.

Arielle picks up the blade and runs her thumb over the ruby embedded into the hilt. "Wrath's downfall," she murmurs.

"Can't wait," Mac snarls. "I can't believe what he's done to Mercy City."

Reign's lips thin, no doubt thinking what the city they both grew up in looks like in the eyes of someone who's been away for as long as Mac has.

Like a supernatural warzone.

"It's some of my best work," comes a smug voice from beyond the vault.

Arielle's hand tightens around the blade as she realizes Wrath is standing in the room, then loosens when she sees he's holding Jilian against him, his hand clamped across her mouth.

"You bastard!" Reign shouts.

Wrath chuckles. "So much anger. I can feel myself getting stronger just being around you, Grail Keeper."

Reign's clenched hands slowly release. He subtly shifts back, giving Arielle a clear line of sight. She adjusts the position of the blade in her palm, frustrated by the way Wrath is holding the Innocent in front of him like a shield.

Jilian's eyes are wide with terror and she screams desperately, but her words are muffled by Wrath's hand. He laughs, pulling her tighter against him as his eyes flash crimson. "It was so easy to lure her out of the farmhouse," he boasts. "One Infinity symbol scrawled beyond the wards and she ran out, screaming that she can fight her own battles."

Jilian mewls and her legs give out, revealing Wrath's shoulder, but he jolts her back up before Arielle can move.

"So close, now," he growls. "Another Gate is about to be opened. Lucifer will be freed of the Cage and the apocalypse will begin with the coming of Eldritch."

"I'm not loving the plan," Reign snaps, jolting into action.

Arielle knows exactly what he's going to do—run at Wrath and try to create an opening for her to use the blade.

But Wrath releases Jilian, throws out a hand, and a black wall explodes across the opening of the vault.

Trapping them.

So that he can escape with the Innocent.

CHAPTER 29

REIGN

Reign roars with fury as he launches himself at the wall of midnight, grunting when he hits what feels like marble. He stumbles backward, prepared to do it again, when Mac grips his shoulder.

"There's a quicker way."

He stops, remembering she's the one who blasted the vault door open in the first place. "You can do it?"

She squints one eye. "This is demon magic, which will be stronger than what was already here." She squeezes his shoulder. "But it'll be no match against the two of us."

Reign's mouth pops open an inch. "The two of us?"

Mac snaps her wings out, although she keeps them tucked in the limited space of the vault. "I always knew we had more in common than being orphaned street rats."

They both have demon blood flowing through their veins.

Reign allows his wings to appear, too. "Although—"

"Yeah, I know, show off. Red was always my favorite color."

Reign reaches up to place a hand on her shoulder, mirroring her. "I'm glad you're back." Seeing her is a reminder that his teen years weren't all bad.

And that being different isn't, either.

"It's good to be back," she says, her eyes shining with the truth of her words. Then she turns to Arielle. "I like what you've done with him."

Arielle shakes her head. "Reign forged every step of his destiny. I'm just grateful I got to be part of it."

"You are my destiny," he says, huskily.

Mac turns to face the black wall trapping them. "Time to shape our future again."

Reign moves so he's beside her, determination settling into his bones. "What do I need to do?"

"Blast the fuck out of it," Mac says grimly. "We have an Innocent to save."

They raise their hands simultaneously, angling their palms at the wall. Reign feels the Mark flare, followed by a rush of power.

Dark power.

Arielle moves beside him, supporting him without even knowing it.

Reminding him of the Light she brought into his life.

Heat builds in Reign's palms in the same moment that a dark glow starts to burn in Mac's. A second later, the same energy appears in his own.

"Let it build," Mac says intently.

So Reign does. The heat multiplies. The power intensifies. He grits his teeth as energy forged in Hell thunders through his veins.

Yet it never reaches his heart. It can't. It's too full of Arielle.

"Now!" Mac shouts.

Reign unleashes the blast in the same moment Mac does. Twin beams of destruction shoot toward the wall and blast straight through it. Onyx shards explode into the room beyond like a meteor shower.

They're running even as the smaller chunks are still skittering over the floor, the gravel-sized pieces crunching beneath their boots. They clatter up the stairs, the sounds of the battle above becoming louder and louder.

"He's taken her to a level above," Mac pants.

Reign realizes she's right. He can sense a trace of the Sin, like a thread as thick as a spider's web. They continue on up the stairs to the second level, then the third.

"He must've taken her to the roof," Arielle says as they pass the fourth level and Mac and Reign register Wrath hasn't stopped.

They race higher and higher, each step counting out the seconds it's taking them to find the Sin. And Jilian.

Reign, Arielle and Mac burst out onto the roof of Mercy City Bank, finding a circle of demons around the perimeter.

And Wrath in the center, standing over Jilian, bound to a chair, slashing a knife straight toward her chest.

One glance and Mac and Reign know what they need to do. They shoot forward like two bullets, coming together, black and red wings mirroring the other, and becoming a tornado of power.

Spiraling together, Reign and Mac become a blur of crimson and onyx as they catapult toward Wrath. Any demon within reach of their wingspan is knocked away, some instantly killed by the razor-sharp edges.

A second before they reach the Sin they split, Reign grabbing Jilian, chair and all, Mac barreling straight into Wrath. He stumbles backward with a roar while Reign twists and propels straight back to Ari. He places Jilian on the ground, then turns, already a blur of punches and kicks as demons swarm them.

"Stay still," Arielle instructs Jilian. "I'm going to cut the ropes."

Mac returns, too, landing beside Reign as they protect Jilian.

A blaze of heat hits them, feeling like a furnace just exploded on the rooftop. They look up to find Wrath engulfed in flames. Flames of fury. The heat coming off him scorches the cement around him, even singes any demons who are too close, yet leaves him unharmed. Even his clothes are intact.

"Step back," Wrath screams. "The Innocent is mine."

He advances, surrounded by an inferno that has his own demons retreating, wrapping their wings protectively around themselves.

It would be suicide to attack Wrath now.

"We need to get back in the building," Reign calls out, taking a step back. To the protection of the Knights and nephilim. It's their best bet of escaping with Jilian alive.

Forming a line between Jilian and Wrath, Reign, Arielle and Mac take a step backward, then another, steadily and swiftly making their way to the door.

Wrath realizes what they're doing and his blaze grows. He drops his chin as he increases his advance.

Reign and the others simply hasten their retreat, walking backward as they don't take their eyes off the burning ball of rage coming at them. There are only a few feet between them and freedom.

"Steady," Mac growls under her breath.

Maybe if they don't make any sudden movements, they have a chance at freedom.

At saving Jilian.

From the corner of his eye, Reign sees Arielle draw the blade out, keeping it out of sight behind him. She'll definitely be making a sudden movement, one to fling the knife at the Sin. But if they get their timing right, then they can also take care of Wrath.

The one Sin who's caused the most destruction.

Sensing they're close to their escape, Reign's about to order them to run, knowing Arielle will fling the blade at the same time, when there's the sound of a zipper tearing open. A few frantic rustles.

Then Jilian barges between Reign and Arielle. She holds the goblet aloft. "Begone foul demon!"

"What are you doing?" Arielle gasps.

Reign reaches out to grip the foolish woman, but Jilian's already running toward Wrath. "You cannot match the power of the Grail!"

She lifts the silver cup even higher, the flames engulfing Wrath dancing over its reflective surface.

Yet nothing happens.

No white light.

No annihilation of evil.

The Innocent is running toward her own doom.

"Jilian!" Arielle screams, flinging the blade with all her might.

Time slows as Reign watches Fate unfold. Arielle's aim has to miss Jilian and hit Wrath.

Before Jilian reaches the Sin and is killed.

The knife spins through the air, the ruby refracting the flames, the blade glinting with malice. It flies past Jilian, perfectly on target for Wrath's heart.

Shock explodes through Reign when the blade unerringly lodges in Wrath's chest, as if a magnet drew it straight there. Yet Wrath is smiling.

Grinning.

Because the blade he launched at the same time, the one he must've hidden like Arielle did, just impaled Jilian.

MAC

It's all too hard to watch.

Jilian stumbling, crumbling, and sprawling onto the cement. Her Grace leaching into the air.

The remaining demons crowing victoriously as they fly away.

And Reign and Arielle simultaneously dropping to their knees, looking broken and ravaged.

Not even Wrath's destruction as inky smoke pours from his bleeding body can counteract the devastation that just eclipsed the rooftop.

Arielle turns to Reign. "We failed. Again."

Wordlessly, he pulls her into his arms and they rock one another, their grief too overwhelming for tears or words.

Arielle tenses, then slams her hands over her ears. "It's happening."

Reign's agonized eyes climb to Mac. "She's seeing the next obelisk break," he croaks hoarsely.

As the next Sin is released onto the world.

There's only one Gate remaining between Earth and Hell.

Which means they can't give up now.

Mac steps forward, knowing she's asking for more from the two who've had so much expected of them already. "I came back because I learned something."

Arielle slowly turns to face her, blinking as if she can't see past the haze of hurt. "Mac—"

"The cult who are part of the Tenth Legion," Mac continues, wishing there was time to let Ari and her best friend grieve. "They worship the Infinity symbol because they believe Eldritch is the true infinite."

Reign is the first to realize what that means. "You think they're working with the Sins?"

Mac nods slowly, wanting them to understand the gravity of this knowledge. "The cult wants the Gates of Hell opened. They're in league with them."

There are humans on Earth aiding the Sins.

Unless someone stops them.

Reign and Arielle look at each other for long moments and Mac finds she's holding her breath. These two deserve a break. They deserve to spend time with just each other, without the end of the world breathing down their necks.

It's too much.

Yet they clasp hands, becoming each other's steading force as they push to their feet.

"We need to find the final Innocent," Arielle says, her voice soft but steely.

Reign kisses their clasped hands. "Together."

CHAPTER 30
ARIELLE

Although the window to Jilian's house has been boarded up, and the door replaced, the interior still looks like a battle between good and evil was fought there. There are holes in the wall, paintings are twisted and broken, and furniture smashed.

Arielle looks around, feeling the destruction here echoes that of Mercy City. And now that Envy has been unleashed, it's only going to get worse. Those who amassed resources fueled by Greed and Wrath are about to be the target of jealousy. The violence is only going to escalate.

Reign pokes a broken vase with his toe. "Let's see what we can find."

Arielle nods, wordlessly walking toward what's left of the bureau. Above is the smudged Infinity symbol, now dried a sickly brown. Learning that the cult is actually trying to bring on Eldritch had been a devastating blow right after losing Jilian. She glances at Reign. Without him, it could've been the final piece of knowledge that broke her.

Instead, it was the reason to get up and keep moving.

To be part of the solution, rather than feeling the problem was overwhelming.

He looks back, eyes soft as if he knows what she's thinking. "Rachel's theory that the Innocents are all connected turned out to be true. Maybe we'll find a link to the next one here."

Tempted to walk over and kiss the mouth that keeps feeding her hope, Arielle nods. That's why they're here. To see if they can find any hints of who Jilian knew. And whether they're the next Innocent.

Arielle returns her focus to scanning the smashed remains of the bureau, eyes narrowing when she sees a broken photo frame partially covered by a half a figurine. Carefully brushing away the shards of porcelain and broken glass, she realizes it's a picture of a smiling Jilian standing beside a man of similar age.

Reign appears by her side. "A boyfriend," he asks, no doubt wondering the same thing she is.

Who is he? And how can they make contact with him?

Reign spins in the direction of the door a second before Arielle hears the crunch of glass beneath a shoe. They both leap forward, ready to fight, adrenaline spiking through her veins.

The young man who just entered Jilian's house rears back, his hand flying to his chest. "Please, don't hurt me!"

Reign and Arielle drop their fists. "Who are you?" he demands, just as Arielle realizes the answer.

It's the guy from the photo.

He lowers his hands. "M-my name's Kilian. I'm Jilian's twin."

Arielle and Reign still. Surely not...

Kilian looks around the room with wide eyes. "What's happened?" His gaze shoots to Arielle, then Reign. "And where is my sister?"

Sweet lord, he wouldn't know yet.

Arielle takes a step forward, compassion tugging at her insides. "Jilian's dead," she says softly, knowing it still won't cushion the impact of the words. "She was killed. I'm so sorry."

Kilian's eyes fill with tears. His lower lip trembles. "Was it demons?"

Arielle almost does a double take. He knows about demons?

Kilian enters the room more fully, taking a seat on the edge of the couch in a way that reminds Arielle of Jilian. "I learned of the supernatural a long time ago," he says hollowly. "I loved to explore just as much as my sister did, just beyond the realms of science."

Arielle moves closer, wishing she could somehow make this easier. "What do you know?"

Kilian looks up, then gasps when he registers the Infinity symbol painted on the wall. "She was killed by the Cultus Infinitialis?"

Reign jolts with surprise. "You know of the cult?"

"I read about them in a book in a library called Veritas. I know they're supernatural. And evil."

Arielle glances at Reign. Kilian was able to enter Veritas, which only the supernatural can do. Could he be the final Innocent?

Reign pulls his cell out of his pocket and swipes at the screen. "Do you know any of these people?" he asks, showing it to Kilian.

Images of Aunt Shell, and Rachel's father, even Norman flit past but Kilian shakes his head at each one. It's only once the image of Evelyn, Rachel's mother, comes up that he frowns. "Yes, I've met her. She came to visit me once, a long time ago. She said something about us both being Innocents and angels. I thought she was crazy." His frown deepens. "Although that's when I became curious about the supernatural."

Reign comes to stand beside Arielle, the same knowledge settling on his face as it is, deep in her chest.

Evelyn dedicated herself to finding the other Innocents.

Arielle kneels beside Kilian. "She was telling the truth. You are an Innocent, with long buried angel powers within. So was Jilian. It was why she was killed."

Reign rests a hand on her shoulder. "And we'd like to help you."

Arielle's insides clench painfully. They've made that offer to other Innocents, and failed them. That can't happen again.

Kilian looks around his sister's destroyed home. He swallows. Then nods. "Okay. I think I need all the help I can get."

ARIELLE STANDS in the living room of the farmhouse, staring at the chalice. Somewhere upstairs, Reign's showing Kilian to his room then talking to the Potentials, Knights, and nephilim about the strongest protection they've had for an Innocent so far.

The collective determination to keep him alive is one of the few things that are keeping her upright right now.

Especially as she stares at the silver goblet, the cup that Jilian put so much faith in that she died for it, wondering how they're going to win this war.

She picks up the cup, once more feeling the gentle hum of power thrumming through it. It killed the hellhound, yet failed to protect Jilian.

Maybe they haven't figured out how to use it. How can they go into battle without knowing for sure?

"You certainly have an affinity for the Holy Chalice." The Professor enters from the kitchen, watching her closely.

She places it down, choosing her words just as carefully. "You don't think it's the Grail?"

He shrugs. "I cannot say." He looks from the cup to her. "But I do know it was forged from Primordial Light."

"In the same way the Grail was?"

"The Grail *is* primordial Light," he responds, as if it's simple.

When it's not. All he's doing is confusing her further. "Why are you here, Professor? What are you trying to tell me?"

"The weapons to kill the Sins were also forged from Primordial Light," he says, not answering her questions. "Reign was able to trace them because his demonic origin is linked to it."

Yet Arielle remembers how pale Reign was when he triumphantly told her he'd traced the weapon to kill Wrath. He didn't say it, but it was clear the process cost him. The Mark's link to the weapons has been poisoned by the obsidian's impact on Hell.

"Lucifer forged the weapons," the Professor continues. "So the Sins could be destroyed."

Arielle glances at the cup. And Lucifer was an angel. "You're saying that the cup can be used to trace the next weapon?"

"I believe it could find the final two blades," the Professor says. "I was once in an Archivist library in Boston and learned that two of the blades were kept together. One can kill Envy, the other Pride."

The remaining Sin who will be released if they fail in keeping the final Innocent alive.

"How?" Arielle asks, urgency thrumming through her blood. "How do we use it?"

"Trust in yourself, Arielle," he says solemnly. "The ability has always been inside of you."

Not entirely sure what he's talking about, she picks up the chalice anyway, once more feeling the undeniable power it exudes. She closes her eyes, not sure what she's looking for, but willing to try as she focuses on the weapons they need to find.

Yes. It is within you.

Arielle startles at Trinity's voice. And what does she mean? But then images of every blade they've found are flashing through her mind.

Dinah providing not one, but two knives to kill Lust and Gluttony.

Her father passing her the one to kill Greed.

The knife to kill Wrath sitting in the vault.

And then two blades sitting side by side, one with a green gem, the other with a purple one. They're in a glass case on a stand, with more around them exhibiting vases or plates or daggers.

Arielle's eyes fly open. She recognizes the place. "The museum!" she gasps. "They're on exhibit at the museum."

The Professor doesn't move, although his eyes smile. "Well done, Arielle."

She looks at him, curious once more. The Professor was right. She was able to tap into the power of the cup, just like she did when Reign was being attacked by the hellhound. He knows more than he's letting on.

"Who are you," she asks, realizing it's the question they should've been asking all along.

Looking alarmed, the Professor steps back. "Just someone who has spent his whole life studying the riddle. I'm not convinced Jilian was right."

Arielle's eyebrows contract as she glances at the cup. "What do you mean?"

"I don't believe Joseph of Arimathea was buried with the Grail."

"But that would suggest..." Arielle stares at the cup as she runs the riddle through her mind, realizing the two middle lines would still be open to interpretation.

Residing in humanity, it transcends immortality,
Resting in red and mortal spread.

She looks up, ready to demand that the Professor stop talking in riddles himself, only to find he's gone. Disappeared. There aren't even footsteps fading away.

Arielle reaches down and scoops up the chalice, shaking away the confusion the Professor left behind. They don't have time to solve riddles. Not when the weapons they need are hiding in plain sight.

"Reign," she calls out excitedly as she darts up the stairs.

They need to retrieve the final two blades.

DINAH

Dinah moves to the next length of shelves, scanning spine after spine as she silently curses the irony that Veritas has so many books, meaning it's the one place she's most likely to find what she needs.

While being the one place that will make it hardest to find as she has to sort through thousands of tomes.

"You!" Dinah looks up, finding Mac standing halfway down the shelves, a book in her hand. "You've got some nerve showing yourself here."

See. They don't trust you. They never will.

Dinah maintains her relaxed posture as she ignores the obsidian. "Also researching the cult, huh?"

Mac frowns. "If anyone else asked me that question, I'd answer it."

How could they trust you? You've done nothing but lie and betray them.

"So far, I know they spawned from the Tenth Legion," Dinah continues. "And that they use the Infinity symbol. And that the Merrick Group of Industries are linked to them."

Mac's mouth goes slack, but she quickly straightens. "Why are you telling me this, Dinah?"

"To show you I'm not the enemy. Caroline Merrick is the leader of the cult. They're tied to all this, to Eldritch, somehow."

"You've been doing your research," comes an appreciative voice behind Dinah. She turns slowly, instantly recognizing it. "Just as I suggested."

And not liking that he's right.

Oliver smiles at her as if she didn't tell him to stay the hell away from her. He nods in Mac's direction. "Hello, I'm Oliver. A friend of Dinah's."

Mac snorts. "I knew I'd stepped into an alternate reality again."

Dinah wonders if she might be right. She never could've dreamed someone like Oliver would be in her sphere of orbit. Let alone her entire life, watching over her as he claims.

His grin widening as if he can sense her confusion, Oliver leans over and grabs a book above her head. Dinah leaps back when she realizes which one it is.

The Book of Monsters.

"Get rid of it," she snaps. "It's dangerous."

Last time it opened, Dinah was sucked into it and was given a tour by Emma, whether she liked it or not.

"You're safe," Oliver assures in a way that suggests he expects her to believe it. "I won't even open it, I promise."

But then he places his hand on top of it, covering the skull embossed on the black leather. Dinah steps away, ready to run.

A glow appears between Oliver's hand and the book, making her more uneasy. Even Mac's looking concerned.

The flash of light is as brilliant as it is short, and before Dinah can react, another person is standing next to Oliver.

"Emma!" Dinah says, shocked.

The small woman smiles. "Hello again, Dinah."

Mac steps in closer, looking between the two. "You two look alike..."

She's right. Both Oliver and Emma have the same brilliant blonde hair, and despite the height difference, the shape of their faces are identical.

Oliver grins. "Ladies, I'd like you to meet my sister, Emma."

Dinah almost does a double take. They're siblings.

Mac angles her head. "There's something else. You look familiar."

"That's because Gabby is our sister," Emma offers. "Half-sister, to be exact. We are all children of Archangel Gabriel."

Dinah's silent for long seconds, trying to understand what that means. And not really getting anywhere.

"She asked us to look after you while she tried to figure out what to do with the obsidian," Oliver says, Emma nodding beside him. "She's trying to find something eternal and impenetrable to contain it."

"Sounds straightforward," Dinah says sarcastically. There's nothing on Earth that could do that.

Oliver grins as if she just cracked a joke. "She thinks she has a lead, but in the meantime, we need to stop the spell the Sins are casting so they can use Pandora's Box to open a Tear."

"And Gabby and Colt have learned that an ancient who calls herself Azura is leading the cult," Emma adds.

Mac lets out a low whistle. "Whoa. Azura is the sister of Cain, Abel and Aclima."

"This goes back to the oldest feud in human history?" Dinah asks, disgusted, but not surprised.

For the first time, Oliver's not smiling. "Which is why it's vital we find Pandora's Box. Azura created the cult for a reason, and she's been planning this for a long time."

Centuries.

Mac's face turns grim. "Maybe it's time we try to trace the bastard using demon magic." She steps past them into the wider space between rows and turns her palms out. "Good thing I learned a thing or two about my heritage while I was away."

CHAPTER 31
REIGN

ithout the Knight Templars and their technology, Reign doubts they'd be able to break into Mercy City Museum after it closes, but they do.

The Knights accessed the floor plan, then the security plan, even hacked into the security company's system and learned the guards locations and movements. It means that as Arielle and Reign slip through the door beside the loading dock along with the Potentials, there's no alarm. No one in their way.

And nothing stops them from making their way to the second floor where the blades are part of an ancient weapons exhibit.

When Ari told him this is where she'd traced them to, he'd been doubly surprised. First, she'd channeled the Grail again. Second, some idiot thought they'd place the two weapons standing between humanity and Eldritch on display.

He's triply surprised when they reach the second floor and they're still not met with any opposition. They slip into the room and duck behind a large, rectangular display case housing Japanese weapons.

Arielle gasps. "There they are."

The blades are close to the center of the room, in a glass case just like she described in her vision, subtle lighting glinting off their green and purple gems.

Make that quadruply blown away. The blades are not only here, but a few, unobstructed feet away.

"It's probably a trap," Simon whispers.

Possibly for the first time since they met, Reign agrees with him. It's too easy.

He scans the area. There are other display cases, some small and square like the ones the blades are in, others larger and taller, housing spears and shields. But everything is spread out, allowing visitors to move freely between them, soaking up the history.

"I'll get them," Reign says quietly. He looks to Arielle, seeing the objection already on her face. "I can fly. And if it is a trap, I can heal."

She snaps her mouth shut even though she doesn't look happy with the logic. He also can't be killed seeing as he's currently immortal. He's the only one who can do this quickly.

And time isn't something they have a whole lot of.

Reign presses a quick kiss to her forehead, then steps around the rectangular case they're hiding behind, every sense alert. There's enough lighting from each of the displays to be able to see most of the room. Large and expansive, it has floor to ceiling windows along two walls, the lights of Mercy City glimmering beyond. It makes him feel open and exposed.

His soft footsteps are the only sound in the room. That, and his thundering pulse. But each step brings him closer to the display case holding the twin blades, so the tension pulling his nerves taut is worth it.

When Reign reaches the glass-topped case, it feels too good to be true. He does a slow turn, surveying every inch of his surroundings. He looks up at the ceiling. Nothing. The

Knights were sure they'd disabled every alarm, but it still feels too easy.

Too many stakeholders want these knives.

But the only movement is Arielle's gaze flicking between him and every other point in the room from where she's peeking over the Japanese weapons display. Then Bryn's purple hair appears, and Simon's spectacled face.

Reign turns back to the blades, every muscle feeling like a tightly sprung coil. The square glass case is the only thing that stands between himself and the means to kill the last two Sins. He moves around it cautiously, but the only way to open it is a small lock at the base of one side. The glass is thick, and no doubt shatterproof. Reign lets out a slow breath. If Marlowe were here, they'd have some nifty secret agent tool that could cut the glass. But he's not.

Which means Reign's about to find out how much force is needed to take the glass from shatterproof to rubble.

He turns to Arielle and the others, mouthing four words. "Get ready to run."

Reign tucks his arm into his chest, digs his feet into the tiled floor, and twists. One turn is all he gives himself to power the blow, so he makes it a fast one. The room blurs, there's not even time to blink, and he whips his arm out. It crashes through the case like a baseball bat, sending glass flying halfway across the room.

The consequences are just as instant.

Blood blooms over the multiple cuts on Reign's arm.

And a horde of demons crash through the windows, shards of glass covering the first explosion like rain.

"Reign!" Arielle cries, leaping around the display case. "We're under attack," she adds, no doubt for the benefit of the Knights and nephilim surrounding the building.

The dozens of demons converge, the blood streaking their

faces and torsos healing as quickly as Reign's arm. He grabs the two blades, tucks them away, and prepares to fight for his life.

He's the one the demons will want. He has the blades.

Reign's wings explode from his back and he leaps high, then slams down on the nearest display case. It smashes beneath his boots and he picks up the small ax inside. He flings it at the demon that's closest, already turning away as it lodges in his chest.

They're in a room full of deadly weapons. It's going to be their advantage.

And their greatest threat.

"Potentials, protect Arielle," Reign calls out.

For once, he doesn't do everything he can to get back to her side. Not when he's the target. He remains in the middle of the room, becoming the center of the bloom of death unfolding around him. The Knights and nephilim rush into the room, cries and grunts puncturing the air.

More glass smashes as weapons are retrieved—knives, arrows, swords, spears. The museum is about to become a bloodbath. Reign ducks when a Japanese fighting star shoots past his head, then kicks a broadsword out of a demon's hands. He uses his wing to knock the bastard out, and he drops onto the blood-slicked floor.

Reign looks up, finding a clear line of sight has been opened to the opposite wall, sneering when he discovers they have an audience. Envy stands near a broken window in a tight, green one-piece. Her thick black hair has been twisted into two goat horns, adorned with emerald ropes. She's watching the battle with relish, looking as if she wants to join in each time someone is knocked down. Yet, she doesn't. She's enjoying the urge, the jealousy. Glorying in it.

A blow from behind Reign has him staggering and grunting with pain. He turns to find a demon swinging the club she's holding back in a wide arc. He blocks it with his wing, grunting again when the wood splinters. One kick and the demon's sent flying backward into a display case, the loaded crossbow within it shooting into her back at blank point range.

Reign takes note of where Ari is. She's using a length of smooth wood to defend and attack any demon who tries to get past, the Potentials by her side along with two Knight Templars. A glance in the other direction reveals he can no longer see Envy past the mass of black wings and battling nephilim.

Leaping so he can kick another demon attempting to slash at him with a curved blade, Reign growls with frustration. He needs a clear line of sight. Then he'll kill Envy, and she'll be dispatched as quickly as Pride was.

"Reign!"

It's Simon's panicked voice that has him turning back toward the Potentials. Envy's moved, and is now standing a few feet to their left, beside a tall cabinet housing spears. And she's already holding one.

"Arielle," Reign shouts, glad to see Bryn leap closer to her side, quickly followed by Tariq.

Yet, it's Reign Envy has her sights on. She lifts the spear, her green lip curling with dark delight. She raises the spear, pulls her arm back, and launches it.

"No!"

Horror washes through Reign as Simon leaps, only to be shoved to the side by Tariq as he launches himself forward. Straight into the spear's path. It hits Tariq with so much force that it propels him backward as it lodges deep in his chest.

"Tariq!" Reign screams, running toward the Potential. Demons try to attack, but he ruthlessly strikes and knocks them away.

Tariq skids to a stop on the floor, smearing blood in his wake.

Beyond him, Envy picks up another spear, green fire smoldering in her gaze. Suddenly, her eyes open wide. Her back arches.

And she disappears in an explosion of inky smoke.

Blaise steps through it, her hands coming to her side as she pants. "She's banished. For now."

Reign maintains his momentum, sliding to his knees as he comes to a stop beside Tariq. Around him are the sounds of wings beating the air as the demon's retreat now that Envy is gone.

Simon drops to his knees with a thud. "No," he whispers brokenly. "He didn't have to do this."

The silence that's left behind only amplifies Tariq's raspy breaths. Reign takes in the blood rapidly spreading over the Potential's chest. How deeply the spear is embedded into flesh and bone.

He has no idea what he's supposed to say. "Tariq," he chokes. "They can't kill me."

Reign's immortal.

Tariq's not.

"They...poisoned you...last time," Tariq gasps. His face twists as he tries to move, then quickly stills.

Reign takes his hand, gut clenching and dropping when he registers how cold it is. "We'll get a medic. Just hold on."

Tariq blinks up at him. "I..."

"Shh, you need to save your breath." Reign's hand tightens, as if he can hold onto life for Tariq. Blood is pooling behind his head like a halo.

But Tariq's brows contract with effort. There's something he wants to say. "We can't...win this...without you," he rasps. A faint smile plays on his pale lips. "Grail Keeper."

277

The Potential's hand goes limp and slips out of Reign's numb one. His eyes flutter closed and his chest sinks, never to rise again.

A sob echoes somewhere behind Reign. He thinks it was Leila or Seiko. The same sound punches through his chest.

Tariq's dead. Killed by Envy.

So he could save Simon and Reign.

He looks up, quickly finds Blaise. "Can you track her?" he asks, his voice as cold as the tiles his knees are resting on.

Blaise nods grimly. "I have her energy signature."

Reign pushes to his feet.

Envy is going to pay for this.

MAC

The abandoned warehouse isn't a large one, which Mac isn't sure whether she likes it or not.

Smaller means less areas to search, less hiding spots for demons to ambush from.

But the walls of the single-story building feel like a trap. Especially when they have no idea what they're walking into.

Yet that's exactly what they do.

In fact, Mac opts to just ram the door down, a little disappointed when the rusted metal just flies off its hinges.

She stalks in, Dinah on her right, Oliver and Emma on her left.

They stop short when they realize they're most definitely not alone.

The warehouse has been gutted, the cement floor covered in nothing but years of dust. In the center of the room is a table.

And on it sits Pandora's Box.

"We found it," Emma breathes.

"And now we're going to get it," Dinah adds, her voice hard.

Except Oliver shoots his arm across her chest, holding her back. "It's protected by a magical barrier."

Mac notices it, too. A gentle hum of cold energy surrounding the box. "And we need to remember it's probably a trap."

There's no way the Sins would've left the Box protected by only a ward.

Dinah stalks forward, her gaze zeroed in on her target. "No magic will stop me from getting my hands on it."

Tension winds through Mac's body. This is why she's here. Why she so willingly decided to join Dinah, whether she has two new angel buddies or not. Especially when she doesn't trust the witch. Mac's hands silently, unobtrusively form into fists.

Dinah has the obsidian inside of her, desperate to reunite with Eldritch.

She's the last person they want to get their hands on Pandora's Box.

CHAPTER 32

ARIELLE

"I'm not sure why we're here," Blaise murmurs as they approach the small warehouse. "This isn't a sacrificial site. They've always been on a confluence of ley lines so the Sins can harness the power of the sacrifice more effectively."

"That's a good thing," Reign growls. "Especially when Envy doesn't have the Innocent."

Arielle moves a little closer to him, the hard edge in his voice making her chest tighten. Reign hasn't said much since Tariq was killed.

But the pain etched into the lines of his face is evident. She's not sure whether it's the grief or sense of responsibility that weighs on him more heavily, all she knows is he'll carry both forever.

She places a gentle hand on his arm. "Tariq died a hero," she says quietly. "For something he believed in."

Reign.

And the Keepers of the Grail.

A spasm of pain ripples over Reign's handsome face. "I just wish he didn't have to make that sacrifice." His agonized green eyes settle on Arielle. "One I never would've asked of him."

She moves closer, her throat tightening. "He knew that. That's why he did it."

Tariq was silent. Strong. Yet unfailing in his loyalty.

A testament to Reign's ability to lead.

The other Potentials move in, too. "We all would," says Simon, further proving Arielle's thoughts.

Simon was Reign's greatest critic. Yet he was also willing to give his life.

Reign nods, his throat working as he struggles to find words. Tears sting Arielle's eyes as she watches the bittersweet moment. The Grail Keepers are uniting.

"Thank you for protecting Arielle," Reign says gruffly. "I know this isn't always what you signed up for."

Bryn shrugs. "Your way's working, Reign. Tariq realized it, too."

He gave his life for it.

Reign straightens but before he can answer, Blaise steps forward, frowning. "I can sense someone inside."

Arielle and Reign tense as they turn. "How many?" Reign asks.

"I'm not sure." Blaise angles her head as the frown deepens. "I can only sense a few."

Yet they learned at the museum that Envy and her demons can hover beyond the periphery of detection, waiting until the moment they want to attack. Arielle brushes her hand over the knife tucked into her belt, noting that Reign does the same with his. They can't afford to be taken by surprise again.

And now Reign's carrying the knife that can end Envy.

The Knight Templars and nephilim who accompanied them contract around them. "We'll follow you inside this time," says a scarred Knight. "We work together from now on."

Blaise removes her cell phone and presses a single button. "I don't like this. I've called in for reinforcements."

Arielle suppresses her own frown. They already have dozens of fighters with them, but Blaise doesn't think that will be enough.

"Let's see what we're dealing with," Reign says. "Hopefully we won't need it."

They make their way to the door cautiously, finding it's gone. Reign's the first to enter, with Arielle making sure she's close behind, the others pouring in and fanning out. It takes a few tense seconds for her eyes to adjust to the gloom, but then they widen.

Mac and Dinah are here with two others. And so is Pandora's Box.

Mac spins, propping her hands on her hips when she discovers they have company. "This place is small enough, we don't need all of you jamming in here, too."

Reign strides toward her, but stops quickly, glancing over his shoulder at Arielle and the Potentials. His protective streak has his gaze roaming over the warehouse, reaching the same conclusion Arielle has. It appears empty.

He turns back to Mac. "You found Pandora's Box?"

She grins. "I'm pretty amazing, aren't I?"

Blaise moves right, as if she's giving the Box a wide berth. "It's surrounded by a protective barrier," she observes.

"Yeah, we realized the same." Mac indicates to Dinah, her gaze settling on Reign. "Dinah believes she can break through it."

Tension bunches around Reign's spine. "I'm not sure that's a great idea."

"Especially if it's a fake," Blaise says.

Arielle joins them, conscious the Knights and nephilim continue to spread out around the warehouse. "You think it's a trick?"

"There's no way to tell." Blaise studies the silver box. "Not until we break past the ward."

"Which is exactly what I'm about to do," Dinah snaps.

Arielle frowns. "What will happen if it's a fake?" They need to know what they're dealing with.

Blaise's eyes narrow. "It's hard to tell. It might be a trap, in which case, it would be deadly."

Dinah snorts. "My favorite sort."

She takes a step forward, but Reign reaches out and grabs her arm. "We need to decide this together, Dinah. We have to be careful."

"We don't have time for this," Dinah snaps back. "Envy and her demons are nearby. I can sense it."

Arielle instinctively looks around. Dinah has the obsidian inside of her. She's probably far more in tune with the Sins.

"Or you're lying, Dinah," Mac says. "Because you want Pandora's Box for yourself. So the obsidian can open the breach."

Dinah's shoulders draw up as she glares at Mac, then Reign, then Arielle. "What do I have to do for you to trust me? Can't you see I'm trying to help?"

Arielle stares back at her. She can hear the desperation in Dinah's voice. See the pleading in her eyes.

But Arielle's also carried the obsidian. She knows how manipulative and evil it is. That it may not be Dinah speaking.

"We can't take the chance," she says, wishing it were otherwise. "Too many lives depend on this, Dinah."

"Intruders!" shouts one of the nephilim.

Reign is instantly by Arielle's side, calling the Potentials to join him. The adrenaline that had barely abated spikes all over again.

Arielle's mom rushes in, Gabriel by her side, just as ready to fight.

It takes a second, but everyone lets out a breath of relief. Arielle's mom rushes to her, engulfing her in a hug. "It's good to see you're okay." She startles when she sees what else is in the room. "Is that...?"

"We hope so," Arielle says. "We were just deciding who would find out." Her gaze instantly darts to Reign, hoping he's not about to nominate himself again. She doesn't think her heartbeat once as she watched him walk toward the display case with the blades.

It certainly stuttered to a halt when she saw the spear flying straight for his heart. Reign doesn't know it, but the tip was painted green, just like the knife that sent him to Purgatory.

Tariq saved Reign from endless cycles of pain and death. But he also saved Arielle from having to choose between saving the man she loves, or saving the world.

Reign's just opened his mouth to answer when there's the sound of someone bursting through the door.

"I will avenge my sister's death!" Kilian shouts. His eyes widen when he discovers a room full of allies, rather than enemies.

Professor Breckenridge enters at a run, then skids to a stop. "Sorry," he pants. "He followed Sierra and the others. I couldn't stop him."

"What the hell are you doing here, Kilian?" Reign demands, stalking toward him.

He holds his ground. "My sister was killed by these bastards. I won't sit around when I can do something about it." He lifts his fists. "I used to train at the Phoenix Dojo. I know how to protect myself."

Surprise shoots through Arielle. The Phoenix Dojo belonged to Rachel's father. Kilian was more connected to the other Innocents than they'd realized.

Which is all the more reason to protect him.

Arielle walks forward, determined to convince Kilian he needs to return to the farmhouse, when there's a screeching, tearing sound above.

A large piece of the roof is torn away and Envy drops into the warehouse.

"No! Kilian!" Arielle and Reign shout simultaneously.

Envy throws her arms out wide and a thick, impenetrable black smoke pours out. It billows and grows so fast, it swallows Arielle before she can take another step. She waves her arms blindly, her heart a jackhammer against her ribs. The smoke is so thick, she can't even see her hands.

"Kilian!"

The sound of shouts and coughing are her reply. The inky smoke is so complete, it almost feels like a suffocating weight.

"Arielle!"

"Reign," she calls back, unable to place the direction it came from.

A blast of wind pushes the hair from her face and Arielle instinctively shuts her eyes. When she opens them, the warehouse is clear once more. Blaise is standing a few feet away, her arms falling to her side, energy still crackling along her fingertips.

Although there's no time to thank her. Arielle frantically turns to where Kilian was standing only seconds ago, already knowing he's gone, but still feeling like a white-hot knife just slammed into her gut when she finds the space empty.

"Dinah!" Reign roars.

Arielle turns, still reeling from the loss of the Innocent, gasping when she sees what has Reign sounding so panicked.

Dinah has her arms out, her palms open as if she's pressing against a glass wall. A thunderous *crack* snaps through the warehouse and electricity sparks like lightning over and around Pandora's Box.

"Finally," Dinah murmurs.

"No, Dinah!" Arielle shouts, running to stand beside Reign. "Don't touch it!"

Dinah glances over her shoulder. "Don't you see, Ari? I have to. This is the only way I can make everything right. The only way I can prove to you I'm on your side."

She lurches forward and picks up Pandora's Box.

The impact is instantaneous.

Dinah's head is thrown back as she cries out. The Box blazes bright enough to make Arielle squint, then disintegrates into ash.

It was a fake.

Dinah goes very still. With measured, almost calculated, slowness, she returns to looking forward, her gaze roaming over every person in the warehouse. A few people gasp. Most freeze.

Her eyes are an endless, terrifying black.

"No," Oliver moans. "The obsidian has complete hold of her."

Dinah's lip curls. She looks up. Then shoots straight through the metal roof, leaving behind a torn hole.

Arielle's gaze finds Reign's, her whole being too shocked to move.

Envy has the last Innocent.

And now the obsidian has Dinah.

Eldritch has never felt more inevitable.

Reign holds her gaze as he speaks. "Blaise, trace Envy again." His whole body seems to tighten, even grow. "We have the Grail. This is a battle we won't lose."

CHAPTER 33
REIGN

E nvy has prepared well for this final battle.

Their contingent of angels, Knights, and nephilim could see the field they're approaching at a distance, even though twilight has blanketed it like a bruise. There are seven blazing piers circling it, and Reign would bet his wings they're in the formation of a pentagram. The light from the seven burning pyramids flickers and writhes, illuminating the army Envy has amassed.

A seething horde of demons.

They're spread out over the field, red eyes flashing and black wings twitching.

"Envy's in the center," Mac growls. "I can feel her."

So can Reign. She's no longer masking herself. Her arrogance fuels the powerplant of fury that's building within him.

Too many lives have been lost. The Innocents. Angels and Knights and nephilim.

And Tariq.

The Potential who will never live up to his title—he'll never know exactly what he could've been.

The barely banked rage has Reign's wings appearing as they

come closer. The area around the field is largely cleared. There are no houses in the vicinity. Only a road that leads in and out.

They progressively fan out the closer they are. Reign and Arielle, Mac and Blaise, Oliver and Emma, the Potentials and the Professor, Gabriel and his angels, the Knights and the nephilim. They've brought their own battalion.

Because they don't intend on losing.

Reign meant what he said to Arielle. It doesn't matter how hopeless things appear. How many wins the Sins have had.

Each has simply cemented the determination that they need to win.

It's how they'll ensure each death was not wasted. That each loss won't always slice so deep.

And it'll prove that evil never stood a chance against all the things that have risen from the ashes of destruction, time after time.

Friendship.

Faith.

And love.

"Here," Reign says to Arielle, passing her the knife that can kill Envy. "She knows this is personal now. She'll expect it to come from me."

She looks like she's about to object, but then nods. "Okay." She hefts the backpack carrying the Grail, adjusting the straps.

"I'll cover you," Reign says, the words a promise. "You finish her."

"Together," Arielle vows, her beautiful face full of the courage and grace Reign can't imagine facing this without.

"Always."

They turn and face the restless mass of demons. Release a joint battle cry.

And break into a run.

The echoing roar from the demons is deafening as they

surge forward like a swarm of death. Reign plows into the first one, killing it instantly with a powerful swipe of his fist. Arielle slashes at another with a knife, its cry quickly turning into a gurgle.

The two demons are instantly replaced by four more. Reign strikes and blocks and strikes again, never letting more than a couple of feet grow between himself and Arielle. Above them, Mac takes to the air along with Oliver and Emma, several angels and nephilim joining them. Beside them, the others fan out, creating a wall of fighters advancing on the demons.

As Reign ends another enemy, he glances around. Sounds of grunts and cries and abruptly-ended screams are coming from every direction. As Reign drops, picks up an abandoned knife, and impales it into the nearest enemy, a nephilim falls to one knee as she's struck by boot to the gut. She never has the chance to rise again. The attacking demon crushes her face with one blow.

Reign winces at the loss. Although more will be inevitable, it doesn't make it any easier to accept.

He leaps, in part to swipe his foot across the jaw of a demon, but also to assess what they're up against. The flames from the surrounding pyres flicker over the bad news stretched out ahead.

The distance between them and Envy is yards deep, every inch covered by demons. They're making progress. But it's slow.

Each second is one where Envy can end Kilian.

He moves behind Arielle and scoops her up, knowing they need to get to the heart of this battle. Killing Envy will end the death toll.

"Mac," he shouts over the battle. "Cover us."

Reign launches into the air, Arielle in his arms as she holds on tight. Just as he suspected, a dozen demons do the same, creating a wall between them and Envy.

Mac appears with Oliver and Emma and they shoot forward simultaneously. Reign dips low as one demon comes at him, then twists left as another tries to slash them with her claws. Mac dispatches the first by breaking one of its wings, then the second by scorching it with a fireball. Below them, a blast of heat shoots through, razing any other demons who were about to leap and join the fray.

"Keep going!" Blaise shouts, sending off another sweeping burst of magic.

Reign aims high, wanting to be away from as much of the violence as possible while he's carrying Arielle and limited in his ability to protect them. Oliver shoots past, his white wings a stark contrast to the black savagery they're facing.

"Look what I have," calls out a triumphant voice.

Reign looks down, feeling Arielle's gasp as much as he hears it. Envy stands in a clearing at the center of the battle, holding Kilian high by the throat. He struggles, his hands wrenching at Envy's, his legs kicking wildly.

"Jealous?" Envy shouts.

Laughing at Kilian's attempts to be free, her blazing green eyes glare at Reign and Arielle. Without breaking her gaze, she powers her arm down.

And slams Kilian into the ground.

The Innocent crumples like a doll. And goes deathly still.

"No!" Arielle screams.

Just as a blow hits Reign between his shoulder blades. Pain explodes down his back and along his wings, robbing him of breath for precious seconds.

Precious seconds where they're sent tumbling through the night, propelled straight into the waiting claws and hungry arms of the demons below.

Somehow, despite the flashing sky, ground, sky, ground, Arielle wraps her arms around Reign's neck, clamping onto him with all her strength. Gripping her, knowing she'll always be the center of his universe, the one who will always ground him, he quickly rights himself. One pump, two, and they're soaring back into the sky.

"Kilian might still be alive," Arielle whispers. "We have to get to him."

A demon slices through the air from their right, but Gabriel appears behind him before Reign can take evasive action. The archangel grabs the demon's legs and swings him straight into a nearby pyre. The flames explode, blasting orange light over the bloody scene and engulfing any demons nearby.

Gripping Arielle close, Reign powers forward, angling so the radiant heat hits his wings and protects Arielle. They cover the remaining distance in a few seconds, landing in the open area Envy's standing in.

The demons surrounding them surge forward, but the Sin lifts a hand. "They're mine," she growls.

Her arrogance only feeds Reign's fury.

But it also means the demon's step back, snarling with discontent.

"He's still breathing," Arielle gasps, her gaze on Kilian.

Reign doesn't take his eyes off Envy, although relief that they still have time is like a tide sweeping through him.

"I'll take care of her," Reign mutters, not caring if the Sin can hear him.

He powers forward before Arielle can answer. Or Envy can react.

Two bounding leaps and he's before the Sin, a flurry of strikes and kicks. Envy blocks every one of them, proving she's not going to be an easy foe to defeat.

Then again, all the greatest victories are hard won.

Reign tucks his wings in tight, spins, and unleashes another volley of blows, aiming for wherever he gets a flash of green.

The chest, abdomen, legs. Envy ducks and weaves, then whips out a fist the first opening she sees. It slams into Reign's temple, snapping his head to the side, quickly followed by his body. He staggers, shaking away the grenade of pain that just exploded inside his skull.

"Kilian, you need to get up!" Arielle cries.

There's no response.

Envy chuckles as she advances on Reign. "Did you know the Innocent is jealous of you, Reign?" she sneers. "He wants the loyalty you have. The authority. The ability to lead."

Reign lifts his fists, noting that Arielle's trying to shake Kilian awake.

Envy's green wings snap out, blocking his view. "Which is ironic considering how many people have died under your care."

A cry sounds somewhere to their left. "No, Bryn!"

Envy's smile grows. "This Innocent will be next."

Reign releases a roar of rage, allowing every loss to power his forward momentum. He ducks as Envy swipes at his head, then smashes his fist into her gut. She grunts, grabs him by the shoulders, and slams him down on the concrete altar waiting for the sacrifice. His head hits the hard surface, and he instantly feels warm blood gush down his scalp.

"Reign!" Arielle cries.

But he can barely hear her past the ringing in his ears. He blinks, the motion feeling slow and heavy. Envy appears above him, grinning maliciously. "Do you think the Innocent will be jealous that you'll be killed on the altar first?"

She jerks forward, her eyes widening so much there's more white than green. Screeching, she stumbles back, spinning around.

And revealing the knife wedged in her back.

Reign sucks in an excited breath. Arielle's killed Envy! He distracted her enough to give her an opening!

But it's the Professor who steps back, breathing hard. One strike from Envy and he's sent sailing. She yanks the blade out as he crashes onto the grass, arms and legs crumbling like they're suddenly dislocated. Reign scrambles off the altar, ignoring the wetness trickling down his spine. Even if it wasn't already healing, it wouldn't stop him.

He watches as the Professor tries to push up, only to collapse. His face morphs and shifts, and Reign expects to see the aged, ancient man they first met. A man who isn't likely to survive what comes next.

Yet the features that appear are ones Reign recognizes. Ones he's seen before.

Joseph of Arimathea catches his gaze. He mouths two words, his lips and teeth bloody. "The Grail."

The cup they can't guarantee will make a difference. The one Joseph himself should've taught him about.

Reign sprints toward Arielle, who's desperately trying to lift Kilian. Maybe Reign can carry them away. Keeping the Innocent safe is all that matters right now.

The pain that explodes between his shoulder blades has him involuntarily crying out. The knife that lodges in his back hits him with such force that he stumbles forward, hands scraping through the dirt. Envy just used the same knife that Joseph attacked her with.

"No, Reign!" Arielle cries.

"Stay with Kilian," he shouts.

As Reign looks up, his breath stutters. Although Arielle hasn't left Kilian's side, her focus is on him. It means she doesn't see Kilian sit up, grab the knife that can kill Envy, and run at the Sin.

"No!" Reign screams.

Kilian slashes at Envy the moment he's close enough. His aim is strong, and he's clearly skilled with a weapon, yet he's no match for a Sin. Envy sidesteps, her movement so fast she's little more than a green blur, then her arm shoots out. She grabs Kilian by the throat, tightens her fingers, and snaps his neck.

Her face alight with victory, she throws the Innocent's limb body onto the altar. Withdrawing a knife tucked into her scabbard, she lifts it high. Swings it down.

And impales it in Kilian's chest.

Reign blinks. His world goes silent. All he feels is disbelief.

They've lost.

The last Innocent is dead.

The remaining Gate of Hell was just opened.

CHAPTER 34

REIGN

T he knife flies as fast as a bullet, impaling Envy's chest, but Reign doesn't bother to watch the Sin disintegrate into black smoke. He's barely conscious of the army of demons screeching as they retreat to the skies.

He turns to Arielle, his mind reeling. And yet it's more still than it's ever been.

Everything makes sense.

Why she was always connected to the obelisks and the Innocents.

Why she could channel the Holy Chalice.

And why he's always been driven to protect her.

He's the Keeper of the Grail. She's the freaking Grail.

She smiles tremulously up at him. "It was me all along," she whispers, sounding as astounded as he feels.

Reign steps forward, banishing the space between them and cups her face. "It's always been you," he breathes.

Their connection was fated.

Their love was destined.

How could he have not seen that?

Arielle's hands come to rest over his. "We can stop this,

Reign. The power of the Light is within me." Her smile turns rueful. "I don't exactly understand it all, but I can feel it."

Reign's throat is too tight to speak. His mind is too overwhelmed with everything he feels. Of course the amazing, beautiful, courageous girl who was his savior is going to be the key to defending humanity. There are no words to encapsulate the enormity of that.

So he shows her. He leans down and brushes his lips over hers. The touch is brief. More of a caress. But it holds everything.

Love.

Devotion.

A hint of the passion that's always existed between them.

And a reverence that he's here, experiencing this, with her.

Arielle pulls back an inch. She smiles up at him, her blue eyes shimmering. "I'll always love you, Reign."

He draws her into a fierce hug, vaguely aware that there's cheering around them. "I'll always love you, Ari," he vows.

They hold each other tightly, and Reign knows they've just become the beacon of hope for every being surrounding them. Arielle is the Grail. She's the one who can save them all.

Which means his role in the battle of good against evil has become clearer than ever.

If the demons know Arielle is the Grail, they'll want her dead.

And it's his sworn duty to make sure they never succeed.

CHAPTER 35
ARIELLE

Arielle's unable to move. She can't even breathe, her body is too frozen in shock.

Kilian's dead.

They've lost.

Her eyes slowly scan the war they were never destined to win. Angel and Knights and nephilim battle demons. Black-winged corpses litter the field, but there are almost as many white-winged beings and humans. Blood has turned the Earth black, the flames from the pyres flickering over it, making it glisten.

Reign's devastated face is next. He tears his gaze from the image of Kilian sprawled on the altar, a knife embedded in his chest, focusing on Arielle. A single tear tracks down a smudged cheek. Yet it's the devastation that weeps from his eyes that has a sob fracturing through her chest.

Visions of the final obelisk cracking and crumbling sear her frozen mind.

They've lost.

A faint groan has Arielle turning to the other body sprawled in the clearing. She knows without a doubt that the man who saved Reign's life is Joseph of Arimathea. The gray-haired man pushes up on his hands. He's the only one not looking at Kilian. His gaze is intensely focused on Arielle.

He's also the only one who doesn't look like the world was just failed by those who were supposed to protect it.

His lips form two words. "The Grail."

They hit Arielle like a battering ram.

The Grail!

There is a way to stop this!

Yanking the chalice out of the backpack, she runs toward Envy. The Sin has her back toward them, her arms extended as she calls out a spell in Demoniac.

One to tear open the Cage and release Lucifer.

"No!" Arielle screams. Earth will not become a battleground for angels. Humanity will not become collateral damage to the battle between Michael and Lucifer.

Except a circle of soil is crumbling away around the altar, expanding fast and forcing Arielle to stop. Envy slowly turns as she hovers in the air. A slow smile spreads across her face just as the altar sinks into the black pit that's appeared.

"Winning feels good," Envy purrs. "I bet you never thought you'd be jealous of me."

"I'm not," Arielle shouts. She holds the goblet up. "Because you haven't won."

The pit opens wider, a white light beaming up from its depths. The ground begins to shake. The fighting stops and the field goes silent.

An apocalypse is trying to be born.

Arielle throws the cup with all her might, watching as it shoots into the blackness. There's a small burst of light. An ear-splitting screech from Envy.

And the pit closes up.

A roar of victory bursts from the angels, Knights and nephilim. Elation explodes through Arielle. Reign joins her, wide-eyed and awed, and a smile bursts across her face.

They've won!

Arielle's about to hug Reign when a cackling laugh erupts from Envy.

"Fools!" She opens her arms wide, laughing at the dark clouds still moving above. "That cup wasn't the Grail. If it was, I would've been pulled into Hell."

Along with every demon still standing on the battlefield.

Arielle's once more speechless. But the pit! It's closed!

"The chalice is obviously a conduit of Light," Envy says. "But it is not the Grail." She points at Joseph. "He knows I'm right."

Joseph's head is hanging between his shoulders. He's the picture of loss and desolation Arielle and everyone else was feeling only moments ago.

"Yet he's cursed to never speak the truth," Envy cackles. "He can never tell a soul where the Grail is."

Arielle's knees go weak. Her chest feels like someone just excavated it.

The Gates of Hell are still open. The final Sin has been released.

They've failed. Again.

Joseph slowly raises his head. His eyes plead as he looks at her. "Remember," he mouths.

She blinks, trying to understand. Remember what?

Their last conversation flickers in her mind.

I'm not convinced Jilian was right. I don't believe Joseph of Arimathea was buried with the Grail.

And he *is* Joseph of Arimathea. He *knows* he wasn't buried with the Grail.

Which also means the riddle hasn't been solved.

Residing in humanity, it transcends immortality,
Resting in red and mortal spread.

Suddenly, Arielle's vision fades. She fights it, not needing to see the last obelisk break, but it's not one obelisk that she sees, but all seven. All nothing but rubble. And at seven points are the seven Innocents.

Shell. Rachel's father and mother. Norman. Renata. Jilian, and even Kilian.

The Innocents slowly raise their arms, each pointing at Arielle as she stands in the center, and a soft moan climbs up her throat. This must be her punishment. To see each of the lives she failed to save.

She feels something brush her feet and she looks down, finding a river of blood rushing over them. A river of red.

Arielle's about to cry out, when a voice stops her. The river disappears.

Remember.

"Trinity?" she asks in a whisper.

Believe.

Arielle looks back up, finding the Innocents are still pointing at her. But there's no blame or judgment or pain on their faces. They're nodding. Shell is smiling.

Residing in humanity...

Resting in red... Like a vein.

The moment the possibility enters Arielle's mind, she feels it. Power rises within her. Rushes through her.

The same Light that she experienced when the hellhound attacked Reign.

She looks up, eyes wide, her heart filling with the truth.

It's you.

Arielle smiles. Her gaze falls on Envy and the Sin is smart enough to look nervous. She reaches a hand out and the blade Kilian had taken from her flies into her palm.

A heartbeat hasn't passed before she throws it at Envy, shouting the words that will change everything.

"I am the Grail!"

EPILOGUE

SIERRA

Sierra wants to pace. But she doesn't want to leave Ryder's side. He shifts in the armchair, rests his hands on the armrests, then pulls them back into his lap.

He's as nervous as she is.

Arielle wipes her hands down her jeans. "Are you ready?" she asks, glancing between her father and her mother.

Ryder glances up at Sierra. "It might not work," he says, and not for the first time.

She gives him the same answer she has every other instance. "We have to try."

"I may not remember," he warns.

According to Cain, his mind may no longer exist.

"I don't believe that," she responds, not sure if she's trying to convince him or herself.

"Neither do I," says Reign, even crossing his arms for good measure.

Sierra smiles faintly at him. Who knew that the precious baby she tearfully left with David would grow up to be everything she imagined—a Grail Keeper worthy of the title—but also so much more than that.

He's the light of Arielle's heart.

The light of the girl who *is* the Light.

Sierra almost shakes her head, something she's done so many times since the battle two days ago, she's lost count. Arielle is the Grail. Which means, Sierra once was, too.

The very thing she was searching for. That Ryder was searching for.

They created with their connection.

Sierra turns back to Ryder. Which is why this has to work. This picture isn't complete without Ryder back in her life.

Cain said the Grail had the power to remove the Mask and break its hold on the man she loves.

Which means Arielle can make this happen.

"I don't exactly know how the Grail works," Arielle says, wiping her hands down her jeans again. "Only that it's no longer dormant within me."

"All you can do is try," Sierra says, not wanting to put pressure on her daughter.

Even as she wants this so badly.

Arielle draws in a breath, then approaches her father. He stills, watching as her hands draw closer to his face. Yet, he doesn't draw back. Xeven is willing to die if it means ridding himself of the Mask that's tortured him for almost twenty years.

Arielle's hands gently cup either side of his scarred, twisted face. She closes her eyes. Her breathing evens out. Ryder's own eyes flutter closed.

At first nothing happens. The fragile flame of hope in Sierra's chest flickers painfully.

She hadn't considered that this would fail. That Ryder would remain Xeven, a living reminder of what she's lost.

But then white light glows at the tips of Arielle's fingers. The pinpoints grow, the pure ivory looking strangely warm. It spreads out, arcing around Ryder's face. The outline of the Mask quickly appears among the ridges of his face.

Reign instinctively moves closer. He lived up to his role as her protector even before he knew Arielle carried the Grail within her.

A smile spreads over Arielle's face, and it's one of the most beautiful expressions Sierra's ever seen. The glow in her daughter's fingertips seems to echo deep within her, making her skin luminescent.

There's a faint sound of wood fracturing and the Mask cracks, lines spreading over the surface like veins. White light beams from them, as if it's radiating from beneath.

Suddenly, the light explodes out, blinding Sierra. Relegating her to a world where there's no color, yet it feels like everything is existing, all at once.

It's gone as quick as it appears, making her wonder if she imagined it. The euphoric sensation was so short-lived, she's not sure it was even a thing.

But then it doesn't matter.

Ryder sits up, looking around in a daze. He pushes his fingers through his hair. Scratches his chin. Sierra's knees almost give out as a sob bursts past her lips.

Her Ryder is there. A little older, a little leaner, but most definitely her Ryder.

He blinks, his gaze coming into focus. "Sierra?" he gasps.

He doesn't get to say another word, because she launches at him, wrapping her arms around his neck and pressing her lips against his.

It's the most beautiful sensation Sierra's ever experienced.

The warmth, the softness, the frisson of heat, are all so achingly familiar. It's like they were never apart.

And yet it's something she never thought she'd feel again.

Sierra pulls back, regretting they have an audience, but also conscious it's time for Ryder to meet their daughter.

Except Arielle and Reign are gone, leaving them alone.

So that almost two decades apart can be erased by a love that never died.

CAIN

Cain enters his sister's office, cautious about what he's walking into. In the following minutes, she won't be Mayor Virginia Goodstone.

She'll be Aclima. His twin. The one who's been determined to punish him for his mistake all those centuries ago.

But it's not his sister who is the first to greet him.

It's Abel.

His younger brother regards him steadily. Once, Cain could've read him, no matter how inscrutable his features.

But too much has passed. He killed Abel for siding with Michael. He became the first murderer.

And Abel got his revenge by killing Cain in the frozen tundra of Alaska.

Cain has no idea where that leaves them.

Abel nods once, his gaze heavy with meaning.

Cain nods back, also willing to acknowledge everything that's passed. The pain. The mistakes. The fact that none of it can be changed.

Aclima rises from behind her desk. "Great, now that we've got that out of the way, we have something to discuss."

Abel turns and Cain follows him to the desk. They stand

side by side for the first time in thousands of years, facing their sister.

Aclima opens a drawer and pulls out a photo. She slides it across the desk, facing them. "Seems you weren't the only one to hitch a ride out of Purgatory, Cain" she says grimly.

Cain feels the ripple of recognition move through his brother in the same moment it shakes his own foundation.

The brown-haired girl isn't one he's seen since the day of Abel's death, but it's a face that is as familiar to him as Aclima's or Abel's.

"Azura," he murmurs.

"What does this mean?" Abel demands.

Aclima leans back in her chair, although she looks far from relaxed. "It means, brothers, that it's time to set aside our differences. We now have a common enemy."

Azura.

The sister who was hell bent on destruction long before any of them were.

Ready for the next instalment of Keepers of the Grail?
Check out Gates of Hell!
https://mybook.to/GatesofHell

GATES OF HELL

The truth about the Grail has been revealed. Along with the price to close the Gates of Hell.

Now, choices must be made.

Arielle and Reign face the end of the world as they know it. Untold horrors wait to ravage Earth, angels and demons are at war, the apocalypse is near. And as the Gates of Hell crumble one by one, the ultimate battle to save humanity has begun.

Their love has given them the strength to fight every obstacle. But with the overwhelming odds, they're about to find out if it's enough.

GRAB YOUR COPY HERE
https://mybook.to/GatesofHell

THE KEEPERS-VERSE IS ALWAYS GROWING!

The Keeper Chronicles will continue to grow, with each new addition adding to its epicness. Each interlinked series will have you falling for unforgettable characters, being swept away by captivating romance and thrilling adventure, and re-visiting old friends (you'll discover all your favorites popping up when you least expect it!).

Dive in at any series!

Keepers of Excalibur
A fated love. A cursed wolf.
A supernatural war only they can stop.
Check out Book 1, Wolf Marked, HERE

Keepers of the Chalice
A vampire. A huntress.
A cure that will change everything.
Check out Book 1, Vampire Unleashed, HERE.

Keepers of the Light

Angels and demons have battled for millennia. Their inevitable war has begun.
Check out Book 1, Hidden Angel, HERE.
http://mybook.to/HiddenAngel

HAVE YOU READ THE KEEPER CHRONICLES PREQUEL?

As an exclusive for my subscribers,
you can download it for free!!

When Sierra sneaks out, determined to escape her over-protective family, she stumbles across a young man covered in blood. His last words are a plea. *Find the Grail Keepers. Warn them.*

Ryder is the young cop who was last seen with the murdered victim. Sierra doesn't trust him, no matter how drawn she is to him. Except it turns out they're both looking for the same thing—the Holy Grail.

They're quickly drawn into a dangerous hunt involving cryptic clues, a mysterious stone, and a Grail that hasn't been seen for centuries. One that leads to more questions than answers. Can Sierra trust her impulsive emotions? Should she believe Ryder's words or the truth she sees in his eyes? And ultimately, should she follow her heart?

Especially when every decision will decide the fate of countless lives.

CLICK HERE TO DOWNLOAD FOR FREE!

ALSO BY TAMAR SLOAN

PRIME PROPHECY SERIES

He failed to shift like every one of his ancestors.

Until he met her.

KEEPERS OF THE GRAIL

The legendary Holy Grail is real.

Yet everything known about it is a lie.

KEEPERS OF THE CHALICE

A vampire. A huntress.

A cure that will change everything.

KEEPERS OF THE LIGHT

Angels and demons have battled for millennia.

Their inevitable war has begun.

KEEPERS OF EXCALIBUR

A fated love. A cursed wolf.

A supernatural war only they can stop.

DESTINED DEMIGODS

Love that defies the gods.

Powers that define destiny.

ELEMENTAL GAMES

Elemental powers. Deadly Games.

No escape.

THE SOVEREIGN CODE

Humans saved bees from extinction...and created the deadliest threat we've seen yet.

THE THAW CHRONICLES

Only the chosen shall breed.

ZODIAC GUARDIANS

Twelve teens. One task.

Save the Universe.

ABOUT THE AUTHOR

Tamar hasn't decided whether she's primarily a psychologist who loves writing, or a writer with a lifelong drive to make a difference. She must have been someone pretty awesome in a previous life (past life regression indicates a Care Bear), because she gets to do both. She divides her time between helping families and writing emotion driven YA stories set in amazing imaginary worlds that surprise even her.

The driving force for all of Tamar's writing is sharing and connecting. In truth, connecting with others is why she writes. She loves to hear from readers. Find her on all the usual social media channels or her website, www.tamarsloan.com where can download one of her books for free.

(Seriously, I LOVE hearing from you guys!)